hOWL

hOWL

HOWARD JACOBSON

JONATHAN CAPE
LONDON

1 3 5 7 9 10 8 6 4 2

Jonathan Cape, an imprint of Vintage, is part of the
Penguin Random House group of companies

Vintage, Penguin Random House UK, One Embassy Gardens,
8 Viaduct Gardens, London SW11 7BW

penguin.co.uk/vintage
global.penguinrandomhouse.com

First published by Jonathan Cape in 2026

The verse quoted on p. 287 is from 'Espenbaum' ('Aspen Tree')
by Paul Celan, translated by Pierre Joris

Typeset in 12/14.75pt Bembo Book MT Pro by Six Red Marbles UK, Thetford, Norfolk
Printed and bound in Great Britain by Clays Ltd, Elcograf S.p.A.

The authorised representative in the EEA is Penguin Random House Ireland,
Morrison Chambers, 32 Nassau Street, Dublin D02 YH68

A CIP catalogue record for this book is available from the British Library

HB ISBN 9781787336445
TPB ISBN 9781787336452

*To my long-gone, beloved grandmother, Andy, who kept
to the old ways, asked for nothing, and trusted
all her short life that the Almighty would protect us —
a faith to which, out of love for her, I go on clinging*

I saw the best minds of my generation destroyed by madness

Allen Ginsberg, *Howl*

PROLOGUE

This is what will happen.

On a sunny day in 20—, in the umpteenth week of the Peace Marches, Dr Ferdinand Draxler MBE, FRSA, headmaster of Strawberry Fields Non-denominational Primary School, Streatham – Sir to his pupils, Ferdie to his wife and close acquaintances – will get lost in the middle of London, a city he has lived in all his life. He will remove the Lenin cap he wears at weekends to hide his bald spot and will scratch his head.

The driver of a tuk-tuk decorated to look like a discotheque will honk his horn. Draxler will jump and drop the bag of churros he is carrying. The tuk-tuk will be playing 'Waterloo' by ABBA. Am I in Bangkok, Barcelona or Stockholm, Draxler will wonder.

He is lost all right.

'Let's get lost' was an expression he and those teenage friends who knew him as Ferdie used when London was their playground. It meant let's get drunk. Let's shed our inhibitions. Let's forget our way home. But he isn't lost in that sense today. Today he is lost in the sense that what used to matter doesn't and that what used to be true isn't.

Caught in the ferocious crossfire of peaceful protest, Draxler will stumble and fall.

Not impossibly he will have been pushed. Not impossibly he will have been struck by a heavy object. It is reasonable to ask if, either way, this is what he will have been hoping would happen.

PART I

THE WORLD TURNED UPSIDE DOWN

THE DAY BEFORE THE DAY AFTER

This being the story of how the world lost its mind and also – not incidentally – of how I, Ferdinand Draxler, lost mine, it makes sense to begin at a time when both of us had a mind to lose.

6 October – the day before the massacre in the Negev Desert – is as good a starting point as any.

What was I doing on that day? Fortunately, my wife, Charmian, an actress and so someone with a trained memory, was able to tell me. It was Charmian who looked after the remembering part of our lives. Without her this would be an even more chaotic tale than it might turn out to be. 'We were in Oxford, darling,' she reminded me. 'With Zoe.'

Yes. We had visited Oxford with the gift of a food processor and cake-mixer for our daughter who had moved into new digs in Queen's Lane, directly opposite New College's celebrated gargoyles – grotesques with hooked noses and lascivious expressions. The three of us had strolled through the college arm in arm, I – I don't mind admitting, a man there was no reason to look at twice – proud to be flanked by my two tall, flame-haired, flamingo-like women.

Charmian suggested we go into the chapel to light a candle for her late mother. Zoe lit one too. I stood admiringly, and just a small bit anxiously, to one side and watched them. What would they do when my mother died, I wondered. Zoe hardly knew her. She had found her frightening when she was little and I, who also found her frightening when I was little, and still found her frightening now I was big, allowed that fear to meander into coldness. It's what I do – I let things take their course. We shouldn't force belief or affiliation or even family affection on our daughter, Charmian believed, and I went along with that. Weren't the offspring of a mixed marriage advantaged in having the best of both worlds? Not without envy, I watched my wife and daughter close their eyes in unison and show their fine profiles to the candle flame.

Afterwards we repaired to Zoe's rooms for tea and seed cake.

'Zoe, there's a fly in my cake,' I said.

Zoe looked at my plate in pretend consternation and waved a napkin over it. 'There's no extra charge for the fly,' she said.

I took her wrist and kissed it.

'You smell of cake, candle wax and chapel,' I said.

'Is that a compliment?'

'I mean it to be.'

Something made me say, 'Grandma Agata was a great cake-maker. Baking cakes for Nazis kept her alive in Belsen.'

'I know,' she said. 'You've told me. Several times.'

'Perhaps you could take her one of your cakes. Show that the skill lives on in the family.'

'Do you think she'd like a fly in hers?'

'My dear, do you make any other kind?'

She turned her face from me. Did that mean she'd had enough of teasing? She who had an answer to everything?

I rose and strode around her room, pausing at her book-shelves. 'I don't have all my books here yet,' Zoe said.

I wondered if that was her way of telling me not to look for my briefly seminal pamphlet on the Fool in Shakespeare, my thesis being that Shakespeare's fools and clowns were, without, exception, Jewish. I had presented Zoe with a copy the moment she was old enough to read. That it wouldn't forever be her prized possession, I accepted; but I couldn't help but look for it on her shelves whenever I visited her. Couldn't she, out of love, bring it forward if only for the duration of my visit? Supposing she any longer had it, that is.

'Ferdie,' my wife called, 'come and look out of the window.'

Charmian knew what a trouble I could be around books – anybody's books – unable to read a spine without passing derogatory comment; but around Zoe's books, she had told me several times, I was the Grand Inquisitor.

I ignored her, taking one volume after another off Zoe's shelves. 'Oh, God, not *Orientalism*,' I exclaimed.

'It's a course book, Daddy,' Zoe said.

'I bet it is. What's the course – *Peevishness and Revolution*?'

'Don't rise, darling,' Charmian said. 'He won't even have read it.'

'I know that,' Zoe said. 'I am used to arguing with him about books he hasn't read.'

I flicked the pages. 'Now I've reread it,' I said.

'Do you like it any better this time?' she asked. 'A second read is said to bring out things you missed the first time.'

I shook my head. There was a dedication on the flyleaf. *From Osman*. Did it say *with love*?

I replaced the book on Zoe's shelf and finally did as Charmian suggested, looking out of the window at the grotesque spouts and downpipes that seemed so close they could have been in the room with us. 'I'm surprised you can sleep with those Jewgoyles looking in on you,' I said.

Zoe compressed her lips, making a small, sad aperture of her mouth. 'I draw the curtains,' she said, exchanging looks with her mother.

'But you must still know they're there.'

'Daddy, I'd still know they were there if I lived in Tel Aviv.'

Is there a word for feeling uxoriously about your own daughter? I loved it when the women in my life held their own or even bested me in these games of my devising. 'Don't patronise me,'

Zoe often said, but the pleasure I took in her cleverness and grit wasn't patronage. It was naked pride.

Later, I would wonder at the coincidence of Zoe bringing up Tel Aviv quite out of the blue, just the day before the massacre. Tel Aviv had never been any sort of reference point for us. Was Zoe possessed of some seventh sense, like Miriam or Deborah or another of the Five Prophetesses of the Old Testament?

I had given up hoping I would one day be the wonder of Our People. Zoe, on the other hand . . .

On the drive back to Streatham, Charmian and I discussed our daughter.

I thought she looked tired and tense.

'Well, you can be hard work, Ferdie.'

'Me! What did I do?'

'You did to her what you often do to me. You disparaged her.'

'I did not.'

'You don't know yourself, Ferdie. You send out small arrows of provocation and expect her to deflect them all. Well, she can't. She's still a child. She isn't as robust as you think she is.'

'I don't recognise myself in your description, Sharm. I was playing, that's all.'

'Jewgoyles! Playing?'

'I wasn't suggesting she knock them down.'

'Just because you weren't suggesting it doesn't mean you'd have minded if she had. And knowing Zoe she'll be thinking about it this minute. She's a serious daughter.'

'I'm a serious father.'

'You are a relentless father, Ferdie. As you are a relentless husband. I don't complain. We are lucky to enjoy your attention. But you've often talked about what it must have been like to be Adam and Eve, watched over by a God who couldn't leave them in peace. *And they heard the voice of the Lord God walking in the*

8

garden in the cool of the day . . . You're the walking fucking voice, Ferdie. You are a test we have to pass and I'm not even a fucking Jew.' She put her hand on my arm. Was she frightened I was going to crash the car? 'Don't get me wrong, darling. That doesn't upset me. I knew what I was letting myself in for when I married you. And I don't mind failing. I judge myself by different criteria. But, other than in looks, Zoe is more your daughter than she is mine. She seeks your approval more than you realise.'

I drove the rest of the journey in silence, upset by the accusation but at the same time pleased to learn how much I mattered to Zoe.

Then came the massacre in the desert . . .

A NEW MNEMONIC OF HATE

I learnt of what had happened in stages, as though a cliff I'd been
walking had begun to crumble without my noticing.

Charmian and I had risen early to meet friends for Saturday
breakfast at the Rookery Café on Streatham Common. We had
not seen a paper or listened to the radio. After ten minutes waiting for our friends in the café we checked our emails and found
a message of condolence. 'How shocking! So sorry. We won't
trouble you at such a time but if there is anything we can do, just
ask. All the love in the world.'

At such a time?

'My God,' Charmian said, 'Zoe.'

My heart jumped in my chest. 'Ring her, for God's sake,'
I said.

Charmian was already on the phone. 'What do you think I'm
doing?' she shouted.

Zoe did not answer her phone.

'Keep trying,' I said.

'I'm keeping trying.'

Charmian rose and walked away, as though she needed to be
alone with the phone.

'Well?' I asked when she returned. 'Well? Well?'

Charmian shook her head. 'She's not picking up but she's all
right.'

'How do you know she's all right if she's not picking up?'

'She's left a message.'

'She could have left that at any time.'

Charmian breathed hard. 'No. This is a new one.'

'How do you know it's a new one? What does she say?'

'It doesn't matter,' Charmian said. 'We'll talk about it later.'

Before I could ask any further questions, I had to take a call myself. It was from an old pupil who was also distant family, a second cousin or something, I didn't know or care what – a jumpy Jew who sent me Christmas cards. He was ringing from Eilat.

'I can't imagine why you're in Eilat,' I said. 'But this isn't a good time to speak. My emails are going crazy. Can we talk another time?'

'I haven't rung for a chat, Uncle Ferdinand. Something terrible has happened over here . . .'

'In Eilat? Can anything more terrible happen in Eilat?'

'Than what?'

'Than being in Eilat.'

'Ha, ha. But listen. I rang to tell you what I know before you start hearing false rumours.'

'Leonard, are you weeping?'

But the line went dead. Leonard had either dropped his phone or thrown it away.

'Listen to this,' Charmian said, handing me an earpiece. Her phone was like a battlefield command centre. She had an app for everything. This was the BBC World Service.

I listened in silence.

'Jesus Christ!' I said at last.

That evening, the occupants of numbers 31 and 33, across the road, spilled out into the street and started dancing. Bottles of prosecco popped. The air was filled with scented vape steam. The electric blue light of a hundred television screens – on each one the same clips of rifle-fire and screams and blood flowing – gave the gardens a ghastly aspect.

'Gas the Jews!' someone shouted.

I ran out into the street, clutching my head. Gas the Jews —
here! In Strawberry Fields, Streatham! 'Hey,' I shouted. 'What
the fuck!'

No one heard me.

'Hey,' I shouted again.

A couple of the dancers looked up. What?

Good question.

I took a moment to shape my objection. 'Could you tone
it down a bit?' I said at last. 'My wife's not feeling well and is
trying to sleep.'

'Sorry,' someone said.

He conveyed my message to the others, putting a finger to
his lips.

'Gas the Jews,' they whispered.

Charmian was waiting at the front gate. I expected her to
throw her arms around me. *My hero!*

But she did no more than kiss my cheek and ruffle my hair.

'That's telling them,' she said.

Strawberry Fields Primary was closed over the weekend but I was
there early Monday morning. It was unnervingly calm. Many of
the staff had not yet fully taken in what had happened. Afraid of
a copycat attack, a couple of Jewish parents were there to discuss
taking their children out of school. I told them I thought that
unlikely. Streatham was a long way from southern Israel and we
weren't a specifically Jewish school. But of course it was up to
them. I didn't make light of their agitation. If anything, I'd have
liked more panic than there was. I wanted to see people rending
their garments. I wanted the sheeted dead to come howling out
of their graves. Normality was an insult to the slaughtered.

My deputy, Max Axelberg, rang to say he'd had a puncture
and was late getting in, but wondered if I was going to address
the school. 'And say what?' I wondered.

'Well, you're the headmaster,' he said. 'Something in solidarity.'

Solidarity! By any measure, solidarity was the wrong word. Shock, yes. Sympathy, yes. Sorrow, yes. Solidarity, no. You don't show solidarity with the dead. Or the living when they're murderers. I thought I knew Axelberg's politics, but what had happened was surely beyond politics. What had happened was the Devil's business. Was Axelberg asking me to show solidarity with Satan?

I slammed the phone down on him, locked myself in my office and turned on the radio. From the great world came the ululations of delight.

I tried another station. Here too, wild protestations of pride. 'Resistance is the only answer,' someone called out, again and again. I wondered if I was tuned into Radio Riyadh until one of the joyful told the interviewer in an Irwell accent that she was a student at Manchester University. Saturday, she went on, had been the best day of her life. Since dead Jews did it for her, I was only sorry she hadn't been alive to see the crematoria of Belsen at full bore. As a rule, I didn't believe in invoking the death camps, but today I felt I owed my mother a mention of Belsen.

The longer I sat at my desk with the lights off and the radio on, the further I was from making sense of anything. I didn't know this room. I didn't know this school. I didn't know the hands that fluttered to my mouth. *My* mouth? Had I screamed, would the screams have been mine?

I was a man like other men, but I couldn't punch the air in celebration of the murder of innocents had my own life depended on it. But I hadn't been listening. There were no innocents. Only Jews, Israelis, Zionists. JIZ – a new mnemonic of hate.

I couldn't have said how many hours I remained locked in my office, listening to increasingly frantic footsteps in the corridor, but it must have been just before lunch when Isabel Lester, our art and handicrafts teacher, hammered at my door, begging me to let her in. She had with her a disturbing cray-oned drawing that showed a clothesline with severed babies' heads hanging from it by their ears. The artist was a five-year-old Turkish girl. Irmak. I asked Isabel, who was shaking, to ring Irmak's parents. 'Those weren't babies,' Irmak's mother laughed. They were cheeses. Irmak had only recently watched her grandmother hanging out bags of küflü katik peyniri. Delicious on flatbread.

'Is that like labneh, do you think?' I asked Isabel.

'I don't know what I think,' Isabel said. 'I've come to you to find out what you think.'

I told her to take the rest of the day off, but she lived alone and couldn't face her own company. 'Then stay in here,' I said, leading her to a sofa and covering her with my coat.

I wished she'd offered to do the same for me.

I, too, was unable to clear my mind of that clothesline of babies' heads. My phone did not stop ringing. Wild rumours were swirling. There'd been a pogrom. There'd been a Holo-caust. Thousands were dead. Jerusalem had been taken. Eilat had been stormed. I rang to check on Charmian. She had been listening to the radio and watching television. I could hear that she'd been weeping. 'It's because what we do know is so ter-rible and yet so sketchy,' she said, 'that deeds more terrible still invade one's thoughts.' That sounded like Shakespeare put into modern English, I thought. But I agreed with her. Who else but Shakespeare had words for what had happened? The gates to hell had been opened. Anything was now possible. No report was untrue. Each side put nothing past the other.

I decided not to tell her about the bags of labneh on the clothesline . . .

As, I would later learn, she decided not to tell me what Zoe's voicemail message said. You protect those you love.

★

The massacre was one thing. The minutes, hours and days that followed – the speed at which morality went into reverse – shocked me far more. Murder made its own sense. You killed. You outraged. You were caught. You said sorry and promised never to kill again. The rent in the fabric of civil society was mended, the guilty were punished, the innocent mourned, and everyone went back to believing in the possibility of justice. What was said and done in the hours and days following the massacre in the Negev, however, did not remotely conform to this pattern. Why, for example, if Jews had been slaughtered, were my neighbours across the road calling for the slaughter of more? Wasn't it a mark of civilisation to call for the slaughter of fewer? I didn't recall my mother ever mentioning crowds gathering outside Belsen on the day it was liberated, shouting for more Jews to be incinerated. Who ever heard witnesses to a fatal road accident asking the driver to reverse and run over the victim a second time? When it came to killing, wasn't humanity unanimous in thinking once was enough? Wasn't that the essential compact by which everybody lived – that the killing was to be rationed: just one per person?

Yes. But that was before the massacre of teenage partygoers and kibbutzniks gave men the licence to demand more.

This was a time like no other. Days emptied of all remorse followed days when it was argued that dismembering Jews was not the same as dismembering anyone else because Jews were excepted from the rules governing hate. Don't get me wrong. Barbaric adversaries were no surprise to me. I grew up hearing my mother speak in matter-of-fact terms of the ovens of Belsen. What was new to me was the educated esteem in which the old familiar barbarism was held. Teach people and Belsen will never happen again, the world said in 1945. We forgot that it depended on *what* we taught. We missed what should have been obvious:

15

that a university with the appropriate curriculum could be the perfect prep-school for a second Belsen.

In the history of hate, had there ever been anything like this rush of clerks and scholars to embrace savagery? Handsome Harvard professors with beautifully coiffed silver hair, little curls dancing into their shirt collars, appeared on television to explain that as it was morally allowable to kill a colonialist and, since Jews were colonialists, it was morally allowable to kill a Jew.

'Five minutes ago, Jews were detested because they were refugees,' I shouted from my armchair. 'Now they're detested because they're colonialists. Make up your fucking mind.'

He wasn't listening. Like Leonard in Eilat, he had a number of lies to refute. Such as that there'd been any sort of attack on Jews, qua Jews, at all. 'Didn't happen.'

'What about decapitating Jewish children to make labneh?' I shouted again.

This time he must have heard me. 'Zionist propaganda,' he said.

Again like Leonard, he had tears to shed. The difference being that his were tears of joy. Who knew, before 7 October, what would make so many people happy!

I stayed up all night to argue with the television until Charmian threw a sheet over it.

'You could have just switched it off,' I said.

'I wanted to suggest something more final. That's a winding sheet. The television's dead in this house.'

'For how long?'

'Dead's dead, Ferdie.'

'Not any more it's not,' I said.

We looked at each other. 'I'm sorry,' she said. Not to me. To more than me.

We lay awake in the dark, listening to each other breathe. That was something.

A few days later, on her suggestion, I cried off school and went to look at the pelicans in St James's Park. Take in a painting at the National, she said. Buy a bag of churros. Change the subject. Change yourself.

So that was what I did. Sat in the drizzle, watched the pelicans, read Montaigne. *Que sais-je?* My most favourite sentence in all literature. In fact there were some things I did know. Such as that humanity had lost its mind. That it had succumbed to bloodlust. That bloodlust begat bloodlust. And that its victim would eventually be me.

In the drizzle, *Que sais-je?* began to lose its allure. I was wary of the pelicans in case they were concealing grenades in their beaks. I couldn't get into the National Gallery because of a small demonstration on the steps. Inside, watched by a police cordon, a couple of activists had glued themselves to Rubens' *Samson and Delilah* a) because it was in Gaza that Samson pulled down the temple of the Philistines, which made him complicit in genocide, and b) – not impossibly – because they confused Rubens the painter with Reubens the delicatessen in Golders Green.

I tried to edge my way slowly through the demonstration and almost got to the top step of the gallery where I was spotted by a protestor, two of whose children were my pupils.

'Dr Draxler,' she said. 'It's so good to see you here.'

Fortunately, I recognised her – one of the creamy-skinned milkmaid mothers of our age, more girlish in their gymslips than their daughters. 'It's good to be here, Mrs Costello,' I said.

She touched my wrist. 'I'm Melody.'

'And I'm Dissonance,' I didn't say.

I looked around in order to depersonalise the encounter. Her innocence was hard not to focus on.

'So good that you're here,' she repeated.

'I love this gallery,' I said.

'So do I. But I mean so good of you to join the demonstration.'

'Oh, I'm not really here for that,' I said. 'I hope the painting is all right.'

'It will be. We are very careful which works we draw particular attention to. We don't choose paintings that might suffer permanent damage.'

'Draw particular attention to for what, exactly?'

'The succour they give to illegal regimes. A great work doesn't excuse a great crime,' she said.

No, I said, it doesn't, though I thought yes – taking the long view – it probably does.

I tried to avoid Melody Costello's eyes which blazed with the piercing white light of someone who'd seen God. I feared that if she ever allowed herself to look long enough at a painting the pureness of her gaze would strip away the paint.

She asked if I came to many such protests and I said no, I wasn't a protest kind of guy. She laughed a thin laugh. Did she think I'd invented an impossible category – a non-protest kind of guy?

'Our organisation enjoys good relations with many Jews,' she said.

I stiffened.

'Jews love their art,' I said.

She stiffened.

'What's your organisation called again?' I asked.

She gave me her card.

Melody Costello
Director
Artwashingtheoccupation.org

I thanked her and asked if she'd been glued to any artwork herself recently.

She shook her head. A lovely flower on a fragile stem. 'Not

for a while, unfortunately. Administration tends to keep me at my desk.'

'You must miss the fieldwork, Melody,' I said.

She looked around to be sure no one was listening. Then she half whispered, 'We'll be at the Whitechapel next week.'

'Who will you be glueing there?'

'Chagall.'

'For giving succour to Judaism?'

I'd taken her for a vestal enthusiast but she was not put out of countenance by my mockery. 'Might you come, Doctor?' she asked.

I held my breath. 'Yes,' I lied. 'I might.'

What else could I say? She'd called me Doctor, perfuming the word with her unsullied fragrance. She was a student of painting, whatever her politics. She knew what Delilah had achieved. And therefore she was a student of Jewish men too. She brought her face close to mine and then, God help me, we kissed. Chastely, a mere brushing of cheeks, but not, I feared – since we were enemies of sorts – anything like chastely enough.

I left her hurriedly, pushing my way through the protestors on the gallery steps. Had I only been strong enough I'd have done a Samson a second time and pulled the Temple down on the lot of them.

A CHOICE JEW

I had hoped, when I first took over the headship of Strawberry Fields Primary, to incorporate some of the suburb's vaunted multicultural liberality into the school's curriculum. I changed the school's motto from KNOW THYSELF to KNOW THYSELF BUT KNOW OTHERS BETTER. I invited representatives from every ethnic group to attend classes and comment on the school's teaching methods. Tailors from Bangladesh and bead-workers from Nairobi gave courses on their professions. Writers from Syria and Armenia read extracts from their memoirs at school assembly, while quilt-makers from Pakistan hung their work in the corridors. There is no Third World, I would say whenever the phrase popped up in conversation. There is only Our World.

The sweet mutual understanding of South London that had originally inspired me did not extend to the small group of ultra-Orthodox Jews who, it was true, kept themselves to themselves but did not attack members of other faiths in the streets, did not pull their hair or spit at their babies, did not throw bricks through their windows, did not climb into their cemeteries to upend their gravestones, did not break into their places of worship and pour water (let's say it was water) on their sacred texts, did not drag produce from the shelves of the stores, did not shout FASCIST at them as they went about their business or paint the word MURDERERS on their walls.

Though I had never been enthusiastic about this sect of believers whose default position on every decision was to defer it until the coming of the Messiah, I called out for their protection in

articles I wrote for the local and Jewish press. It was cruelly iron-
ical, I said, that though they were routinely paraded as trophies
on any march dedicated to proving the illegitimacy of all Jewish
claims to anywhere or anything, back in Strawberry Fields they
were treated as pestiferous Jews again.

Maybe they didn't mind. I conceded that. Maybe the trophy
march was worth it.

In short, though these brushstrokes of Jew-contempt spoiled
somewhat the idyllic picture of mutual respect I'd tried to paint,
Strawberry Fields Primary did a good job of keeping alive the
delusion of all-faith togetherness and curiosity – delighting in one
another's difference – in whose name I'd been awarded an MBE.

Until the school janitor, who had been away on vacation,
returned in unusually high spirits, running down the corridor
that divided the five-to-sevens from the eight-to-tens, waving
his mop in celebration of the recent ravaging of his enemies,
crying God is Great. Though I had done all I could to keep the
school free of partisanship, I saw at once that short of locking
him in the broom cupboard I would not be able to hold back the
tide of pro-Hasheen sentiment once it took hold.

'Go, Hasheen!' the nine-to-elevens shouted excitedly as he
danced in the schoolyard. Reports even reached my ears that he
had emptied a bucket of dust behind the bike shed and drawn
a map of the Holy Land with the handle of his broom. Here
the river, there the sea, and there – look! – his countrymen and
women struggling to be free.

'No,' I said, when I called Hasheen into my office. 'That, I'm
afraid, is a no-no.'

Hasheen looked downcast. 'It was my ambition to be a geog-
raphy teacher in my country,' he said. 'I like making maps.'

I explained that Strawberry Fields Primary was a proudly
free-speech school but I couldn't permit him to redraw the
map of the Middle East in the playground in celebration of the

presumptive or prospective slaughter of one ethnic group by another, however happy the slaughter made those who were made happy by it. It would confuse the children, I said.

The janitor looked puzzled by my choice of the word slaughter to describe a slaughter, explaining that it was God he was praising, not acts of violence.

I get that, Hasheen, I told him, but praising God for assisting in acts of extreme cruelty against another people was still performing acts of extreme cruelty against another people.

Those were filthy lies, Hasheen said.

'You're saying it didn't happen?'

'None of it. No sir.'

I rubbed my bald spot. 'Then what exactly are you celebrating?' I asked.

Hasheen's English wasn't perfect but he employed the past conditional tense with great expertise. 'I am celebrating what we did had it been true we did it,' he said.

In this, it has to be said, his thinking was no more byzantine than that of many better-educated commentators from around the world who argued that the Jews had asked for whatever hadn't happened to them.

God is peaceable, Hasheen insisted.

And a subtle grammarian, I thought.

'Then why are you making martyrs of murderers who haven't murdered anybody?' I continued.

But even his head was now beginning to spin. He flashed me his sweetest smile. 'You must ask the Jewish,' he said, 'why they have stolen our land.'

'The Jewish,' I replied, flashing him the sweetest smile in return, 'don't see it that way.'

And there with a shake of hands, we left it – the Arabic and the Jewish, each not seeing what the other saw.

★

I had no way of knowing whether Hasheen had publicly voiced dissatisfaction with me, but the morning after we'd exchanged words, my usually effervescent Jamaican secretary fell silent and, in the afternoon, tended her resignation.

'I feel I have nothing to say to Jews today or in the foreseeable future,' she wrote.

'This isn't a Jewish school,' I reminded her in person.

'I am not speaking to you,' she said.

'We don't have to speak,' I told her.

She kissed me on both cheeks before she left but put a finger on my lips. Not only didn't she have anything to say to Jews, she didn't want to hear anything Jews had to say to her.

'Only hear me out,' I cried as she quit the building carrying her papers in a cardboard box.

'I am not answering,' she shouted without turning around.

'That is an answer,' I called.

This time she put her free hand behind her back and showed me two fingers.

It wouldn't be long before the international community did the same.

For all the determinedly ecumenical spirit in which I'd so far run the school, I didn't see how I could put off addressing the Jewish members of my staff much longer. Hasheen was still running wild, radicalising toddlers, and no new replacement for my Jamaican secretary had yet been found. In fact, no one had even applied for the job. Was I an anathema? Had the school been proscribed? I had no choice but to call a meeting.

'Welcome, everybody,' I said, opening my arms as though to a great horde, though we were only six or seven in number and seemed, even in my cramped office, far fewer.

'This is like a gathering in the waiting room of fate,' said Elaine Muller, Special Educational Needs Coordinator.

'We are here to control our own fate, Elaine,' I rejoined. Rich, coming from a fatalist, but I was captain of a lurching ship. 'We must seriously put our minds,' I went on, 'to the likely effect both on our pupils and ourselves of what's happening, especially given the wildly different interpretations of the massacre that are already in circulation.'

'Almost all of it Zionist propaganda,' someone rejoined, 'beginning with the word *massacre*.'

I say 'someone' but I knew full well who that someone was. Max Axelberg, head of Drama and Creative Writing and my deputy. No one else put every other word I spoke in italics.

Max Axelberg, né Tony Evans – a 'Jew by Choice', he called himself by way of reversing the idea that Jews were chosen of God – was a convert to a form of Judaism whose distinguishing feature was an intense dislike of Jews who'd got to Judaism any other way. Jews like me, for instance. Jews who'd been born Jews. For which, if I understood his position correctly, we had either to apologise or perish. Ask what we had to apologise for and he would roll his eyes and look at his watch. Max Axelberg was, in my view, the person most likely, by virtue of his slow-burning inflammatory pacifism, to cause World War Four. World War Three, between Jews and those who opposed their presence in the Holy Land, was not concluded yet, and couldn't fairly be blamed on Axelberg whom it predated by several decades. But the flames of World War Four – between Jews and Everybody Else – he could claim a degree of credit for fanning. Some days it seemed that only I – in the environs of Strawberry Fields Primary School, at least – stood in the way of its starting in earnest.

It would be hard to say which of us hated the other more. But he rattled the bars of my self-confidence far more effectively than I rattled his. He'd been vouchsafed the truth, I – though I expressed myself vehemently – felt I had to find the truth

24

anew every time I spoke or wrote a word. What else was my vehemence but a palisade of sharpened pencils to keep the likes of Axelberg – the pious, the vouchsafed, the imperturbably certain – at arm's length. He made me feel flashy and superficial. I'd merely been born a Jew. He brought to being a Jew a lifetime of being something else. We owed him our gratitude. He could have chosen another people to harry. He had read and prayed his way to a confounding new truth about being Jewish – that you only were if you weren't.

We had met at school where he combined a love of theatre with devout Christian faith – 'Riches I heed not, nor vain empty praise,' he explained to those of us who were sceptical of all belief. At fifteen or thereabouts he was entrusted with a school production of the Gospel According to Matthew – think *Jesus Christ Superstar* without the music – for which I auditioned, hoping to get the part of Barabbas the firebrand.

'Not Judas, Draxler?'

'No, not Judas, Evans.'

'Then I have only two of the Three Wise Men and the Donkey left to find and I don't think you'd be right as a Wise Man. Which leaves only . . .'

'Yes, I know,' I said, 'the Donkey.'

'It's an honourable role, Draxler. It bore Our Lord into Jerusalem. I can see you making a lucrative career out of playing dumb animals.'

'I'm not looking for a career,' I told him. 'Riches I heed not, nor vain empty praise.'

'Your choice, *Draxler*,' he said.

Draxler!

He couldn't say my name without making it sound exotic. I should have been grateful. The other boys called me Drexler. He rolled a wet tongue around the soft syllables of my name and knotted his teeth around the x as though to double it. *Dthraxxth-ler*. Sure, there was contempt in the way he lisped it, but was it fantastical of me to hear envy, even the panting of hidden desire in it too? He wants my *x*, I thought. I am an adult film to him. I am the Christian equivalent of trayf. For which compliment I almost forgave him the donkey.

There was a truism I learnt at my mother's knee: those who hate the Jews most, most want to be them. I hadn't known for sure what Tony Evans thought of me at school. At that age you take things at face value. But it would come as only a small surprise when I found out he had remade himself as Axelberg, presumably because Draxler was already taken.

I lost track of him for a few years after we left school and only learnt of his transfiguration from his own lips at the opening party for a play by Arnold Wesker in which my wife Charmian had a minor role. Tony, as it turned out, was reviewing it for the *Jewish Chronicle*.

'Small world, Evans,' I said when I saw him.

'Axelberg,' he replied.

'You've got the wrong man,' I said. 'I'm *Draxler*, remember. Donkey Draxler.'

He shrugged. 'I know who you are,' he said. 'Axelberg, *c'est moi*.'

I feigned surprise. 'You mean as in *I'm Spartacus*?'

'No, I mean as in I'm Axelberg.'

I didn't ask how come. I knew in my bones how come. He had always had an eye on the spiritual main chance. I didn't blame him for wanting to be where the excitement was. Jesus was done. Jews were where it was at.

'Mazel tov,' I said, offering to get him a drink.

'Jews don't drink,' he reminded me.

All things considered, it was a good joke. Or would have been had he been joking. I laughed anyway. Whereupon he removed a folded yarmulke from his jacket pocket and placed it, with clumsy deliberation, where yarmulkes are meant to go. It was so big a yarmulke it covered his eyes. I reached forward. 'Let me show you how to wear that,' I said.

He stepped back. We might both have been Jews now but we weren't on touching yarmulke terms. Not that I was wearing one. I wasn't a yarmulke Jew. Except in the presence of the dead, I had always felt a fool in a yarmulke.

'So spill,' I said. 'Was there a blinding light? Did you encounter Moses on a pilgrimage to Bethlehem? Tell me.'

'So you can scoff?'

'We are no longer schoolboys, Tony.'

'Max.'

'Max! No more Tony?'

'Max.'

Another *x*.

'As you please, Max,' I said.

'As I *chose* . . .'

I didn't ask why he hadn't chosen Xerxes in case that was now his middle name. 'Whatever,' I said.

'See.'

'See what?'

'You're scoffing already.'

'Far from it, Max. Life is serious now. Look about you. We're in a room of actors who don't know where their next job's coming from. We are all characters in a tragedy, even when we think we're in a comedy. My scoffing days are over.'

In fact, I would have liked to thank him for choosing to be a Jew, but how do you do that unironically?

He eyed me suspiciously, from underneath his yarmulke. But, for the convert, the need to relive the miracle of found faith trumps all precautions. It began in Atlanta where he'd been a guest at a week-long convention of Gospel singers, writers, painters, directors. How to make spiritual art in an unspiritual age. On the third morning he suffered a sudden dissatisfaction. He woke with a bad back. His coffee was weak. His eggs were cold. The laces in his trainers broke. He took a taxi to the airport and caught the next flight to New York. At once his spirits lifted. It was while crossing Fifth Avenue without taking due care that a yellow cab hit him. (I imagined him walking with his head in the clouds, humming 'What a friend I have in Jesus'. Which he might have construed as scoffing.) He was in a coma in Mount Sinai Hospital for five days, attended by the best Jewish brain surgeons, and came to speaking Hebrew.

'So now I'm probably more Jewish than you are,' he said, pushing back his yarmulke and looking pityingly at my wine glass.

'Had I known we were going to be in competition,' I amicably quipped, 'I'd have got myself baptised. But I'm pleased to learn I might have been in some small way an influence on your conversion.'

'You weren't.'

Did that hurt? Yes. 'A real Jew, a nice, proper *menschadik* Jew,' I told him, 'would have expressed himself with more grace.'

'If we are to talk etiquette,' he corrected me, 'it is not the thing to accuse a convert to Judaism of not being the real thing. A Jew is a Jew is a Jew.'

It was at this point that my wife walked by carrying an empty glass. I called her over and introduced her to Max.

'Ah, the critic for the *Jewish Chronicle*,' she said.

He bowed, spilling his yarmulke. You have to learn how to wear these things. You can't just wake up from a coma in Mount Sinai Hospital speaking Hebrew and think you know how to manage the headgear of Judaism.

'Max is a recent convert and thinks he is more Jewish than I am,' I told her.

From her great, laconic, Gentile height, she looked him up and down. 'How secure do you feel in your Jewishness?' she asked.

'Entirely,' he said.

'Then you aren't what I'd call a Jew,' she said, wandering off to get another drink.

Whether that was the reason he reviewed the play badly we never found out.

How long he remained a drama critic for the *Jewish Chronicle* I don't know. Perhaps reviewing one Jewish play for a Jewish publication was enough to prove his bona fides, along with finding himself an already Jewish wife who had already Jewish children, a Jewish tailor, a Jewish hat-and-yarmulke maker and a Hebrew teacher who taught him the order of the Shabbes service so well that he could have led it in any synagogue in the country had the resident rabbi taken ill.

I lost touch with him until he applied to be my deputy. A post for which, though I thought him entirely unsuited, I couldn't oppose, given his impressive CV – a degree in Theology, Divinity and Religious Studies, experience in amateur theatricals, two publications, which was one more than me, and a far greater knowledge of devotional literature than my own. He'd published a short history of famous converts to Judaism and an even less successful graphic novel about Jamil, a Palestinian orphan who'd been brought up by a Jewish family in East Jerusalem, became a Nazi hunter and then joined Hamas when the Israelis accused him of forging evidence in order to gain preferment in government circles. It ended with Jamil learning that a bomb he'd planted was about to go off on a bus in which his adopted Jewish parents were travelling. The last drawing shows him throwing his own body on the bomb. To make up for poor sales, Max worked part-time at a small tefillin factory in Whitechapel.

Whatever he had been doing, he was not a person you'd have expected to find teaching drama at a primary school in Streatham, but by the definition of the Judaism he woke to in Manhattan, he was bound to seek out the company of innocent children, stand up for the oppressed, and practise humility. Besides, Strawberry Fields had a good drama department. Before my time, Harold Pinter was said to have taught here for a fortnight. Was that what attracted Max to the job, or did he apply solely to teach humility to me?

Here we now were, anyway, the choirboy and the donkey, together again. But this time as fellow Jews, no matter that one was born that way and on bad days wished he hadn't been, and the other had to prove his attachment to a religion that wasn't his by sporting a giant floppy scarlet skullcap that most resembled a blood-soaked dressing for a shocking head wound. If anyone looked as though he had that minute walked out of a massacre, Max Axelberg did. But he still held firm against the word.

'Just to be absolutely clear, what's your objection to it, Max?' I asked. 'A Jew is a Jew is a Jew, you once told me. Isn't a massacre a massacre a massacre?'

'What I have against that description is its certainty.'

'How, then, would you describe what happened?'

'At this present moment, I wouldn't.'

'But only recently you counselled me to get the school to show solidarity. What would we have been showing solidarity with?'

'A people's struggle to achieve self-determination.'

Whenever he used the word people, he meant people who weren't Jews.

'Would you mind terribly,' I asked, 'if I expressed it otherwise, as an act of unimaginable depravity? We're not that far apart.'

'Your judgement presupposes a great deal, Headmaster.'

'Such as humanity? Judgement always does.'

He brought out the worst in me. A flippant, ill-considered clever-dickery. Face to face with Max Axelberg I had only one tune to play. My excuse is that our arguments were well tried and well trodden. The very terrain carried us along.

'Inhumanity has been shown on all sides,' Max said.

'I doubt whether teenagers fleeing from a music festival can be charged with inhumanity, Max.'

'Such events don't happen out of the blue,' he said.

I felt a great weariness descend on me. I hated Max Axelberg. I hated his stolen name even if it was in essence mine. I hated his eyes, blinking back tears of ahistorical sanctimony behind faux-owlish spectacles. But above all I hated having to hate him. I was a teacher. I couldn't choose who I taught. Jews or non-Jews – they were all the same to me. But a volunteer woodlouse Jew who'd moved into Judaism only to gnaw away at it from the inside was a call on my resilience too far.

'I thought the civilised view on rape, Max – to choose one barbarity out of many – was that no circumstance can justify it. Or is rape not rape when the victim is a Zionist attending a music festival on disputed land?'

Axelberg adjusted his yarmulke. 'Not disputed, stolen. But I'm not going to defend a statement I didn't make.'

'Didn't make or wouldn't make?'

'You talk of rape as though you witnessed it, Headmaster. You weren't there.'

'I wasn't at the Rape of the Sabine women, either.'

'History has had the time to make up its mind about the Sabine women.'

'You think we should give it that long before we call the rape of the Israeli women rape?'

'Well, I certainly haven't got that kind of time,' said a retired

31

religious-education teacher who was said to have fought in Israel's war of Independence as a teenager and was welcomed into the staffroom to read the papers and snooze in the warmth; his faltering voice carried an other-worldly authority that brought a brief halt to a conversation in which neither party could be said to be conversing with the other.

After a break for biscuits, Max wondered if it would be fruitful to start again, say from the Balfour Declaration which, if we would permit him to remind us, many anti-Zionist Jews resisted.

'Isn't that in the nature of their being anti-Zionist?' I asked.

'I simply note the commonality of their dissent, Headmaster.'

'There are Jews who will oppose anything, Max,' I said.

'That doesn't nullify their opposition.'

'Nor does it validate it.'

'Here we go again,' someone said.

There being a pause, I asked, 'So from what stage in your Jewishness do you date your own dissent, Max? Are you pre-Balfour or post? It's a chicken and egg question. Were you a Jew before you were a dissenter or a dissenter before you were a Jew?'

A man more easily hurt now that he was Jewish than he had been before, Axelberg lowered his head. 'Your sarcasm isn't lost on me, Dr Draxler,' he said.

'You would be no Jew if it were,' I answered.

If anything proved that he was indeed no Jew, it was how ineffective he was at meeting sarcasm with sarcasm. On the other hand, that he had the Jew's over-readiness to blame his own people might have told in his favour as a Jew had Jews only been his own people.

I could not myself, as his headmaster, go so far as to accuse him of passing himself off as something he wasn't, but Elaine Muller did bring him to the brink of tears by wondering if he had only become a Jew the better to express anti-Jewish sentiments.

'Explain to me, Elaine,' he was able to say at last, 'why I would take upon myself the sorrows of the Jews only to add to them.'

'I don't know why you want to be a Jew, Max,' Elaine said, wrapping herself in her two cardigans. She cultivated the air of being an old lady though she must have been no more than fifty. Zionism had declined somewhat from its frontier days. The frumpiest of Jewish women were now its most fervent adherents, as though in defiance of the modishness of being anti-Zionist. 'But if you think you're doing us a favour, you aren't. We already have enough faint-hearts of our own, thank you very much.'

'Are you telling me to shut up, Elaine?'

'I might be.'

I should have stepped in at this point. I hadn't been awarded an MBE for running a madhouse. But where wasn't a madhouse right now? Where did any of the old rules apply?

'Well, if you won't call order, Headmaster, I will.'

At the sound of Gillian Wallenstein's bass-baritone, the staff-room windows shivered, as did I. She was an overqualified English teacher with an MA in Critical Race Theory – wasted, like most of our degrees, in deconstructing *Janet and John* in a Streatham primary school – a helmet of steel hair, and eyes that bored through whoever was fool enough to meet her stare. She wore long skirts denoting freedom from all assumptions as to femininity and shoes so flat they made her shorter than she was. Come upon her suddenly and you felt she towered under you.

Somewhere between sermon and song, between psalm and sarcasm, Gillian Wallenstein intoned her reprimand. 'As I see it, Mr Axelberg has nothing to apologise to Elaine about. If anything, it's the parochial Zionists among us who should be apologising to him. They forget why our civilisation has prospered for so long. To be Jewish is to love the world and move freely among all its peoples, not to dwell in ghettos of the mind with guns between our knees.'

'Amen to that,' said Axelberg.

'And what the hell would you know about carrying a gun between your knees?' an antique voice, quavering yet authoritative, called out from a chair beside the radiator.

The room fell quiet.

The little colour in Axelberg's face drained clean away.

Got you, I thought. You are too new a Jew to bear the scrutiny of an old.

'The Lord has spoken,' I said. 'I now call this meeting to an end.'

On the way out, the mild and reverent Elaine Muller, a woman who never missed an occasion to burn candles for the Jewish dead, who kissed every book she touched in the synagogue, and would never hurt a fly because the Torah forbade it, tore off Max Axelberg's skullcap, cast it to the floor and stamped on it.

'Sorry,' she said.

In the wake of one of the most terrible tragedies to have befallen Jews in more than half a century, opera buffa had come to Strawberry Fields Primary.

MUTTI

'There was a strange relief in it,' I told Charmian. 'It was all I could do not to stamp on it myself.'

'Perhaps you should have.'

'A Jew cannot desecrate a yarmulke.'

'You say Elaine did.'

'She's a woman.'

'Are you telling me Jewish law decides what is or isn't desecration on gender grounds?'

'I'm telling you that as leader of the school's Jewish minority it's my job to interpret the law. As it is to set an example of decorum. Call me the patriarchy.'

'What about an example of indecorum? It can't all be catastrophe, Ferdie. Even the Greeks knew they had to alternate their tragedies with comedy.'

'The Greeks weren't Jews.'

'That's no reason why Jews shouldn't be Greeks . . .'

My mother would have been too young to know about such things when she pissed into Hauptsturmführer Kramer's chlodnik soup. As I picture her doing it – which I know I should not – I see her laughing immoderately, obeying an instinct for vengeful mischief that needed no knowledge of classical theatre or familiarity with the conventions of opera buffa to justify it.

She was thirteen or fourteen and had been working as a nutritionist in the kitchens of Josef Kramer, commandant of Bergen-Belsen, for a couple of years, give or take, depending on what version of her biography she was relating and to whom.

Kramer almost certainly took liberties with her, and those I do not allow myself to picture. Chlodnik is a cold Polish beet soup which happened to be Josef Kramer's favourite dish in the whole wide world. Whether or not in search of the best chlodnik soup the camps had to offer, Kramer had progressed from Dachau to Sachsenhausen to Mauthausen to Auschwitz before settling down in Belsen where he tasted my mother's and begged the Führer never to move him again.

On the eve of the arrival of the British army at the gates of Belsen, my mother made chlodnik soup in the knowledge that it would be Josef Kramer's last. She wanted him to go to his certain death thinking of all that he would never taste again. So this night's chlodnik was to be the finest she ever made. There are people to whom she has told this story who have accused her of pandering to a Nazi. Alternatively, of disrespecting the Holocaust. On the eve of liberation, of all days, how could she lift her skirts and urinate in a camp commandant's supper? She has always replied that her only intention was to make a chlodnik to end all chlodniks.

I have a personal interest in this as follows:

Years later, safe in London, my mother gave birth to a baby boy who blew bubbles through his nose when he cried, whose chubby, clumsy appearance – as red as a German beetroot on the outside, as sodden as the River Fuchsmoorgraben within – brought back such intense memories of her greatest culinary triumph that she gave the boy the nickname Chlodnik – pronounced as though to cough up a week's worth of Baltic phlegm.

Ch – Ch – Chlordneek.

I was that baby boy.

I make no complaints. I could have shed the name earlier than I did. In strict confidence, I liked it – not for its associations with Hauptsturmführer Kramer, but for all it conjured of the Polish, Carpathian, Austro-Hungarian history I'd never known but which fermented, as it were, in my bloodstream. Not a history of intellectual or bodily attainment but of knockabout farce. To my ear a chlodnik was a clown, a chancer, a nudnik, a hayseed, a trickster, a shyster and blasphemer who brought the peasantry to God and cheated the Cossacks of their quarry. In the word 'chlodnik' could be heard the whole history of holy Ashkenazi impudence that had spawned mirth-makers and counterfeiters from George Burns to Philip Roth, from Karl Marx to Sigmund Freud. Had Sigmund changed his name to Chlodnik who's to say he wouldn't have garnered a wider readership? Would Chlodnik Marx have had fewer fanatical followers than his brother Karl?

I wish I had kept my nickname, is what I'm getting at. As Chlodnik Draxler MBE, FRSA, I'd be better placed to make a mockery of those who will dismember me in the desert the minute the opportunity arises. Ridiculing our enemies until they have no recourse but to pull their rifles on us is what we do; laughing the witless murdering lying literal-minded self-glorifying sanctimonious bastard racist Jew-dismantling sons-of-bitches out of business.

Thank you, Mutti. You gave me the opportunity. It wasn't your fault that I didn't grab it.

It was time I saw her. I had put off my usual weekly visit. That she hadn't rung me was a sign, I thought, that she didn't know what had happened. For many years her house had been a fortress protecting her from unwelcome report. She had the internet and radio and television but kept them switched off. What more do I have to learn about the world, she used to ask. As it turned out, quite a lot. She had to learn that Holocaust Denial in which, when all was said and done, she had an interest, had been superseded by a crime still more iniquitous. It was so crooked that no straight word yet existed to describe it. They don't deny atrocity, Mutti, they welcome it. Instead of *Never Again* they hang out a sign saying *Please Repeat* and then party in the desert when the pill's gone down. They can't get enough of killing us, Mutti. If you ask me what I think – and, with good reason, you never do, Mutti – there are more people wanting us dead today then there were when you were pissing in Josef Kramer's soup.

And telling her that would be of use to her how exactly?

Charmian was always anxious when I visited my mother. 'You come back more like her than she is herself,' she said. 'Anyone would think you'd been in the camps yourself.'

'I was,' I told her. 'Just because I wasn't born yet doesn't mean I didn't spend the last year of the war as a germinating idea inside her. Ask me what it was like in Belsen and I'll tell you. I can describe Josef Kramer's well-fed, hog-like face and the way he tucked into my mother's food. I can remember the smell of him. He was hanged in Hamelin prison in 1945. Albert Pierrepoint pulled the lever. I heard Kramer's neck snap. 1945 was one of my better years.'

'There are times,' Charmian said, 'when I wish you'd stay there.'

'At Mutti's, or Belsen?'

Dared she say it? Yes, she dared. 'Is there a difference?' she asked.

I kissed her. It wasn't fun being married to me.

It was my custom to take an unexpected present to my mother whenever I visited her. Not flowers. She didn't get the point of flowers. Not rare fruits or exotic chocolates. She couldn't taste them. And not a book. Once I gave her a signed first edition of *Schindler's Ark*. 'Why the hell do you think I might want to read this?' she asked.

This time I bought her a shredder.

'For me?' she asked, smiling her most acid smile.

How old was she? Ninety? Ninety-five? She had to be older. A hundred then? Older, older. A hundred and ten? I had done the sums a hundred and ten times and couldn't make them add up. The camps did this to time. They warped it. There were people yet unborn who would one day be sent to Auschwitz. And people long dead who were surviving it.

That said, I was, by temperament, an obfuscator. I wanted not to know anything for certain. I liked to live in the margins of doubt. Not knowing was a gift to my imagination. I could think things worse or better than they actually were. Worse, preferably. Imagining lent mystery to what was otherwise mundane. It pleased me to shroud my mother's mysterious life in more mystery still. A shredder might seem to contradict the logic of this. Wouldn't a shredder clear out what I wanted to stay congested? Yes, except that the very necessity of shredding implied there were shames and falsehoods to shred.

Whatever the maths said, when she smiled her caustic smile she could have been a beautiful, bitter thirty-five-year-old.

'Don't dismiss it out of hand, Mutti,' I said. 'A shredder could make all the difference.'

'What to?'

Not having the courage to say, 'What's left of your life,' I gestured generally at the letters on her table and the ancient invitations on her mantelpiece and the bankers' boxes on the stairs.

Did she not need all this to show future historians and scholars?

No. They had been through her possessions a hundred times. She had written memoirs. She had been written about by biographers. Every item she owned had been photographed and catalogued. What I wanted her to shred were the lees of her life. The bills. The begging letters. The abuse.

Me?

'There's so much of it, Mutti.'

'Which is why there is not enough space for a shredder,' she said.

'That's like saying you are too ill to see a doctor.'

'And what exactly do you think ails me that a shredder can fix? Constipation?'

Ails me! You could tell she was a reader. Talking to my mother, I thought, was like talking to Jane Eyre. It was she, by the way, who gave me *Daniel Deronda* to read long before it cropped up on a university course. 'I hope you're taking some of this with a pinch of salt,' she said.

'You mean the Zionist sections?'

'No. The non-Zionist sections.'

Well, she claimed the English nineteenth-century novel saved her.

From what?

From the twentieth century.

Except that it didn't, did it?

Nothing did, I knew. Nothing saved anybody.

Some got away, was the best anyone could say. Some escaped. But to escape is not the same as to be healed.

To be healed one needed time, and between the twentieth and the twenty-first centuries there hadn't been time enough.

I believed you had to make your own time – forget, look away, destroy the evidence and the memories, change your nature, change your attitude, change your profession.

And change your name?

It had crossed my mind. Where's Draxler from? people asked. Drexler I'd been called in school. Which the even wittier kids sophisticated into Fred Dreck. There could be no doubt I'd have fared better as Davenport or Drinkwater, though when I looked in the mirror I didn't see a Davenport or a Drinkwater.

A Deronda yes, but that would not exactly have made me more English. In the end, if it had been good enough for my mother to stay Draxler – she never married my father and so never took his name – it was good enough for me.

Mutti, Mutti . . . She had a fierce, embattled face with which she had held me captive since I first opened my eyes upon her half a century before. She couldn't produce her own milk – she had Belsen to thank for that – and so fed me from a bottle which she jammed into my mouth like a petrol pump. I cried. A problem child in my first week. Bubbling through my nose. A true Chlodnik.

In my early teenage years I tried to outstare her. I rarely lasted five seconds. She didn't blink. She was afraid of nothing, least of all death which appeared to have forgotten she was still alive. I carried a photograph of her as a young woman around in my wallet. It wasn't necessary. She remained young in the flesh, glowing, not loving exactly – well, not loving at all – but fiercely, egotistically protective. A warrior mother, great-grandmother to the race.

What was hers she would kill to protect.

Was it because I was overawed by her that I wanted to shred her?

Or was it because I was in love with her?

She had enjoyed fame as the author of a controversial memoir, *Trauma*, and then again, more widely, as the Nutritionist of Belsen, the real-life heroine of a botched 80s miniseries subtitled *The Girl who Fed the Nazis*, with which she'd refused to have anything to do. After which she faded from view, only to be wheeled out every Holocaust Memorial Day both as a living witness to horror and a testimony to the resilience of the Jewish people. It infuriated her to be turned into a relic. 'I live in the here and now,' she told journalists who did their once-a-year exhumation job on her. 'I can't commemorate as past something that is present. The camps are of today, and so am I.' She cited the Austrian philosopher Jean Améry who refused to get over Auschwitz, who declared himself against forgiveness and vowed to keep his wounds undressed. I do the same, she declared.

In my heart I applauded her. Live it all as though it's still happening, Mutti.

So why the shredder, in that case? If it was all still happening, none of the evidence should be removed.

Allow me to be a contradiction. I was a peace-loving headmaster who made his pupils shake hands after the most trivial fallings-out, a bolshy melancholic with a clown's nickname and ambitions who found nothing funny, a father who upset his daughter and a son who applauded what he opposed.

And besides, when they came for my mother again, things would go easier for her if she had a clean sheet to show them.

'It's time for a clear-out,' I said.

She sat in her chair, her back straight, watching me tear open the box the shredder came in. For a second, she closed her eyes. Was this the secret of her sempiternity – a thousand infinitesimal catnaps a day?

'Then you can start by clearing out that box,' she replied, opening her eyes.

'Mutti, there's no space to breathe in this house. There's no air here.'

'Then open the windows.'

'How? These windows have been screwed shut since Suez.'

'A sensible precaution, wouldn't you say? So far no one's been able to get in.'

'And nothing's been able to get out. Mutti, I'm worried about you.'

'So you've bought me a shredder?' She eyed it hyperbolically. She could have been a great comic actress, I thought, had she not chosen to be a great tragic one. In a hyperbolic eyeballing contest with my wife there was no saying who would come out on top.

What was it with me and actresses?

It was wrong of me to use that word 'chosen' even to myself. What choice had she exercised, a little girl in Josef Kramer's kitchen? What choice did I have as that little girl's little boy, still wondering in middle age what sort of Jew to be?

But I was sticking to my guns. There was always a degree of choice. Screwing down the windows was a choice. Not poisoning Hauptsturmführer Kramer, commandant of Bergen-Belsen, with a vegetarian blutwurst that a fat rat had twice shat in was a choice. Pissing in his chlodnik soup was a choice.

'Just be patient,' she said. 'I'll be gone soon.'

We both know she wouldn't ever be gone. History had embalmed her, like an Egyptian queen.

'Look,' I said, once again throwing my arms wide, a gesture that embraced the folders of correspondence under the dining-room table, the Babel towers of cuttings from newspapers and magazines on the sofa, interviews, profiles, articles by and about her, photographs, reels of film, videos, and the files of complaining letters and legal threats she'd sent to editors over the years along with the smaller number of replies. 'Dear Agata Draxler, Thank you for your . . . etc. . . . please be assured . . .'

How many letters had she written? How many had she got me to write for her when I was small? How many was my brother, poor oscillating Isak, still writing in the Orthodox Jerusalem bedlam to which, for his own safety, he'd been confined? Letters to me, letters to her . . . *Get me out of here.*

('Ech, Isak?' she would say whenever one arrived, written in red ink on purple paper with references to Isaiah. I the same. 'Ech, Isak.' He was a *tsedraiter*, a nutter. We had no time for *tsedraiters* in our family. Our history had been too grand. We

43

had suffered on an international scale. Isak's parochial nuttiness brought us down. No one made him grow sidelocks. He was his own decision – and that decision reflected badly on us. I put him in brackets even now ('Ech, Isak') hoping that no one will notice him.)

But my mother was right to suspect it wasn't Isak but her history of being immured inside herself I wanted to shred. Not because that, too, diminished us – on the contrary, it contributed to our grandeur – but because I wanted to lighten its burden. Too much, Mutti. There's too much in there.

It hurt my own heart that hers would never be well, that her brain would never be still, that I couldn't give her a holiday from herself.

'I just think this place needs decluttering,' I said.

Decluttering! She put her head to one side and looked at me with one eye, like a rare parrot that had just flown in to learn the art of euphemism.

I stared back at her, though I doubt my eye had any of the sardonic savagery of hers. In silence we imagined a world shredded of her presence.

'The *world* needs decluttering,' she said at last, by way of concession.

'Yes, but we have to clear our own space before attacking anybody else's.'

'Then start by taking that horrible contraption out into the garden.'

'Mutti, you don't have a garden.'

She closed her eyes.

She knew what I was thinking the minute I thought it. *You don't have a garden Mutti, because you had only to look at a flower to kill it.* With her children she had second-hearing. She heard if they skipped a heartbeat. Family for her was a continuum of blood. If one spilled a drop, they all spilled a drop. Family had no beginning and no end. Hence no forgiving, no forgetting, no shredding.

Agata had never told a child of hers she loved it. But she would know if he had cut his finger anywhere in the world.

She tossed her rich abundance of hair. A horse's mane. To go with her teeth. Was she showing me why there couldn't ever really be another woman?

She was wrong but I was glad she tried.

I had never had much hair myself. I was born already receding. She knew when she first saw me that I would not be a warrior in her great cause. I introduced interfaith classes in my school. I made the children learn about Jesus and Muhammad as well as Moses. She was not at all Orthodox but she'd have liked me to be a synagogue-goer with a dozen Jewish children. And a Jewish wife. And thick hair. It was her unshakeable belief that the thin-haired were cowardly and disloyal. 'Don't you think it's time to forgive and forget?' her thin-haired, common-law English husband said in 1950. 1950! Measured by trauma-time, 1950 was a mere ten seconds after she'd served the beast of Belsen his last ever chlodnik, yet my poor gutless father thought it was time to forgive and forget.

She didn't bother to answer him for the final twenty years they were together as the last of his hair fell out a strand at a time. Name an apostate who had good hair.

She closed her eyes.

'How's your spikey daughter getting on?' she asked suddenly.

'She's your granddaughter, Mutti.'

'Who'd know?'

'Mutti . . .'

'And stop calling me Mutti.'

'*Mutti*'s what I grew up calling you. It enfolds me. It makes me feel protected.'

'You're too old to need to feel protected. You sound just like

45

your father. You've got his hair. I handed you both the eternal torch of justice and you both dropped it.'

'It's the eternal torch of fury, Mutti.'

Why did I say it like that? What did I have against getting even? What had pacifism ever done for us?

She made a distasteful sound through her teeth, like ski blades cutting through ice. Tsk, tsk. Teeth that were all hers. Such teeth. Such a jaw. Samson slew a thousand Philistines with the jawbone of an ass. With my mother's jawbone he could have slain a thousand more. Was it any surprise that it was asked of her, this precocious young woman who taught the Nazis how to chew their food healthily, 'Whom did she bite?' – *Wen hat sie gebissen?* – to get where she got. Looking at her, I felt what I had felt all my life – that she was magnificent in her obduracy. Beautiful and hardened, like a sword of steel. The beauty of someone who had passed through flames.

Whereas I? Ferdinand the Moderate, a Prufrockian headmaster of a liberal, multifaith primary school by Streatham Common, what fires had I walked through?

'Go on, say it, Mutti. I am no son of yours.'

'Of course you are a son of mine, just not the one I expected.'

'And the shredder?'

'Take it away.'

She might as well have said the same of Zoe about whose welfare she briefly enquired without bothering to wait for an answer.

We parted without kissing. There had never been kissing. Charmian had to teach me how to kiss my daughter. Now she was probably kissing the man who had signed her copy of *Orientalism*.

It had turned dark outside. It made no appreciable difference. Neither the curtains nor the windowpanes had been washed since I grew up here. The books and bankers' boxes gathered dust inches thick. The settee was threadbare, the cushions flat. The carpet had been hoovered down to the brown boards beneath and now wasn't hoovered at all. The Stannah stairlift was long unused, the proof that no attempt to make life easier was welcome. 'The gloom is a necessary adjunct to my state of mind,' she told me once.

Even Josef Kramer would have hesitated before daring to switch on a light.

I let myself out and then, as I had done for the whole of my adult life, let myself quietly back in. A charade by which I silently showed my consideration for her. And by which, in her non-acknowledgement of it, she showed her consideration for me.

It was more than consideration. It was love. But we were wary of the word.

'Mutti,' I heard her call up the stairs faintly, as though not expecting or wanting to be heard. 'Mutti, darling.'

Long after her mother had died, she went on calling up the stairs for her.

'NOTHING WILL COME OF NOTHING . . .'

'How would you have responded,' Zoe asked me once, 'had God told you to do that to me?'

'Do what darling?'

'Cut my throat.'

We were sitting in the chill-out area of the local gym – Zoe's idea that I accompany her there, try to lose a little of my podginess on an exercise bike while she signed up for Yoga and Pilates and Zumba and whatever else sixteen-year-old girls did to keep themselves trim and beautiful. We were drinking raspberry smoothies. 'The colour of blood,' I joked.

'Human sacrifice is no laughing matter,' Zoe said.

Some months before, I had taken her to St Petersburg, where Charmian was filming, to see the ballet, visit the Hermitage and eat food which she found disgusting. It was there she told me I had to lose weight. Of the paintings that caught her attention in the Hermitage the one that engrossed her most – though she was silent about it at the time – was Rembrandt's depiction of the Old Testament story of Abraham agreeing to carry out God's will and sacrifice his son.

'Christ, Dad, what kind of father was he?' Zoe asked on the plane home.

'God or Abraham?'

'I was thinking of Abraham but, since you ask, both.'

We went through the usual hoops. Young person appalled by

authority and obedience, old person engaged by the subtleties of loyalty and love . . .

'Sticking with Abraham, if I may, Rembrandt paints him as exquisitely solicitous, covering Isaac's face with his hands to spare him the sight of what he is about to do . . .'

'And to spare himself the look of terror in his son's eyes. It seems to me he is as concerned for his own feelings. If he cared so much about his son, he'd have told God where to stick it.'

'Oh, Zoe, you and your theological subtleties. There is also an angel in the painting, about to stay Abraham's hand. Like you, God wants Isaac spared.'

'And had the angel not appeared?'

'We don't know. We are not meant to know. What makes the story so terrible is that uncertainty.'

'What makes the story so terrible, Dad, is Abraham's willingness to put his love for God before his love for his child.'

'We are witnessing a moment in the history of humanity,' I suggested, 'where precisely the issue of competing acts of devotion is on the table . . .'

'What's on the table, Father, is the body of a young boy who trusts his dad.'

'A young boy who is about to be spared.'

'At what cost to his psychology? At what cost to the trust a child is meant to have in its parent?'

I kissed her. Lovely lucid Zoe whose mental safety in this world of crazy ideologues I, like a thousand fathers, now feared for. 'I won't be sacrificing you, Zoe,' I promised her.

'We'll see about that, won't we,' she replied. 'But it's good to know that if God orders you to, you'll cover my eyes so that you don't have to see the fear and sadness in them.'

And now, here we were again, in our gym clothes, drinking blood-red smoothies, and worrying about Isaac's mental health.

'And yours,' Zoe reminded me. 'Only a deranged father would have agreed to this.'

'It's a fable, Zoe. It's an interrogation of our faith.'

'No thank you. *Your* faith.'

'Your mother's faith is scarcely less bloody.'

'That's because the Jews plays a major part in it. Didn't I once hear you say that Christianity was Judaism interrogating itself? You like that phrase, obviously. I can see why. Interrogation's a nice euphemism for murder.'

'No Jew kills anybody in either story.'

She laughed. 'It's all killing, however you justify it. Killings are us. Correction – killings are *you*.'

'Ending killing is what we have always been about, Zoe. If anything, we've ended too much. Thou shalt not do this. Thou shalt not do that.'

'Those are just self-pleasing words. If there's one "thou shalt" the Jews should have been given it's thou shalt not bang on about thy virtuousness. Thou shalt shut the fuck up about thine ethics.'

'Zoe!'

Her laughter had turned to anger. The secondary emotions didn't suit her. They shrank her face. 'I'm going for a swim now,' she said.

It was clear to me then that she was going to be trouble. Letting her go to Petra on an archaeological dig was a risk we should not have taken. She was bound to meet someone who would influence her for the worst. Unless she would turn out to be the one who malignly influenced him.

'Sit down,' Charmian said, a few weeks into the new deranged world we now inhabited. It was more an order than a statement. 'Sit down, Ferdinand.'

Ferdinand not Ferdie. 'Ferdinand' was reserved for serious business.

I sat down.

'Prepare yourself,' Charmian said.

'Prepare yourself' was reserved for tragic business.

Prepare yourself, Ferdinand, meant someone dear to us had died.

'Zoe!' I cried.

'She's all right. She's not ill. She's not been harmed.'

'What is she then?'

'You remember that morning on the Common when we heard what had happened. Over there. In Israel.'

What had happened? Why didn't she call the massacre a massacre? Television presenters couldn't say the word 'terrorist'. My wife couldn't use the word 'massacre'. How long before we'd be referring to that sunny day when some nice Arabs crossed over from Gaza for a tea party?

'Of course I remember. It's not a morning I will ever forget.'

'And you remember how I rang Zoe to see if she was all right, and I told you there was a message on her phone?'

Why did I go cold? Why did a rivulet of icy water trickle down my back?

'And?'

'I don't know how to tell you this . . .'

It was my turn to worry about Charmian. She couldn't look at me. I took her hand.

'What did the message say, Charmian?'

'*Good morning, freedom.*'

'Anything else?'

'*The resistance rises.*'

'Anything else?'

'*I share my exhilaration with the brave people of Palestine.*'

'That it?'

'I put the phone down.'

'Have you rung her since?'

'I'm too frightened of what I might hear.'

'Should I ring her?'

'Only if you want to suffer a cardiac arrest.'

'So what do we do?'

'Allow her to express her feelings.'

'How about disowning her?'

'How does that work, Ferdinand? She has already disowned us.'

'So we sit on our hands?'

'What else?'

'And wait for the tantrum to blow over?'

'It's more than a tantrum, Ferdinand.'

'I'm her father. I know a tantrum when I see it. She's in a tantrum because I was willing to sacrifice Isaac.'

'I don't know what you're talking about, but we have to grant her the right to express what she believes.'

'Even if what she believes is drivel.'

'If saying that helps you, say it. But it doesn't help me. And it certainly doesn't help Zoe.'

'So we do nothing.'

'Nothing can be something.'

'Explain that, Charmian.'

'Nothing doesn't make it worse.'

'There is no worse.'

She shrugged.

But since I had no better solution I too put my weight behind nothing on the grounds that nothing could be something.

THE SHIRT DRAWER

It was to be a few weeks before I spoke to my mother again in person. She'd kept me away on any number of pretexts – she had a cold, she could hear I had a cold, she had an article to write, workmen were digging up the street. Then, quite uncharacteristically, she rang to ask if I could come over. In that time the Carnival of Gore had upended the world. Morally, we were living on another planet. I passed people on the street who had green faces and one eye. Some had eleven fingers. Many had turned themselves into placards. You couldn't move from your house and not know we'd been taken over. My mother had long since stopped going out so I didn't have to worry that she'd see or hear things that would make her heart stop. The giant Georgian housekeeper who came three times a week kept the house the way she knew my mother liked it. Doors fast shut. Windows impenetrable to light or change. Whatever Margalita knew about what was happening outside my mother's four walls, she kept to herself. She had the build of a bouncer. News would not have dared to push in past her. 'You are so big,' my mother said the day she employed her. 'You make so much noise. I'd like it if you went about with bare feet. And when I want conversation, I'll tell you.' Yes, Mrs Draxler. So not a word was exchanged. The television was never on. Newspapers were delivered but not read for weeks. The telephone was not answered to anyone but me. So whatever word of the insanely disordered world reached my mother's ears came from my lips only.

There was, though, something discernibly different in the way she greeted me on the phone this time. Indeed, there was something discernibly different about her ringing me at all, asking me to come over so soon after my previous visit. 'I like to measure out my pleasures,' she'd said drily when I remarked on her reluctance to see me more than once or twice a month. So why now?

'I assume you want me to come over to collect the shredder,' I said, pausing to give her time to say there were more important matters to discuss. Such as telling me she loved me.

'Yes, yes I would like you to get rid of that monstrosity,' she said, as though that monstrosity was the last thing on her mind. Couldn't a mother and son just exchange pleasantries once in a while? I asked if she was well. 'Ech, well! You?'

'You know,' I said. 'Well enough.'

'Well enough for what?'

'For talking to you, Mutti.'

'That's good. There are a few changes here I'd like you to know about.'

'Changes?'

'Personnel. Sleeping arrangements . . .'

'Mutti, you aren't getting married?'

'Chance would be a fine thing,' she said.

I laughed. 'I don't believe any Austrian woman has ever said that.'

'I certainly haven't.'

'So what then?'

There was a long pause. 'Your brother is here.'

'Isak?'

'Do you have another brother?'

'From Jerusalem?'

'Where else?'

Didn't that have to mean he'd told her about 7 October? Quite possibly he'd flown over from Israel for no other reason *but* to warn her. '*Mutti, pack your things, it's happening again . . .*'

'And when you say *here?*'

'Here. With me.'

'Is there space?'

A thought occurred to me. Had I known in my bones he was coming? Did that explain my purchase of the shredder – to clear the house for him? Or *of* him? It was part of the disordering of things that prescience should be in the air. What promised to be the future had happened aeons ago. Everyone was a seer.

'I thought I'd put him in Mutti's room,' my mother continued.

She waited, as though expecting me to protest *'And what do you intend to do with your Mutti?'* For a moment I wondered if she feared I didn't know Mutti's Mutti had left the house in an oblong box more than thirty years before. Had the pretence been for me all along? Did my mother worry I didn't have the strength to cope with my grandmother's death? Every now and then the world struck me as a place in which everyone felt bound to protect me from pain and sorrow – poor thin-skinned, bookish, fragile Ferdie. Everyone except Zoe to whom I was Abraham, God's executioner.

Funny. There was a sense in which I preferred to be seen as Zoe saw me. A daughter who hates you at least spares you the insult of pity.

It briefly occurred to me to wonder if my mother knew about the massacre and was keeping all mention of it from me. A perfect circle of leaving the unsayable unsaid.

'Do you need help getting the room ready?' I asked.

'It's ready,' she said. 'It's been ready a long time.'

Her words shocked me. Ready a long time for whom? Isak? Had she always been hoping he'd return? Longing for him to return, even? Or had she been keeping the room for me? For when Charmian threw me out? *Here's your son back. I'm up to here with all the Jew talk. He's your doing. You Holocausted him. You called him Chlodnik. Your turn to live with both of them now.*

55

Or – or! – she'd readied the room when she dreamed the massacre the year before last.

'So—?'

'So come over. Isak is keen to see you.'

'You mean he's here?'

'I just told you.'

'I didn't think you meant *here* here.'

'Well he is.'

I held back for three, maybe four days. The killings had sent me into slow motion. I had suffered no personal loss but the space I moved in, like the air I breathed, had acquired a different density. At times I felt I was moving backwards. There was nothing ahead of me I wanted to reach. All the good things were behind me. 'What is there to say?' I asked people who were good enough to enquire how I was. In truth, there was a lot to say but I lacked the words to say it. The language I'd been reading and speaking all my life assumed a common enterprise of imagination and compassion. Words were there to help us navigate our way to truth. But not any more. Suddenly words subverted truth and what before had been a horror had become a blessing. It was as though God had decided without warning to throw in His lot with the Devil.

Other people had moved on to the inevitable next stage. Our killing them. But I wasn't ready for that. We hadn't done with their killing us.

Charmian was watching me, as though afraid of what I might say or do. Zoe had gone missing and was living wild, wherever those who had started to take to the streets decanted at the end of a march. I had gone back to work but had not yet addressed the school. It was as though I'd morally retired. Had someone offered me work on an allotment I'd have taken it. And as for Isak himself, well, Mutti said he wanted to see me, but I wasn't sure I wanted – or was ready – to see him.

Up until this moment I had supposed him to be in Jerusalem forever, in what wasn't quite a yeshiva and wasn't quite a mental hospital and wasn't quite a care home and wasn't quite a bench overlooking Temple Mount where all the Messiahs sat waiting for the call. In my mind, I pictured wherever he was living or studying or rotting or having visions as a madhouse, which doubled as a description of the inside of his head.

Unkind of me. Let me come clean about the obvious: he wasn't the brother I wanted, in so far as I had wanted a brother at all. He wasn't the sort of Jew I admired. He wasn't a good advertisement for our people or my family and, by extension, he wasn't a good advertisement for me. To understand that you need to know how family works for Jews. It is the rock of our faith, the knot intrinsicate that binds belief and behaviour, self-realisation and self-worth. It is the metaphor enabling us to speak about ourselves as a people. We are a people because it is through our kin that we come to a realisation of ourselves. If family has done a better job than God in keeping us together in the worst of times, it has also driven us apart in the best. Family can abash us as no God ever can. Who is ashamed of their God? We can drop Him when He doesn't deliver, but we don't say that, by the words He utters and the company He keeps and the clothes He wears, He demeans us. Whereas you can and do say precisely that about your brother Isak – who looks nothing like you and yet does a bit, and who thinks nothing like you and yet, in all likelihood, does a bit. Is this what motivates Jews who march with people who openly seek their extermination? Are they so ashamed of their provincial Zionist uncles and so desperate to prove they bear no relation to them that they would rather resemble their murderers?

He was three years older than I was but cut off from me, in a world of his own, from as far back as I could recall. We shared a bedroom and a bathroom though I never saw him bathe. This is more an observation about the selective nature of my memory than it is about his personal hygiene. I blacken his name and his body with every recollection. Though I do remember, for sure, that in his teenage years he masturbated into his shirt drawer, a location chosen partly because the chest of drawers had a mirror above it in which he could see the repugnance in his face as he spent his seed, and partly, I think, because he thought that spending in his shirt drawer kept the act out of the sight of God. When I was too young to understand, I asked what he was doing. 'Expelling all the devils in my body,' he said.

'So why do you do it every day?'

'Because the devils keep coming back.'

Since then, I've thought that expelling the devils in one's body is a good description of Onan's curse.

This horrified Charmian when I told her. 'You Jews!' she said.

'I can't help what I am.'

'Listen to me. If you had devils in your body I'd have been the first to know.'

I laughed. 'Could your not knowing be because I had expelled them all?'

'The only devils in you,' she said, 'are in your head.'

Shame there's no Onan of the brain in our literature, in that case, to teach me to expel foul thoughts.

After what I've said about Jews and their too-too-close relations with their families, you will understand why my brother shamed me. His habits, it seemed to me, were clearly marked on his face. Aside from the obligatory maniacal ringlets – the *payos* – he had nibbly, hamster's teeth, a wet mouth, and that premature moustache all religious Jews seem to have from the earliest age. Did I look like that? I didn't regard myself as a religious Jew, but what if I was even more fanatic than my brother under the skin? Could passers-by have seen that I didn't bathe and masturbated into my shirt drawer?

I doubt he was the cause of shame to Mutti and Vati that he was to me. They were past wondering what people thought of them – the voluptuous Austrian survivor and her bare-boned, stuttering English civil-servant companion – by the time he was born. They packed him off to some sort of seminary run by Haredim in the holiest corner of Jerusalem, more to allow him to be with like-minded Jews than to wash their hands of him. But he was a mystery to them and I could feel a weight fall from the house when he left. 'Now let's sort you out,' I remember my mother saying to me.

I couldn't decide whether that meant I'd be easy by comparison, or hard.

He had chosen a bad time to be back in London. It was my duty to warn him not to wander about the streets as he'd been free to saunter through Mea Shearim in Jerusalem, reading a battered prayer book and muttering to himself. There had been no orchestrated attacks on plain-sight Jews in London yet, but there had been individual insults and assaults and shops selling pickled herrings had been daubed or broken into. Cut your *payos*, Isak, I planned to say. Or stay indoors.

Ha! If one of us was going to be attacked in broad daylight, it was me. The Isak who rose to greet me in my mother's kitchen bore no relation to the Isak I hadn't seen for twenty years or more. The ringlets of religious observance were gone. So was the black hat and the regulation rabbinic suit. He wore jeans and a T-shirt showing the dates of a recent Rolling Stones concert. Would I have known him had my mother not told me he was here? In my bones, perhaps, but not with the sensible and true avouch of mine own eyes.

'So,' he said. 'No kiss for your big brother?'

'We don't kiss in this house,' I reminded him.

'Then it's time we started,' he said, taking me in his arms.

He didn't smell. Funny, but I felt bad about that, as though he was lesser than himself. He'd been odd, uncouth, wispily Messianic, marked out for madness. He stood out. Today he could have been any man who'd been to the gym.

I told him he was looking well. So well, I wondered if he'd taken up surfing or roller-skating. Breakdancing. Bodybuilding even. This was my tactful way of saying I no longer saw in him the boy who grimaced in the mirror above his shirt drawer. 'Looking well' was probably overdoing it a bit. With his accustomed beard gone, his skin had that sickly whiteness of creatures that live under stones. His lips, too, were drained of colour. Soft. A lover's lips even.

He showed me his biceps. On one was a delicate tattoo of a butterfly. I was right. He had been working out. For a dread moment I thought he was going to lift me up.

'Impressive,' I said. Meaning the biceps.

'And the tattoo?'

'Pretty,' I said.

'It's to show I'm out of the chrysalis at last.'

Yes, of course, that was what his whiteness reminded me of — a pupa.

'I get the significance of the tattoo,' I said. 'But I'm surprised.'

'With my choice of a butterfly?'

'That you have a tattoo at all.'

'Because of that Leviticus shit?'

He meant the injunction against cutting or marking or otherwise desecrating our flesh. I agreed with Leviticus. 'No,' I'd told the teenage Zoe when she asked for money to be scrawled on in a backstreet of Soho. 'You will not desecrate the beautiful body you were born with. You are perfect as you are. I am the Lord thy father and I have spoken.'

Would I have still objected had she asked for a butterfly like Isak's?

Yes.

I admit it. I am an absolutist. Call me Leviticus man. No cutting of the flesh. No marks. Show a bit of respect. If not to God, to your father. And if not to your father, to yourself.

Never mind Abraham: was my denying Zoe even the most delicate butterfly, the real reason she had given space on the chaste canvas of her half-Jewish body to portraits of Islamic terrorists?

I skipped the Leviticus shit to ask Isak what brought him to London. Was he done with Jerusalem or was this just a flying visit? I didn't ask if he'd come over just to show off his butterfly.

He looked, I thought, a little shamefaced. 'I've been here,' he said, 'some time . . .'

'So how come you only show up at Mutti's now?'

'I wasn't sure of a welcome.'

'You want a welcome?'

'That isn't what I mean.'

'So what have you been doing? Where have you been?'

'Here and there. Getting the lie of the land.'

'For what?'

'Just seeing how everything feels . . . And, you should know I'm here with a woman.'

'Mazel tov,' I said. Whoever the woman, she had to be better than his shirt drawer. 'Is it serious?'

'*She* is.'

'And you?'

'I want to be serious but I'm not sure I know how. How did *you* know how?'

'I don't understand the question. You meet someone and you love her – or him – or you don't.'

'But how do you know if you love her? I wasn't taught. Who taught you?'

'It's just in you, Isak. Who taught you to love God?'

'I never did. Looking back, I think I must have hated God.'

Something wicked whispered in my ear. Did he see the face of the God he hated every time he opened his shirt drawer and did the thing he did there?

No. That thought was too depraved even for an age in which feminists applauded rape.

'And now?' I asked.

'Now I love no one and hate no one. Respect no one and . . . what's the opposite to respect, Mr Headmaster?'

'Disparage?'

'That'll do. I love no one and disparage no one. Where I've been there was too much disparagement. Too much of the chosen-people shit.'

'Whom did you disparage?'

'You name them, we disparaged them. Everyone was unclean except us.'

I didn't ask if that meant he'd bathed more in Jerusalem. But I did say, 'It works both ways, Isak. They think we're unclean too. I was called a dirty Jew at school. Isn't that just how enemies talk about one another?'

He took a moment to think about that. 'I'm not sure it's just the enemy thing,' he said. 'I think God's to blame. All Gods. It's only believers who think they're cleaner than anyone else. I've lived among them, Ferdie. All that apartheid shit.'

I breathed out hard enough to blow away his little butterfly. 'Not you too, Isak!'

'You have to call it for what it is, Ferdie.'

'But you don't have to call it for what it isn't.'

'When were you last there?'

'I've never been.'

'Never? Not even a brief visit?'

'Never.'

'So how do you know?'

'I just know. I was in Cape Town once for a conference of headmasters. Apartheid was over but still lingered. You could smell it in the air. Blacks still didn't dare look at you. Or, if they did, they looked with the legacy of terror in their eyes – vengefully. No one describes Israeli society that way. War is not apartheid. Neither is a wall. Be honest with me, Isak – do you fear contamination when you pass an Arab in the street? I bet you feared mixing milk and meat more.'

'Right this minute, little brother, I wouldn't want to meet the rage burning in any Palestinian Arab's eyes.'

I lowered my head. Right this minute I didn't want him to see the rage burning in mine.

We fell quiet, then he returned to marvelling that I'd never been to the country in which he'd missed out on the godless, carefree youth I'd enjoyed and on whose behalf I had a lot – far fucking too much, if you asked him – to say.

'You don't visit an idea,' I said.

'What do you do with it?'

'You entertain it.'

'I've tried that. I entertained the idea of God.'

'But you won't entertain the idea of worldly love.'

'On the contrary. It won't entertain me. It thinks I'm unworthy.'

'Of love?'

'Of anything.'

'Even of being a Jew?'

'Especially of being a Jew.'

'Isn't that an indulgence right this minute? Shouldn't you postpone your Jew-unworthiness until there are fewer Jews feeling it?'

'That's like telling a pacifist to fight a war.'

'It is. Some times are better than others to be a pacifist. This is a bad hour to be a wavering Jew.'

'When will a good hour be?'

'You'll know.'

'What if I don't want to wait that long? I was a good Jew for more than thirty years. I did everything a good Jew was meant to do. I obeyed all 613 mitzvot twice a day. Now I'm ready to break them all three times a day. It's my turn to be the bad Jew, Ferdie. Next week I'll be going on a Shabbes peace march. I've even learnt the words of a song the kids sing. *From the river to the sea . . .*'

'Tell me you aren't going to sing that.'

'What would you like me to sing – the "Hatikvah"?'

'Why not? It's a stirring tune. I used to cry when they sang that at weddings.'

'You would.'

'Then sing "God Save the King" if the "Hatikvah" is too sentimental for you.'

'Don't know the words.'

'But you know the words of "From the River to the Sea"?'

'Those are the words.'

He made as if to kiss me again. 'No,' I said, 'not until you promise not to sing it. Sing nothing for God's sake? If you've had enough of being a Jew, couldn't you just be a non-Jew for a bit? The opposite to fanatic fucking Jew doesn't have to be fanatic fucking Jew-hater. There's going quiet. There's indifference. There's staying shtum. There's shutting the fuck up, as Zoe used to say.'

Now it was his turn to wax sentimental. 'Ah little Zoe. My favourite niece.'

'You've only got once niece. And you've never met her.'

He paused. 'Blood's thicker than water, bro.'

'Then try to remember that when you're marching with people who want to spill ours. Stand to one side, Isak. Cultivate fucking moderation at least.'

'Can't. I was brought up on all-or-nothing platform. As were you. Jews can only do extremes. Even moderate Jews have to be extremely moderate.'

'Then be extremely moderate.'

'Let me tell you something, Ferdie boy – Israel is the worst thing that could have happened to the world, for the Jews, for everybody, not because it's been a disastrous failure but because it's been a roaring success. Too many people never wanted it to go that way. Jews have been put on earth to demonstrate the shortcomings of mankind. We invented a God who regretted our creation from Day One and never stopped thinking of new ways to destroy us. Loyalty to that idea of human failure makes it impossible for people – Jews especially – to applaud Israel. On the other side are those who believe there is no other way for Jews to survive but this, and in pursuit of that survival grow hard-hearted. Call it a war between Good and Evil.'

'Which is which, Isak?'

'You tell me.'

We paused. Had I known where, among her papers, my mother hid her teapot, I'd have made us tea.

'So,' I said, 'how long are you staying?'

'For as long as Mutti will have me.'

'Well, she's hardly going to turf you out.'

'She might. I was never her favourite.'

'She didn't have a favourite.'

'Oh yes she did . . .'

It was at that moment that Mutti strode into the kitchen to see how we were getting on. I do mean *strode*. No stick. No shuffle. Her back straight. Her head high. The matriarch.

'Like a house on fire,' I said.

Was that a smile I saw? There's a Yiddish verb that all Jewish families have recourse to – all families but mine, that is. To *kvell*. To take inordinate delight in someone – as a rule, your own children. We were too far gone in sourness to take inordinate delight in anybody. But I could have sworn my mother was *kvelling* over us – her two boys, united at last.

I gave him my hand. He smothered my face in kisses. 'More of this anon, then,' he said.

'Anon? You mean the next world?'

He squeezed my hand. Hard. Yes, he had definitely been spending time in the gym.

I let myself out then, automatically, let myself in again, expecting to hear my mother calling up to her Mutti. But Mutti's Mutti was gone. My *tsedraiter* brother occupied her place now.

I knew what he should have sung on those self-flagellating marches he joined in order to become a bad Jew: 'You Can't Always Get What You Want'.

PEST CONTROL

To anyone versed in the semiotics of groupthink, the Banksy that appeared one morning on my mother's security gate wasn't entirely a surprise.

The city had been growing more fiercely factional by the day. Wherever there was a college, small encampments flying black, white and green flags had been growing up. The atmosphere was reminiscent of Orientation Week. Some sold Turkish coffee. Though the weather was mild, the campers were dressed for a severe winter. Banks and businesses routinely deemed to be complicit in the occupation now had accusations of apartheid, ethnic cleansing, infanticide and a dozen more offences painted on their windows. While the posters on street furniture expressed entirely familiar opinions as to the rights of Zionists to be where they were and the rights of Jews to be anywhere, I sensed a greater virulence in the invocations of the Nazis, whether as heroes who should have gone on killing those they'd been killing, or as monsters with whom it was reasonable to compare those they hadn't killed enough of. This greater virulence, I surmised, was a direct consequence of the massacre. Permission to slaughter had been given, which fed the appetite to slaughter more.

The new moral logic of the universe – kill once and you have to kill again.

A Banksy, though, was of another order of public trolling. A Banksy holds your attention. That this one held mine, to the degree that it left me gasping for air, can be explained by its appearing on the street side of Mutti's aluminium security gate.

It hadn't been there when I called on her. I say 'security' but a child could have kicked it open. My mother, who'd had enough of gates and fences, preferred her protection to be nominal. There, anyway, when the tin can of a gate swung closed behind me, the Banksy unmistakably was, startling in its minimalist reduction of all meaning to a single, slightly smudged, stencilled newsprint image of an Arab street-sweeper shovelling Stars of David into a rubbish bin. *Keeping the World Clean* was its title.

We were back to that.

The phrases 'Pest Control' and 'Gloria In Excelsis' were clumsily hand-painted where a signature might have gone, had Banksy ever signed his work. 'Pest Control' I got. I'd read somewhere that that was his company name and I could see that it gloved nicely with *Keeping the World Clean*. No need to ask who the pests were. 'Gloria In Excelsis', however, defeated me. But then a good work of art is meant to do that.

I say it was *unmistakably* a Banksy, by which I mean unmistakably a forgery of a Banksy. I cannot claim to be an aficionado of street art in general or to know anything much about Banksy in particular other than that he took the populist side when it came to the politics of the Middle East. I also knew it was his practice to turn up suddenly like the Scarlet Pimpernel, whip out a stencil and a spray gun, execute his work at speed, and be gone. And this must have been executed at speed indeed, because it had not been there when I'd arrived to meet my brother an hour and a half earlier. Unless, which I thought unlikely, I'd been so agitated by the prospect of the meeting that I hadn't noticed it – a Banksy! – on my mother's iron door. Nothing else, I have to say, persuaded me I was looking at the real thing. Hard to be sure with a stencil, but somehow, though the conceptual side of it rang true, the draughtsmanship didn't. It lacked the verve. It didn't come shouting off the door the way Banksys were said to come full-frontally off a wall. The street-sweeper looked half-hearted and even just the smallest bit Jewish. Nor did it seem at all plausible that the famous artist would choose Abercrombie Villas in Brondesbury to show his latest work.

I don't mind admitting that I needed it not to be a Banksy, since I wanted it removed quickly before my mother saw it, and I didn't want to be worrying about how much it was worth or leaving it there long enough for Banksy lovers to slap an order on it and demand it stay *in situ* until my mother finally gave up the ghost or every Jew had been swept into the trash. Let it be a Banksy – let it be Banksy at his best – its sentiments were still odious and I wanted it gone.

But Banksy or no Banksy, there remained more troubling questions to be asked. Why had my mother been targeted for abuse? Who knew she or anyone else with Star of David associations lived here? Her door had been erected as a half-hearted nod to security, but even when she was in the public eye no one knew where she lived. All that aside, she was hardly a precipitant of the rage starting to be expressed all over London. She had not pronounced publicly on Zionism and this was not a Jewish area. Nothing Jewishly distinguished her house from the other high-gabled late-Victorian mansions in this garden cul-de-sac except, perhaps, a discreet mezuzah and the degree of its anonymity. It was not a house that looked out. It was not a house whose gaze you could meet. Could that have been clue enough? Target every dwelling that had a metal door and whose blinds were down and by the laws of chance you were bound to catch one of the Hated People. I quickly scanned the nearby houses to see if any others had been graffitied but none had. I could reach no other conclusion than that the would-be Banksy was meant specifically for her – a woman whose only possible politicisable crime was that she'd been in Belsen.

I had only one word for the sick, effronterous fuckers who had done this. But I was still looking for it.

There was no point calling the police to follow up on an incident they would almost certainly see as a prank. And even if they were to investigate, I didn't want my mother disturbed by their questioning. She was afraid of nothing but that was no reason she should be tested. Not *Der Stürmer* art again. She never did think humanity had learnt its lesson or ever would. 'I will not waste my time saying *Never Again*,' I recall her insisting. But that didn't mean she wanted her bitter pessimism confirmed as irrefutably as this. *Keeping the World Clean*!

Only people with verminous minds see others as rats and lice.

I found a paint shop on the high street round the corner and bought a can of paint – I rather liked Agreeable Gray by Sherwin-Williams, agreeable gray being the colour of my mother's door – a giant distemper brush and, in case that didn't do the job, a couple of spray-paint guns. 'Gun' might have been one of the words I'd been searching for.

How long did it take me to walk to the shop, buy the weaponry and walk back? Thirty minutes? If the Banksy had gone up in ninety minutes there was no reason why it couldn't come down again in thirty. Down it was, anyway. Not a trace of it remaining. The door wasn't even wet.

So had I imagined it?

Because I considered Charmian to be the custodian of my mental health, I rang to tell her what had happened. 'I need you to assure me I am not losing my mind,' I said.

She asked me to describe the circumstances. I began as the day itself began with my seeing Isak.

'Who's Isak?'

'My brother.'

'Did I know you had a brother?'

'Yes. He even saw you naked once.'

'That must have been a long time ago.'

'Nothing's a long time ago. In the blinking of an eye I'm a filthy Jew again.'

I had to explain that.

She listened in silence. Then wanted to be sure she'd heard me right. 'And it was a Banksy?' she asked.

'Well, you know. *Generically* a Banksy . . .'

'On your mother's door.'

'On it and then off it.'

'A Banksy?'

'Like I say . . .'

'I think you should come home right away,' she said. 'I'll have a hot bath ready for you and a couple of paracetamol. Unless you want me to drive over and collect you.'

'Best not. I might be gone when you get here,' I joked.

'Gone where? To heaven?'

I thanked her for the feed. 'Hell.'

She was outside our door, waiting for me. 'See what you've started,' she said, pointing out what had been deposited on our drive – vacuum-cleaner dust it looked like, bags and bags of the stuff, a disagreeable gray.

'How is this my fault?' I asked. 'Other than in my being who I am?'

'Who are you?'

'Oughtn't you to know that by now?'

'For the purposes of what's going on, let's just say you're your mother's son. And you've never yet come back from seeing her without bringing something dark back in with you.'

From which it will be apparent that my wife and my mother did not have a good history.

'If you mean I don't as a rule return in light spirits after an hour or so with a survivor of Belsen . . .'

'Come off it. She's survived it better than you have, Ferdie.'

'And as for today—'

'I know – it's Belsen all over again.'

I coughed melodramatically. 'Let's go inside,' I said, 'I'm choking on my own ashes.'

'It's vacuum-cleaner dust.'

'That's not a very metaphorical interpretation of what's been dumped on us, Charmian.'

'So you're choking on a metaphor now. What's it a metaphor for?'

'I'd have thought it's obvious. The dust denotes all that's left after the Arab street-sweeper has done with throwing us in the garbage. In case we'd allowed ourselves to forget, this is to remind us we're the sweepings of history.'

'So you're saying this is Part Two of what was painted on your mother's door.'

'Isn't it obvious?'

'By which reasoning this is also a Banksy installation.'

'A *forged* Banksy installation.'

'How do you know that?'

'Just a hunch. I've not heard of Banksy emptying vacuum-cleaner bags on people's lawns.'

'Whatever you have or haven't heard of, oughtn't we to get it valued?'

'The dust?'

'The idea of the dust. The intention. You don't need me to tell you how conceptual art works. The less tangible the better. A memory trace will do.'

'Then put me on the market . . . But before you do, I think there are a few more serious questions to ask. Such as how they know where my mother lives and how they know where we do. Are they spying on us?'

'And who do you think "they" are?'

I shrugged. 'You know them. Random anti-Semites.

Fourth-year students from SOAS. A gang of Oxford professors of Settler-Colonial Studies going round on motorbikes, armed with Dysons. There's vile stuff going up all over London. You'll probably find everyone with a Jewish surname has had their garden dusted.'

'I said we should have changed from Draxler.'

'What to? Kibosh?'

Why were we joking?

Because we couldn't believe that our enemies were really our enemies or that anyone really saw us as no better than vermin.

I say we, but Charmian was only a little bit Jewish by virtue of marital airdrop. I was her nearest device.

Leaving her out of it, how much more evidence did I need that the old revulsions were storming back? Why wouldn't I accept that people meant it when they said they wanted the world cleansed of us?

Arrogance. How could anyone be revolted by me?

This is called refusing to learn a lesson.

Never Again? Ha! To those who do not learn, 'again' is the most common of all occurrences.

Later that afternoon I had a phone call from Margalita, my mother's housekeeper. 'Mr Draxler, there is message on Mrs Draxler's front door.'

'When you say a message do you mean a picture?'

'No, a message. In spray-painting. Like you see from train.'

'What does it say?'

'I whisper to you so Mrs Draxler doesn't hear. *Death to Jews.*'

'Anything else?'

'Yes. *Stop* – word I can't pronounce.'

'Spell it for me.'

'*J.e.n.o.s.i.d.e.*'

'You sure?'

'Sure. I can photograph with camera.'

'Thank you. You are right to say nothing to Mrs Draxler.'

'Shall I wash off?'

'No thank you. I'll come over and see to it.'

I could, of course, have got Isak to do it. That he hadn't seen any of this himself or made his own efforts to remove it I ascribed to my mother's not wanting to let him out of her sight. Was there jealousy in my suspicion that she was mollycoddling him? Maybe making him chlodnik soup. How could there not have been? A son who's come back is infinitely more interesting to a mother than a son who's never been away.

I decided, anyway, that I would deal with the situation without mentioning anything to him. I would act stealthily and singly. A man alone. I still had paint. I would redact the offending words with my paintbrush and then hide in my car to see if anyone came to replace them.

And then?

I didn't know, but I did own a small designer toolkit which Charmian had bought me for a birthday long ago, the chief contents of which were a miniature claw hammer, a set of Phillips screwdrivers and a Stanley knife. This I packed into a rucksack along with water, biscuits, a packet of crisps and an alarm clock. If putting an end to this meant sleeping in the car all night, that's what I would do.

I kissed Charmian a warrior's farewell. 'Don't cut anyone's throat with the Stanley knife' were her last words to me.

Margalita had been right about genocide. *Jenoside*, for Christ's sake. I couldn't decide which was the greater offence – not knowing what the word meant or not being able to spell it. I could hardly correct it for them. What if the police came by on a routine patrol just as I was dotting the i?

How would that look in the papers? – *Headmaster of a mixed-faith primary school in South London caught spray-painting JENOSIDE on the door of the house he had grown up in. His mother, a one-hundred-year-old Holocaust survivor, was said not to understand her son's motivation. He had always been such a loving child.*

I drove around the neighbourhood for hours without seeing anyone behaving suspiciously. No new defamation of the Jewish race had appeared on my mother's gate. Eventually, growing tired, I parked my car at what I thought was a discreet distance from her house and settled in for the night with the hat I wore to hide my baldness pulled down over my eyes. I turned on the radio, knowing I would get nothing but the latest death count from Gaza. I thought my heart would stop. No buts, no whatabouts, these were bulletins from Gehenna. But there *was* a but. The numbers were relayed as though they were slaps across the faces of doubters. Not doubters of yesterday. Doubters from another age. Doubters from before the ice caps melted. You refused to believe what we told you about the Jews? Now what do you say! Every ruined Gazan family a counter in the game of WHAT DID WE TELL YOU?

It's not difficult to make a Jew feel guilty. What, after all, had we been telling you about ourselves for centuries? Why the Flood? Why Sodom and Gomorrah? Why Babylon? What was our history but one long story of being punished for our sins? With every statistic from Gaza the small part of me that had not yet been chastised accepted guilt. But guilt is a pendulum. You can only go so far in one direction before you must swing back. The worse I felt, the more I resented those who made me feel that way. This is how to harden a heart: first soften it, then leave it out to bake and suffer for too long in the sun. Whoever would make capital out of another's contrition will pay a price for it. Until that consequence, too, recoils and demands a recompense. This is the physical law of guilt, as taught to me, Ferdinand Draxler, by a thousand wise men and women, not the least of them being my mother.

Despite the earlier afternoon nap, I fell asleep. When I opened my eyes, I couldn't see out of the car windows. At first, I thought the vehicle was on fire and the windows had smoked over. It was only when I'd scrambled out that I realised it had been spray-painted white with me in it. It resembled an artwork by the artist who sculpted the memory-trace left by a familiar object when it no longer existed. The words NEXT TIME YOU WON'T GET OUT ALIVE were painted on the car bonnet in letters that dripped red paint like petals. Rather beautiful, I thought. Then I saw that in its purity the car resembled a sealed sepulchre strewn with mourners' flowers.

I walked round it several times before I noticed that the rear registration plate had been painted over. It now read YID 1.

Something else I should mention. The word GENOCIDE – yes, spelt right this time – had reappeared in mockingly formal copperplate on my mother's door. Together with an apology: 'sorry'.

ER IST EIN NAKED YID

In its succinctness, YID 1 worried me more than the verbose NEXT TIME YOU WON'T GET OUT ALIVE. Though maybe not as much as the question of how the graffitist knew a YID was sleeping in the car. The same question kept revolving in my head. I kept a low profile; these days my mother had no profile; who was keeping watch on us? And why?

The 'who' I couldn't answer for so long as they struck in the night with their stencils and paint sprayers, and the 'why' was a question that had defeated interrogation for centuries. Demoralisation seemed as good a motive as any. Converting Jews hadn't worked. Expelling Jews hadn't worked. Killing Jews hadn't worked. If anything, the crueller the envisaged final solution, the more lavishly the problem-people dined out on it as heroes and martyrs. Was it time now simply to wear them down? Harry them. Never let them alone. Just let the drip, drip, drip of contumely and contempt do the work. Keep telling them they were irreparably horrible until they grew irreparably horrible in their own eyes. Disappointment in oneself is the weak spot of the arrogant. The Jews were known for their proneness to self-disgust. What if exploiting that self-disgust until it became habitual – a sort of cancer of the conscience – would reduce and unhouse them as no previous attempt had? Leave it to the Jews themselves, in other words, to wish their own disappearance from the world.

A Zionist, my mother once told me, was a Jew with somewhere to live. Which meant an interior place of self-respect as well as a homeland. Whittle away at that interior place of self-respect as well as the homeland, dismantle the history from which they emerged again and again as defeated heroes, and at last they would be as the dirt beneath their own feet.

Compared to the scale of that ambition, spraying YID on my number plate felt almost affectionate. The word belonged to an earlier, more proletarian period of Jew-baiting. I felt I could work with someone who called me a YID. And calling me YID 1 – well, that gave me something to live up to. Kudos.

Nostalgic for the days when I was the wandering Yid, I drove home in the early morning and slid into bed, not wanting to wake Charmian. But her eyes were open.

'So how did it go?' she asked. 'I've been worried about you.'

'There was no need.'

'So nothing happened?'

'I wouldn't go as far as that.'

'So what did?'

I told her how I'd fallen asleep and woke to find myself immured in white paint with the word YID sprayed on my rear number plate. I forgot to mention the death threat.

She sat up, slapped her forehead, laughed and looked at me, searching my eyes for I didn't know what.

'I like it when people call you a Yid,' she said.

'You shouldn't,' I told her.

'I like it when it's fond.'

'It's never fond.'

'Yes, it is. *Er ist ein Yid.*'

'What?'

She shook my shoulders. 'You were the one who told me I'd once met your brother. Now he comes back to me, shouting *Er ist ein Yid* through the bedroom door. *Er ist ein naked Yid.*'

She laughed, I thought immoderately.

'I'm glad you find the memory of our first erotic encounter funny.'

'The best sex begins badly. Who said that?'

I didn't know but guessed Nietzsche.

'Billy Joel.'

I'd have preferred it to be Nietzsche. But we'd begun badly all right, not the least of our problems being my brother Isak in his flagrant sidelocks and flannel pyjamas, standing shocked outside my bedroom in the flat we briefly shared before his final banishment to the Holy Land. Had I known he was home I would not have brought Charmian back. He was supposed to be in shul, rocking backwards and forwards, apologising to Hashem blessed be He for both our sins. I was embarrassed by what he might have seen. As would Charmian have been had she had an embarrassable bone in her body.

'Let's pretend to be tigers,' she'd said.

'Is this what you do in acting school?'

'In acting school we keep our clothes on. Go on. Growl.'

'Grrr,' I said.

'Is that the best you can do?'

I apologised. 'I'm a very literal person,' I said. 'You're an actress. You know how to pretend. I was brought up to think of pretence as sacrilege.'

'And sex as sacred, no doubt?'

I feared so. She frightened me into flaccidity. Never mind tigers – I couldn't have imitated a kitten. 'I'm sorry,' I said, 'I'm just not up to this.'

She blew out her cheeks and slid off the bed. 'No hard feelings, Mr Ferdinand,' she said almost before her feet touched the floor.

I tried a second Grrr.

She shook her head sadly. I thought she must have been a good teacher. Patient and regretful with her students when they messed up.

I offered her my hand to shake.

'Why are you doing that?' she asked.

I told her it seemed the right thing to do.

'Because you think a drama teacher will appreciate a dramatic gesture?'

'No, because we have shared a human failure.'

She lowered her face and kissed me on the mouth, lips closed, tragically. Cleopatra remembering Antony. *Think you there was, or might be, such a man / As this I dream'd of?*

I couldn't understand why she was having so much trouble landing her first major role.

Before she left, I gave her a book. *Trauma* by Agata Draxler. 'This might explain why I'm so bad at this,' I said.

Whatever he'd seen, my brother Isak had wanted to explain me too. '*Er ist ein Yid*,' he said before shutting the door behind him. And Yids don't make good tigers.

Will there ever be an end to our apologising for all the things which, as Yids, we just cannot do?

MOTHERFUCKER

'I hope you don't see this one as a keeper,' my mother had said the first time she clapped eyes on Charmian, taking me aside but not bothering to keep her voice down.

Charmian and I had got together again — quite tigerishly, as it happened — in circumstances I will relate and were at a dinner to celebrate some cousin's wedding to some dentist at the Grosvenor Hotel in Park Lane, dressed, you might even say decorated, to prove Hitler hadn't won, in the high regalia of a priestly caste, the men in starched white shirts and mirrored shoes, the women wearing the last brocaded cocktail dresses before the Day of Judgement, their bosoms powdered, their lips carmined for seduction or supplication. Only Charmian, thrown together in a floral summer frock and sandals, didn't look as though she'd dressed to change the mind of God. I had done well, I thought, to talk her out of jeans.

I melted, as ever, into my mother's brutal gaze. She'd put me off a dozen women in the past, none as beautiful or as forceful as her. But I was in love with Charmian who was no pushover herself. 'It's a shame you were never in Belsen,' I said to her early on in our romance. 'You'd have made a fantastic survivor.'

I didn't buckle under my mother's scorn. 'What's wrong with her, Mutti?' I asked. 'You don't know a thing about her. You've barely talked to her.'

She arched her pencilled eyebrows. 'What do I need to find out that I can't see with my own eyes?'

'You mean because she's not—?'

'I don't care what she is or what she isn't. Ferdinand – she'll eat you alive.'

'Maybe I want to be eaten alive.'

Mistake. Agata Draxler, the girl-nutritionist of Belsen, clapped her hand over my mouth. Should I have bitten it? Joke or no joke, she did not want to hear one more Jewish man confess his beguiling passivity. Not here. Not again. Not ever.

Charmian saw the exchange without hearing it. But she could guess its import. 'For a woman her age,' she whispered as the dancing began, 'your mother has an amazing figure. I doubt she's wearing underwear.'

'Oh, come on.'

'I'm not kidding. Look at the way she moves her hips. You can see how she might have been able to win deferment.'

'Deferment?'

'Oh, I don't know the right word. Exemption?'

'Exemption from what, Charmian?'

Did she mean the ovens? No, no, she couldn't have meant the ovens.

She danced her fingers up and down my arm, pinching my flesh. 'You must want to fuck her.'

'Are you out of your mind?'

She pulled away. 'OK, if I'm upsetting you. I won't say another word.'

But a year later, at my poor, obscured, forgiving-and-forgetting father's funeral, she returned to the subject. 'What about now?'

'What about what now?'

'You must want to fuck her now.'

'You're crazy.'

'All men want to fuck their mothers at their father's funeral. Especially Jewish men. It's their big chance.'

'Big chance to do what? Take over the family business?'

'No, just to fuck them while they're vulnerable.'

82

'My mother has never been vulnerable.'

'You won't know until you try.'

'You're sick, Charmian.'

'Me sick? I'm a lapsed Low Anglican from Coventry. My parents have made love once. We didn't spawn a whole new science of the mind out of wanting to fuck our mothers – or our fathers . . .'

Let me tell you, I said – or should have said – about the Jews and their taboos. Not only don't we fuck our mothers, we don't *discuss* fucking our mothers, what is more we go to extreme lengths not to allow the word fuck and the word mother to appear in the same sentence. I don't expect such refinement to mean much to a lapsed Low Anglican from Coventry, but if we are to make a go of this relationship I think you should grasp the niceties that underpin my faith. For my part I will make peace with the barbarities that underpin yours.

But as the Philistine women were to Samson, so was Charmian the lapsed Low Anglican from Coventry to me.

LIKE A LAMB TO THE SLAUGHTER

We might have met in a school library that had a formidable collection of early work by Ronald Ridout, the prolific author of English-grammar textbooks, and I was certainly more scholar than wild man, but there'd been passion and surprise enough in the encounter. I'd raised my eyes from Ridout's *Better English* to see a bob of fashionably cut red hair appearing and disappearing from behind the library stacks, as though the person to whom the hair belonged had one leg longer than the other. There was something feral as well as farcical about the movement, like that of a shy creature looking for a book to eat. She emerged at last, loping out into the open on those long thin slightly incurved legs, swivelling her jaw like a giraffe chewing on an acacia leaf. She stopped at my desk and looked me over. Was she wondering if I'd make a good lunch?

Why I had to explain what I was reading and the reason for my reading it I don't know. Perhaps I didn't want her to take me for a schoolboy.

Ronald Ridout . . . Ronald Ridout . . . Yes, no, yes, the name meant something to her, but she didn't appear curious to know more.

She smiled at me in appreciation of my appreciation of her. *Yes, I am, aren't I*, her look implied. *Yes, I am everything you think I am and more* . . .

I danced my eyes at her. *Yes, yes, you are.*

Tall women know who to waste their time on and who not. Most men can't cope, even the tall ones. I was clearly one of those who revere whatever they can't reach.

She was an out-of-work actress doing a bit of supply teaching, and was said to have an easy manner with the pupils to whom she taught acting, dancing, mime, devastating charm . . .

'And anti-Semitism,' my mother surmised.

The gibe came out of thin air. Only in this had I ever found my mother conventionally possessive: she took every woman in whom I showed an interest to be an enemy of the Jewish people. In fact, Charmian came from a staunchly pro-Jewish socialist family of the old school. Her father, a union shop-steward in the motor industry, read novels by Jews and had lived on a kibbutz for a year when he was a young man. That was the best year of his life, he said. It was largely desert but he smelt hope there. 'We have a lot to learn from the Jews,' Charmian remembered him saying. 'They are hard-working, loyal and charitable. And half of them are creative geniuses. You could do worse than find yourself a Jewish husband when you grow up, Charmian.'

And I could do better, Charmian thought. At the age of nine, already a beanpole with her Irish mother's raging hair, she had been a feminist with no intention of finding herself a husband at all. But her father's words stuck. 'We have a lot to learn from the Jews.'

Ten years later the stage beckoned and there they were. The Jews. She ran into Harold Pinter. 'My father says I could do worse than find myself a Jewish husband,' she told him.

He looked her up and down quickly, as though that was all it took.

'Then I wouldn't waste your time with me,' he said.

He suggested she try Arnold Wesker.

Try! She was deeply insulted. What made Pinter think she was *trying* anyone?

They might be hard-working, loyal and charitable creative geniuses, she thought, but they're also fucking rude.

That was Jewish men done and dusted until she met me, a

Jew who had done and dusted himself, so to speak, a suppressed Jew who wasn't exactly in hiding, but wasn't exactly out there either, and for that reason wasn't what she'd been avoiding. There'd been a few at acting school who could have interested her, and who were certainly interested *in* her, but there was an air of self-abridgement about them, as though being Jewish were a serious accident that had befallen them and about which they would rather not talk. A bit like Pinter whom, she guessed, they were keen to emulate. As he punctuated his plays with silences, so they punctuated their biographies with omissions.

'No point being overtly Jewish,' one told her. 'There are no Jewish parts. I'm here to learn how not to shrug.'

'Isn't that itself a Jewish joke?' she asked.

'I'm learning how not to make those too,' he told her.

That was something her father hadn't explained to her about *the Jews*, that their sense of humour was a sort of perpetual carousel: once you'd got on you could never get off. Unless they threw you off.

Beneath the wistfully stylised self-abnegation of the Jews she met in acting school Charmian thought she detected a deeper malaise. They were keeping their heads down, as though hiding themselves. From whom? From their own reflections, Charmian guessed. But then, wasn't that the case with many actors? On the stage you could hide in plain sight.

She talked her thoughts over with her father. 'I don't meet any of those Jews you told me you met on the kibbutz, who danced and sang and made love late into the night. You smelt hope there, you said. When I repeat that to the two Israelis at the school they laugh. What are they laughing at, Dad?'

Retired now and widowed, he sat back in his chair and smoked. 'The word hope, I suppose.'

'Were you romanticising?'

'No. They were. They thought the future was theirs. Not any

more it isn't. I still write to some of the Israelis I met in the early days. Most of them doubt they have a future. They've had the hope knocked out of them.'

'By whom?'

'Who do you think? People who want to knock the hope out of Jews.'

'Why do they want to do that?'

'Ask them. Ask your friends.'

'They won't talk about it.'

Her father sat further back in his chair and closed his eyes. 'I don't blame them,' he said. 'They're dead tired.'

On another occasion he pointed the finger at the Stalinists. They too had admired the philosophy of the kibbutz once, but then changed their minds.

'Why?' Charmian wondered.

'Because they're Stalinists.'

'What does that mean?'

Her father wearily swatted the air with his open hand. He too was tired. He'd fought his battles. 'In a word,' he just found the energy to say, 'Stalinists started out praising Zionists as heroic pioneers. Then they discovered the word "colonist" and that was the Zionist goose cooked.'

'Isn't that what you are?'

'A colonist?'

'A Stalinist.'

'Wash your mouth out, Charmian. I'm a labour man. True socialists never took orders from Moscow.'

Much later, after we'd fallen out and fallen in again, I had to explain to her the difference between Stalinists and socialists. 'And what about Stalinist Jews and socialist Jews?' she wanted to know.

'I'd stay away from both,' I warned her.

'Because?'

87

'Because Jews bring out the worst in them and they bring out the worst in Jews.'

'Why?'

'Because there is a hidden fanaticism of revelation and betrayal in the Jews and a hidden fanaticism of revelation and betrayal in radicals and each reacts chemically to the other's extremism. Sit a Jew and a communist in the furthest corners of an empty room with the order not to exchange a word or a look and within an hour the place will be on fire. Unless they have so much in common they join forces, which is worse. A Jewish radical is a walking stick of dynamite.'

'I admire people of strong conviction,' she said.

'Then spend a weekend at a Jewish Voice for Peace conference,' I told her.

Not that I ever had. I just guessed.

'One more thing,' she pleaded. We were in my narrow bed. I make no secret of the fact that there was nothing roomy or voluptuous about me. On my little bedside table, alongside the regulation number of Holocaust memoirs, including my mother's, were three books by Ronald Ridout, proving my Englishness. In these early days I feared Charmian was with me to bone up on the history of the Jews rather than to bone up on me. I needn't have worried. Her father had recently died of losing hope and she wanted a replacement, that was all. I was a little bit fatherly. And she thought, moreover, that her father would have approved of me. I was her posthumous gift to Daddy. For a man who loved Jews, she thought, here's one from me.

So what was the one more thing she wanted me to help her with? Whether you could be an anti-Zionist without being an anti-Semite.

I sighed. I had lost enough friends answering that.

'Keeping it simple,' I said, 'you can't be anything without

being an anti-Semite. That's a joke. But if you want a serious answer – Zionism was the only hope European Jews had of getting out of Eastern Europe alive. Whoever denies them that is an anti-Semite. Next question.'

After the show-Hitler-he-hadn't-won wedding, Charmian told me she had a trickier question still.

'Go on.'

'Promise me you won't be angry.'

'I promise.'

'Can you hate a Jew's mother without being an anti-Semite?'

I turned over in my cramped little bed and faced the wall . . .

SNOWED UNDER

I tried to dispel all thought of her after that first, failed encounter but couldn't. Failure transfixed me. I couldn't get enough of it. On the pretext of having to do more research, I went back to the school again and again, hoping to see her high head above the stacks. But she didn't appear. At last, I summoned the courage to ask after her, only to be told she no longer taught there. She had only ever been a supply teacher, covering for the head of drama who'd been away having a baby. I sought out the head of drama who said she couldn't possibly give me an address but then went on to say – in God knows what spirit of mischief or prescience – that only that morning, coincidentally, she had received a postcard from Charmian from Kitzbühel.

It seemed that when Charmian wasn't a drama teacher she was a ski instructor.

Let it go at that, I told myself. Leave her alone. Leave yourself alone. She'll want you to bury her in snow and you'll fail again.

But, somehow, I found myself in Kitzbühel carrying a Green Guide and wearing an Alpine bobble hat.

I had never been to a ski resort and had no idea what to expect. Should I just go and stand at the foot of the glacier and wait for her to come flying out of the snow? In my mind's eye I saw the children she was instructing – in a carry-over from her drama teaching, it never occurred to me to think of them as anything but children – following behind her like so many ducklings, their knees buckled, all clutching hold of the rope that was tied around her middle.

'Where's the slope?' I asked the receptionist at my chalet. She laughed and told me Kitzbühel was all slope.

I went to the information centre and asked if they had a list of instructors. They gave me the numbers of several *Schischules* and allowed me to use their phone. That was when I realised I didn't know her surname. I tried them with just Charmian but the name rang no bells. What if she wasn't called Charmian anyway? What if she'd just borrowed the name from Miss Greenaway, theatrically, while she was away having a baby? Such suspicions were groundless but it was like me to entertain them. My suspicions were really about myself as a judge of character.

Is there any time when all the instructors come down on the ski lift, I asked. Say for lunch? But it appeared there were as many ski lifts as there were slopes. So that was that. I hadn't unpacked yet so it would be easy to leave, though leave to where I did not know.

I walked around the gingerbread town in a disconsolate frame of mind.

Snow? What was I to snow or snow to me?

I entertained a half-mystical belief in the persistence of ancestral influences. In my recent Austro-Hungarian past I must have encountered snow. Not impossibly I had skated. Waltzed in Vienna on New Year's Eve. And skied? I shook my head. Skiing was too recent. Further back in my genetic past I rode a camel. If only Charmian had led me back into the desert. We could have raced each other across the dunes. No doubt I would have lost, but at least in the desert I could have made a creditable fight of it; whereas here, in the alien snow, I could only too easily imagine myself lost, the Wandering Jew whom no one would help, a familiar and detested figure to the townspeople, the tragic lover looking for some mythical Charmian, until they found me one morning frozen in the snow, holding a petrified white rose.

And then I saw her, very much alive, coming out of a cocktail bar on the arms of two men.

She was in full après-ski wear, white Abominable Snowman boots, a fun-fur jacket the colour of cognac and the very hat I remembered Julie Christie wearing to entice Zhivago. She didn't recognise me when I called her name, and then, in a burst of crisp white laughter, she did.

'*Er ist ein Yid*,' she cried, clapping her hands. 'And Yids can't be tigers. Does being Jewish preclude you from skiing too?'

'It does.'

'Then why—? Ah, don't tell me you've come to find me.'

'Then I won't tell you I've come to find you.'

'Crazy,' she said.

I smiled my most trystful smile. 'That's me.'

She appeared to be on the point of moving on, then had a thought. 'Listen, we're going for a warming drink or two, if you haven't got anything better to do, why don't you join us?'

This was how I came to go on my first ever pub crawl in the company of Charmian and her fellow ski instructors, Thiago from Baqueira and Berndt from Innsbruck. Though not a drinker myself, I bought more than my share of drinks and passed the time between wondering which of them Charmian was sleeping with. Thiago intermittently held her hand and told her she had wrestler's wrists. 'Be careful not to get on the wrong side of me then,' she warned. Berndt was more the comedian. When Charmian took off her hat, which she'd been loath to do, knowing how well it suited her, Berndt sat it on his knee as though it were a cat. 'My Katyusha,' he purred, stroking it behind the ears. She caught my eye. See what I missed not being a tiger. They talked about their classes, making lewd allusions to learners of both sexes. It was only when Charmian admitted to being just a little bit in love with an American called Paul who had tried all their classes, and Berndt and Thiago admitted to being just a little bit in love with him too, that I woke to the realisation that she wasn't sleeping with either of them.

'I hope you're not hoping we'll try that again,' she whispered as the party was breaking up.

'Going to a pub in a foursome?'

'No. Going to bed in a twosome.'

I lied and shook my head. No, I didn't think it was a good idea. She didn't ask what on earth I'd come here hoping for in that case. But she did offer to give me a lesson in the morning. I thought that wasn't a good idea either, but said I'd like to watch her ski. 'You can't miss me, I'll be head to foot in scarlet,' she told me. I replied, with gallantry, that I wouldn't miss her if she skied in a bin bag.

And so it happened that I waited at the designated time at the foot of the designated slope until she appeared, high up and far away, a lick of flame, like something fiery falling from a star. Her goggles flashed in the sun. The snow sprayed from her skis. The closer to me she got, the less like a meteor and the more like a wounded bird she seemed. She carried her ski poles far from her body, as though afraid she might trip herself up on them. She drove them into the snow spitefully, then raised and seemed to wave them with a strange flapping motion. For a moment it really did look as though she might take to the sky. If she did, she would surely come crashing down. I wanted her to be graceful but had to make do with her being strong.

I was surprised to discover Berndt and Thiago at my shoulder. Something was amusing them. '*Du würdest nicht wollen, dass sie auf deinem Gesicht gelandet,*' Berndt said in a loud aside. The other laughed. I turned to look at them. 'I doubt either of you will ever be given that privilege,' I said. Only I said it in German. Not good German but I'd picked up scraps from

Mutti. Whereupon Berndt said to Thiago. '*Das ist der kleine Yid*.' To which Thiago replied, 'And, if I'm not mistaken, the little Yid is smit.'

Such are the moments when a man discovers if there's fire in his belly. The little Yid should have pushed the little *Schluchtenscheisser*'s face in the snow, but, as I must have said a thousand times, I am a peaceable fellow. I have a theory that it was because Arabs had always thought of Jews as pushovers that they found losing wars to them so hard to take. Losing to a bully twice your size is one thing. Losing to weedy, bespectacled readers of abstruse texts is another. Shame was what made the Arab countries unwilling to treat for peace. First they had to win. Then they'd see. So let Berndt and Thiago take me for a pushover. I'd triumph in the end. I'd walk off with Charmian. This was not quite logical. Berndt and Thiago had no romantic interest in Charmian, more fool them. But the idea of playing a long game, of the quiet, studious Jew finally stealing the girl from under the noses of the godless hoodlums and bully-boys, squared me with myself.

I relegated Berndt and Thiago to the moral sideliness in other ways as well. I needed to bring something to a woman before I could see a future with her. The rabbinic principle of *tikkun olam* – repairing the world – was inscribed on my heart. Even falling in love had to contribute to the spiritual amelioration of humanity. 'That's the burden we Jews carry throughout life,' I would tell my daughter, forgetting that as the daughter of a Low Anglican mother she was no more Jewish than the Archbishop of Canterbury. Watching Charmian fly from the sky to the ironic appreciation of men who did not feel about women as I did, I felt a great protective surge. What she needed above all else, I thought, was protection from herself. She was too big a personality. She needed a reflective, cautious man like me to shield her against the exorbitance that made her striking. If she was not careful she would expose herself at every turn to exactly the sort of ridicule that had diverted her ski-instructor friends. In a word, she needed a Jewish husband.

That she fell and broke her ankle didn't really have much to do with it, even though in later years she would wonder whether, for all she needed me, I brought her bad luck. She came off a bike, once, when I was out riding with her. And fractured a shoulder after colliding with someone in a roller-skating park as I was applauding her efforts. Jews were said to bring bad luck. She wasn't sure she believed that but she wasn't sure she didn't either. I didn't doubt it myself. Jews were walking evil-eyes. But we made recompense with kindness and companionship until the person we were a danger to gave up taking risks and stayed home. Thus, in time, do we repair their world.

But all that was for later. For now, Charmian was in hospital and I was visiting her every day with fruit and flowers.

And so, though we weren't yet a couple in Kitzbühel, we quickly became one when we got back to London.

As for what had welled up in her – there was a word for it. Idealisation. Permit me to see in me what she did. I had my shortcomings – not least of which, to her, was my inability to growl and bite her in erotic play, and of course my mother, who probably would have chewed her face off, given half a chance – but spiritually I was a tower of strength. I had wooed her, lost her, then wooed her again. I might not have been exciting but I was possessed of a quality she was smart enough to know she needed more. I was constant. I would be there in the morning. I had a heart dependable enough for two. She would learn stability from me. I would keep her anchored. And in the end, my unwillingness to savage her in play omened well for our future together. It gave assurance that I would neither want nor be able to savage her in real life.

A Jewish husband! Heavens! She'd never planned to have one of those. But what was there not to like?

Thus did the tigress lie down with the lamb.

A DAY OUT

What she couldn't have known was that there'd be a bloodletting in the Negev and that her husband, with whom, until that point, she had resided peacefully in Streatham, would think of himself as one of the victims.

How many months this had being going on – the Shabbes helicopters, the raging streets, the roars against which, no matter where you lived in London, you had to close your windows and bar your doors – I was the last one to ask. I had entered a second childhood of lying in late under the bed covers and only going out at the weekend if I had to. Who had ever heard of such a thing – a headmaster as unwilling to go to school as his pupils?

Charmian roused me as best she could. Waking me with tea, enlivening me with anecdotes from the invigorating, soapy world of make-believe she inhabited. But as my spirits sank by the day along with my supply of tablets to ease indigestion, palpitations, hyperacidity and non-specific Jew-burn, so her energy levels began to drop too.

'For both our sakes, get yourself going,' she said.

'Where's there to go to?' I asked. I could have been fifteen. I only just managed not to say, 'I hate you, I hate you.' But then I had a daughter who was saying that for me.

I knew that Charmian was right. I had to get going. Confront my fears. Face the enemy. Brave a march. Cheek a policeman. Kick an anti-Semite. That might still sound like the behaviour of a fifteen-year-old but at least, if I did get going, I'd be out of the house. My blood must have been lying in a stagnant pool in my stomach. Just the anticipation of its circulating round my body again made me giddy. 'I need a lie-down,' I told my wife.

'Oh no you don't,' she said.

Thus, psychologically accoutred for war, and carrying a couple of books in case I lost my nerve and had to sit on a park bench and lose myself in someone else's madness, I strode out into the still weak London sun.

This is a piece I wrote about the experience for a leading Jewish paper, changing my name to protect my identity. They didn't publish it. Apparently, every Jew in the country with a keyboard had submitted something similar.

It's as he is leaving Fortnum & Mason on Piccadilly with a box of dark chocolate violet and rose creams for his wife, a stollen for his mother and a brick-sized block of vanilla fudge for himself, that Frank Dexter runs into the fag end of a peace march, which is close enough to the fires for him.

'Not a good idea,' a policeman says, stretching out an arm.

'I agree with you,' Frank says. 'I think that peace marches that don't exude peace are a very bad idea.'

He is — for him — in high, sarky, trickster spirits. I am so limber, he thinks. I could skip out of my skin. Those are not his lines but it doesn't matter. Whatever gets him though.

'No, you,' the policeman says. 'It's not a very good idea for you to join this march.'

'Because I'm laden down with chocolates, do you mean? Must I have my hands free? Just so you know, I am not intending to join it. I am not a fan of marches.'

'What are you intending to do to it?'

'Avoid it.'

'And how are you proposing to do that?'

'By walking in the other direction and minding my own business.'

'The trouble with that idea is that the march might not avoid you.'

'It doesn't have to avoid me. I'm not an obstruction. It just has to take no notice of me.'

'That isn't as easy as it sounds. Your appearance is a bit of a provocation, wouldn't you say?'

'A provocation to what?'

'That is not something I am prepared to speculate about.'

'But what is it about me that people on this march will find provocative?'

The policeman hands him a flyer which he must assume has been given him by a marcher. It is impossible to believe a policeman is distributing such material. In bold letters, it says PARK LANE AND MAYFAIR AGAINST FASCISM and carries the assurance that Refugees Are Welcome Here.

'Very laudable,' Frank concedes. 'Who isn't against fascism?'

The policeman shakes the flyer in his face. 'Read it again,' he says. 'You can borrow my glasses if you like.'

Frank doesn't need them. The war-cry is clear enough. GET RACISTS, ZIONISTS AND ISLAMOPHOBES OUT OF PARK LANE AND MAYFAIR.

'Zionists,' the policeman says, prodding the word Zionist and then pointing to Frank.

'Me! What leads you to the conclusion that I am a Zionist?'

'It's not a matter of what leads me to any conclusion, sir. It's a matter of what conclusion the marchers will reach.'

'And to them I will look a Zionist?'

'To them you will look Jewish.'

'I am Jewish.'

'There you are then.'

'So when they say no Zionists, they mean no Jews?'

'What do you think?'

What Frank thinks is that he wishes he had stayed in bed. Is it really so obvious in this crush and in the midst of so many Levantine faces, that he's a Jew? He is wearing a short puffer jacket and a Lenin cap to conceal

99

his bald patch. He could be anybody. He holds his nose. 'Now how Jewish do I look?' he asks.

'Is that supposed to be amusing?'

'Even the Greeks alternated tragedy with comedy.'

'Well, I hope they were more amusing than you.'

'I'm just having fun, Officer. I've watched Jewish children hiding their noses in the school playground.' Then, fearing he has just outed himself as a child sex offender, he adds, 'I'm a headmaster.'

'Then act like one.'

'Touché,' Frank says.

There is a momentary stand-off as the policeman shakes hands with a marcher he knows. 'Lovely girl,' he says. 'Wouldn't say boo to a goose.'

'But will say boo to me, you think.'

'Sir, I am asking you for your own safety. Go back into the store, buy yourself some more fudge, and wait for the march to pass. You look too openly Jewish to be out here.'

'I'm openly Jewish now?' Frank wonders if he's misheard. 'What constitutes openly Jewish, Officer?'

He takes off his corduroy Lenin cap. Does the policeman fear the demonstrators will see it as a Topol cap? What are the words of the song? When he was a little boy called Chlodnik he would do a jig and perform a nursery rhyme to entertain his mother who took no notice. How would a jig go down now, he wonders. If I were a rich man. Ya ba dibba dibba dibba dibba dibba dibba dum . . . ?

As though he knows there's a song coming on, and probably which song at that, the policeman grabs his arm.

'Am I to assume,' Frank asks, 'that Muslims don't like musicals?'

'I don't know what Muslims like. You ask me what makes you look openly Jewish. It's the books.'

'I've told you – I'm a teacher. It's my job to read.' Frank shows the policeman his copy of England Your England by George Orwell and the pocket Montaigne he takes everywhere. Que sais-je? What the fuck do I know?

The policeman inspects the jackets. Frank wonders what he expects him to be carrying – A Jew's Guide to Organ Harvesting?

'It's not the books in themselves, it's the way you carry them.'

'Are you telling me there's an openly Jewish way of carrying books?'

'I'm not going to get into the aesthetics of your faith,' the officer says as though to suggest that on another day he would be happy to. 'One last time, I am asking you, for your own safety, to find another route.'

Standing his ground, Frank looks around him. He used to love this time of the day in London – the hairspring hour which Jews called havdalla, separating what was holy from what was secular. A good hour to stroll through Green Park or wander into the Royal Academy where, with luck, no protestors would be gluing themselves to innocent works of art. Protestors, protestors. Everywhere you want to walk or look, a protestor shouting 'Shame on you!' to another protestor who is shouting 'Shame on you!' to him.

Frank is sorry for the policeman, having to listen to these inanities all day long. He has a ruddy face, a gentle, gingery moustache and a baffled, disappointed expression. He's from somewhere like Tavistock, Frank thinks. He imagines him sitting in the Wharf watching the Tavistock Players performing Fiddler on the Roof *and joining in the standing ovation for the Tavistock Tevye. Funny how much people like Jews on the stage.*

Something causes the tail end of the march to raise its volume. The music of twenty-first-century London – the repetitive anthems and drumbeat slogans of a grievance that can never be appeased, mingling with technicolour tuk-tuk music and, over that, the occasional siren. Frank finds it frightening. He has heard seasoned protestors describing the joyous, peaceful nature of the marches they go on. But they are describing what it's like to be in the warm companionable belly of a demo, where everyone agrees with everyone. It's at the edges that such marches show their rage, at the point where the marchers encounter people who are not like them.

A marcher wrapped like a sleepwalker in a Palestinian flag looks hard

*at Frank. Remembering his vow to show no fear, to meet hate with hate,
to kick an anti-Semite, he bares his teeth. Grrr! 'Who are you staring
at?' he challenges. 'Never seen an effing Zionist before?'*

*In the scuffle that ensues, Frank hears the blood plashing through his
veins . . .*

What happened next, as I was about to be bundled into a police
van, I considered too private to include in my article – though
as it wasn't published it hardly mattered. Except that it did. It
mattered to my heart.

My daughter appeared. I didn't recognise her at first because
her face was scarfed. But I could hardly mistake her voice – thin
and strident, her vocal cords nothing like strong enough for
all the moral outrage she had set them the task of expressing.
Somewhere between anguish and frenzy, the sound resembled
the ripping of some very fine, tear-soaked material.

'Colonialist Zio pig!' she screamed into my face.

'Zoe!'

Dear, once independent-minded Zoe with the twisted teeth.
Funny we'd called her Zoe. Zoe the anti-Zio.

'Zoe,' I ventured again. I wanted to tell her to stop now. Take
the win. She'd done it. Anyone who didn't know what a Jew was
before, knew now. Her infectious lies had left what remains of
truth to float about the world like dandelion puffs. Blow on the
Jew's good name. We love you, we love you not? We love you
not. Soon, what remained of the Jews themselves would do the
same. One more breath of wind and they'd be gone, out into
the great godless nowhere. What Christianity couldn't quite
manage on its own, Zoe, with her terrorist boyfriend and baby
history of the world, had achieved.

In a twisted universe I should have been proud of her.

What was she doing here anyway? Did she work for Park
Lane Against Fascism? She knew I liked to spend an hour every

Saturday buying chocolates in Fortnum & Mason before nipping across to the Royal Academy. Had she tipped the police off? *Look out for a foolish old fascist in a Topol cap. But don't be fooled by his seeming innocence. He's a child-killer.*

Or was it sheer chance? For any Jewish father of a son or daughter at university, the likelihood of meeting them on the street, wandering from hate fest to hate fest, was high. There were Jewish families who had told their children to stay away from them, be gone, wash your mouths out, and only return when you can make an apology for your wretched pigmy-vocabulary defection. And if you can't? Then stay away from the family you've sold down the river forever.

In my youth I'd heard tell of Jewish parents saying the prayer for the dead over children who'd married out of the faith. Fanatics. How many shiva candles were burning today for children who acted as Zoe did? What was marrying out compared to murdering in?

I shook such thoughts from my head. You don't fight fanaticism with fanaticism. I wouldn't be sitting shiva for Zoe.

It would kill Charmian to lose her. I had to be honest with myself: it would kill me too.

But how was I to get over the memory of her screaming into my face as I was driven away? Colonialist Zio pig! It wasn't just the murderous contortion of her once-beloved face. It was the unadulterated stupidity.

So much, anyway, for going out, getting some fresh air, and kicking an anti-Semite.

THE HONEYSUCKLE HEDGE

Poor, deluded, ill-taught, self-disinheriting Zoe.

I am an educationalist. Ranked high among the literature of education I swear by is Cardinal Newman's *The Idea of a University*. It was in order that Zoe should learn how, in Newman's words, 'to think and to reason and to compare and to discriminate and to analyse', that we encouraged her to go to university. But instead of teaching her *how* to think, those charged with the cultivation of her reason taught her *what* to think. Zoe went into university bristling with animation and curiosity. She will come out of it a zombie. Who will be charged with her lobotomy?

Meanwhile, she was fast becoming the poster girl for the Boycott, Divestment and Sanctions movement, the Palestinian Solidarity Campaign, Jews for Gaza, Jews Against Genocide, Jews Against Jews, Jewish Daughters Who Want to Give Their Fathers Heart Attacks . . .

I'd returned to watching television. If Charmian didn't wrap it in a snowy winding sheet this time it must have been because she knew I needed the sugar rush of rage. The moment I turned it on I saw Zoe marching, mouthing, shouting, jostling, her eyes afire with a burning conviction of right, the snakes of endless fury coiled around her head, a goddess of vengeance with hatred dripping from her eyes.

Not for me the parental pride in seeing one's child on *University Challenge* or *Junior Brain of Britain*.

'Enough. Turn the fucking thing off if only for an hour,' Charmian begged.

'Can't. Sugar rush.'

'Look away, then.'

'I'll still hear it.'

She bought me earplugs.

No good. I still looked at the silent pictures.

A mask.

Still no good. I could make out Zoe's shape and shadow, the coiled snakes, the grimacing, the flames.

I knew her face as only a man who loves his wife can know the face of his daughter. I commemorated that love every time I looked at her. Saw the woman in the girl. Rejoiced in what the union had made possible. Our artwork. Yes, yes, there was a dangerous egoism à deux in that. More than a possessiveness – an appropriation, an avarice of love. But whatever is intense runs the risk of exorbitance. Must I apologise for that? I didn't only want her to be magnificent and magnanimous for me; I wanted her to flower for herself, to luxuriate in what she was capable of.

And that had been crushed, smashed, obliterated, by fanatic brainwashers who took upon themselves the right to think and feel and act for her.

Charmian hid the remote control. But a modern house has more than one remote control. Driven by a disgraceful desire to suffer pain, and as though certain that I would find what I dreaded seeing the moment I pointed the remote at the blank screen, I did just that and there indeed she was – ripping the poster of a hostage from the window of a disused bank and laughing. Laughing! Finally, my incensed teenage daughter had found joy. She wasn't alone. Two other girls, both heavily scarfed, were with her, also richly amused. Three daughters of Hades, in search of a Jew to tear to pieces, in the absence of which – why not? – a poster of a hostage (a murdered hostage, for all we knew) would suffice. Not all the poster would come away from the window. Zoe reached in her bag for a black marker – an eyeliner, was it, or did she carry black markers in her handbag? – and with that she defaced what was left of the picture, scoring it over and over as though to be sure no trace of it would ever be seen again in this world or any other. She knew a television camera was on her but took no precaution to cover her own face. Let everyone see what decolonising looked like. Whereupon even I had to admit I'd had enough. I ran from the room, not wanting to see her blow a kiss of unfathomable spite.

'I have never witnessed a more despicable act,' I said to Charmian who had been watching through closed fingers herself.

'Then you've led a sheltered life,' she said. 'But it was ugly, I agree with you.'

'It was more than ugly. That a child of mine . . .'

'Ours.'

'What?'

'Ours. That a child of ours . . .'

'Fine. Fine. Whatever you want to call her. I thought you'd be only too ready to disown her.'

'That's not how being a parent works, Ferdie.'

'It's not how being a child works, either. That a daughter of ours should plumb such depths of pettiness – Charmian, I'm not sure my heart will take it.'

She sat me down. She poured me a glass of water. She put her arms around me. She wondered if I needed an ambulance. Pills? A rabbi?

'A rabbi's not going to do it,' I said. 'No one below the rank of God will reconcile me to what I've just seen.'

'Then why don't you write to her?'

'I'm not ready for God being a she, Charmian.'

'I mean Zoe.'

106

'I write to Zoe? To say what? You disgust me to the bottom of my soul?'

'Maybe not in so many words. But tell her why you're hurt. Write to her in sorrow, not anger.'

'It would be a waste of time,' I answered. 'She's had sorrow educated out of her. She only knows allegiance and hate.'

But I did write to her. It was that or expunge all knowledge of her from my heart as comprehensively as she'd expunged the image of the hostage.

Dear Zoe,

Your double standards horrify me. You denounce all attempts to silence or remove or even argue with you as assaults on your free speech. Do you know how rich that is, when your every word and action is an assault on the free speech of others? The fact that you hate something does not give you the right to silence it.

Last night, on television, I saw you go further. What you did when you ripped down that poster was deny the person more than her right to speak – you denied her the right to survive.

You tore at her, clawed at her, defaced her. It was an act of extermination. And you laughed while you were doing it.

Who the fuck are you, you little shit, to believe you can pronounce on whether someone lives or dies.

Your father
P S How long have you been carrying a black marker around with you like a firearm?

When I showed the letter to Charmian she wondered if I might tone it down a mite.

I removed 'you little shit'.

'Are you sure you want to send this?' Charmian asked.

'I'm sure.'

'Then I will deliver it.'

'You know where she is?'

'Isn't it enough that I have said I will deliver it?'

A week later she handed me an envelope in which I found an intact poster of a hostage and a flyer showing a dead child on the bombed-out streets of Gaza. Scrawled across the flyer of the dead child were the words 'Geddit now?' And across the face of the hostage the words, 'Who are you, Dad?'

So I thought it was time I told her. And this time, yes, I did tone it down a mite.

Darling Zoe,

I believe you when you ask who I am. No doubt you think I don't know who you are. Could we agree at least to hear what the other says?

When I last encountered you face to face I saw in your eyes the person you saw. The very Devil. The image was so powerful I would not have been surprised to discover I had horns.

Zoe, your father is the somewhat clerkly headmaster of a primary school in South London. I won't say the baby-murdering land-grabbing Jew you march against does not somewhere exist, but he is not me. I am a moderate-minded Englishman. I don't wish the death of anyone, least of all a child. And I am not implicated in the harvesting of organs. Nor am I a member of any secret organisation dedicated to winning worldwide supremacy for Jews. If they could all come to live in quiet in Streatham I'd be content. But Jews fleeing Russia and Poland and Hungary and Morocco and Iran didn't have Streatham high on their list. Rootlessness is painful.

Was it because, as a boy, I feared being blown about the world randomly that – pompous beyond my years, with a stiff burgundy satchel that drew my shoulders to attention and a schoolcap that I alone among my fellows wore pulled down over his brow — I lusted after the rigid systematics of grammar? Remember Ronald Ridout, whose books I taught you grammar from when other fathers were reading their children Thomas the Tank Engine? *He memorably wrote 'The study of grammar helps us to understand the contribution each word, or group of words, has to make to the total meaning we wish to convey by our sentence. If we can understand the work each word or group of words does, we shall be able to express ourselves more accurately, and this in turn will help us think more accurately . . .'*

When I read those sentences as a boy I saw as into the heart of order. Grammar was the image of a perfect republic of language, wherein every individual word contributed, as in a dance, to the coherence and well-being of the polis. Careless expression equated to misgovernance. What I especially loved was the idea that you had to express yourself accurately before you could think accurately, and not the other way round. This described my own mental processes exactly. It was only when I put words in their correct relation to one another that I felt I was thinking at all. Grammar was creative: it was the fecund soil from which thinking grew. People who chaotically spluttered their views, looking for words in which to dress whatever it was they already thought they thought, were going the wrong way about learning to think at all. Ditto, if you will forgive me, people who go on marches expressing banal and sometimes hateful ideas in hand-me-down language.

When your grandmother heard me speak on this subject all those years ago she advised me to stay silent. 'You might sound a little formalist for your classmates,' she said.

I reminded her that my inspiration was a textbook studied by the whole class.

'Yes but your interpretation of it might strike them as a bit . . .'

Her voice trailed off as it always did at this point in any conversation on the subject of him and them. A bit . . .

'Ronald Ridout is English!' I exclaimed in my own defence.

'What you need to understand about the English,' my mother said, 'is that they are funny about their culture. What we admire about them is not always what they admire about themselves.'

The English — weren't we 'the English'?

Yes and no.

The 'no' part could have explained why I was the only one who stayed in during break to finish one of Ridout's syntactical exercises. While the other boys ran around the playground kicking balls and swapping cigarette cards, I, Ferdinand Draxler, your father-to-be, sat at my desk, sucked the tip of my pencil, and began the delicious task of parsing the following:

> *Not twenty yards from the window runs a honeysuckle hedge, and close to the top a pair of linnets had with great cunning built their nest and hatched their little brood.*

I didn't need to be told what to do next. For the sheer joy of it I set about picking

1. *the subject of the verb 'had . . . built'*
2. *the object of the verb 'had . . . built'*
3. *the subject of the verb 'runs'*
4. *a collective noun*
5. *a common noun*
6. *an abstract noun*
7. *a transitive verb*
8. *an intransitive verb*
9. *two adjectives and the noun they qualify*
10. *two conjunctions and the parts of the sentence they join*

I am not going to aggravate the bad relations between us by parsing the banners you carry. Another time, perhaps, we can discuss the confusion between the subject of the verb 'to slaughter' and the object of the verb 'to slaughter' which many of your co-demonstrators perpetuate. Today, it is

*far more important to me that you understand the allegiance to an idea of
Englishness that my love of Ridout's books fostered.*

*As I parsed the sentence about the honeysuckle hedge and the pair of
linnets I could smell the honeysuckle; had I whistled to the linnets they'd
have flown to me; I knew how big their little brood was; they would take
food from my open palm. To speak the words, to use the right collective
noun, and qualify it with the right adjective, was to inhabit the cottage
from whose window these natural wonders could be identified and admired.*

This is not the Devil's landscape.

*The enemy you have identified in me is a political fantasy. As a devil
I vindicate your world view. But world views are invariably misguided.
Better to start at the honeysuckle hedge and proceed gingerly in your
theories — if you must theorise — from there.*

*In recent times, dogma has reversed the grammar of event and so bru-
tally knocked nature off its course that nothing is but what is not. A line
from Shakespeare's* Macbeth *which you might remember I took you to
see not very long ago.*

*My love for you, my dear Zoe, is not subject to this carnival topsy-
turvy of vindictive groupthink.*

What is **IS***.*
Your loving dad

Charmian thought that was a big improvement on the previous letter. It even told her things about me, she said, that she
didn't know. Fancy, for example, my recognising the smell of
honeysuckle.

'Get the grammar right and there's no end to what you might
accomplish,' I said.

She rolled her eyes.

Was I expecting an apology? I am always expecting an apology.
In the meantime, I received an email from my mother. Since

that was unheard of, I assumed Isak had sent it. 'Sorry to see Zoe being an idiot on the box,' it said.

Yes. Isak's locution. My mother wouldn't have called Zoe an idiot when there were words like she-devil available to her.

Also an email from Max Axelberg. It was a list of links to stories in the press proving a) that no one had been harmed on 7 October, and b) that Israeli snipers were positioned on every rooftop on Gaza, picking off toddlers for sport. I binned the email. I wasn't in denial. Not even quid pro quo denial. I just didn't trust the integrity of people who sent me links.

Before we sat down to dinner, Charmian and I performed a sentimental ritual of giving each other a small finding or *objet trouvé* – a song, a joke, a poem or a flower. Accidentality was of the essence. So I thought nothing of the scrap of cardboard she handed me one evening, though her words, before she fully relinquished it – 'I hope you'll take this in the right spirit, Ferdie' – did alarm me. On it was written

> *dear loving Dad –*
> *Grammar is racist and so is you*
> *Z*

I remembered why I'd loved her once.

But still no apology.

THE GREY SUNKEN CUNT
OF THE WORLD

Concerned about my state of mind after the sundry indignities to which I'd been subjected, and feeling unnecessarily guilty for her role in some of them, Charmian invited me to a party that her fellow soap stars were throwing for the birthday of their oldest cast member.

'Get you out of yourself,' she said.

'I like it in myself.'

She refused to believe that. Nobody could like being in me.

'You should try it,' I said.

It sounded sexual. It wasn't. These were not sexual times.

I agreed to go to the party.

'Just one thing,' she said as we were waiting for the Uber to arrive, 'you know what actors are like, they all hate Jews.'

'What!'

'Sorry, sorry, I mean Israelis.'

'Do they know I hate all actors? Sorry, sorry, I mean acrobats.'

'Yes, I've warned them.'

'And you think this is a good idea?'

'Nothing is a good idea. But it's a better idea.'

'Than what?'

'Than you wandering around London with a can of white paint.'

I was not wandering around London with a can of white paint. I was driving to my mother's every morning and if I happened to see something disagreeable on the way I'd pull over and paint it out with Agreeable Gray. What was wrong with that?

It could be thought of as borderline OCD, Charmian said.

No, the person suffering from borderline OCD, I told her, was the person stencilling swastikas.

Charmian disagreed with me. Stencilling swastikas didn't have to denote mental instability. It was quite possibly a wilful act entirely in the stenciller's control. The malevolent were not necessarily nutjobs. Which could not be said for people who rushed to read the Jewish press every morning to check whether there were Jews still alive outside Streatham. Or kept their phones on under their pillows all night in case their daughters rang to say, 'Daddy, you were right all along.'

And that, you're saying, is borderline OCD?

That, I'm saying, is borderline lunacy.

'Those whom the gods love they first make mad,' I said.

Charmian corrected me. 'Those whom the gods would destroy they first make mad.'

'My God is a loving God,' I said.

She snorted. Exactly as Zoe had. 'He has a funny way of showing it,' she said. Exactly as Zoe had.

I lent my ear to a wicked whisper. Was my wife the cause of my daughter's low opinion of the God of Abraham? Was Zoe the price of what Jews of a sort I didn't like called 'marrying out'?

And was such a thought, I asked myself, the price I paid for the Jew-obsession into which I'd let my adversaries trap me. Charmian was right again — out of myself was better than in.

I was glad when the Uber arrived. Upon my agreeing not to start a fight with anyone at the party, and Charmian signalling me to modify my language in deference to the driver's Islamic beard, we kissed like the comrades in arms I still liked to think we were. The driver noted that we were in love. 'I love love,' he said.

114

Perhaps it was 'our love' that distracted him. He had to brake suddenly to avoid hitting a tough-seeming character who had wandered into the road looking at his phone. (Was this what I looked like now, I wondered, forever walking out into traffic holding my phone to my ear for the sound of Zoe.) I expected an altercation. Our driver wound down his window. 'Are you all right?' he asked softly. 'Be more mindful in the future.'

Rather than swear or pull a knife, the pedestrian nodded as though to say yes, more mindful was exactly what he would hereafter aspire to be.

Mindful.

Charmian and I looked at each other. A new concept had entered our marriage.

Asked by Uber to rate the ride, I rated the driver excellent and awarded him a twenty per cent tip. There was nowhere for me to rate his wisdom.

Not for the first time I told Charmian that I thought Jews and Muslims would get on fine if it weren't for universities. And, maybe, Islam.

'And, maybe,' added Charmian, 'Judaism.'

'Then I won't come to the party,' I said.

'Oh, don't be ridiculous,' Charmian said.

'All right, provided you agree to be more mindful.'

'Of what? My grammar?'

'My feelings.'

The party was in an expensively converted Edwardian house in Paddington.

'Nice to see that some conversions work,' I muttered as we strolled up the path.

'Shut up,' Charmian said. She knew I had Zoe on the brain. (In fact Zoe's tearful apology wasn't all I was consulting my phone every half-hour to hear. I was also hoping to be the first to learn of the death of Max Axelberg.)

As far as being head and deputy head allowed, we'd kept our distance since the kerfuffle in the staffroom. I drew up new timetables which ensured we never had to be in the same part of the school at the same time. We communicated by class monitors. 'Tell Mr Axelberg that I would like him to . . .' 'Tell the headmaster I will do my best . . .'

I had conveyed to Charmian my suspicion that it was Axelberg who'd been following me to my mother's and spraying my car. It made no sense that he should do it, but I needed to add concrete charges against him to give body to my airy hatred of him as a turncoat against his own people who weren't even his own people.

Had I not liked our Uber driver I'd have indulged the wish that Axelberg had converted to Islam, so he could have shown Muslims the fealty he was showing Jews.

Charmian put her finger to her brain and turned it like a screwdriver. She was right. I did have lunatic-level OCD. Axelberg obsessively and compulsively disordered me.

As ever, Charmian intuited it all. 'Do you want to go back?' she asked.

I shook my head. Absolutely not. I needed a break from teachers and family. I wanted to meet actors even though, in the matter of hating Jews, they were worse.

The moment of entering a party – any party – had never been easy for me. I put this down to the early years of my mother's notoriety when people wanted to see what the son of a survivor looked like. But this was long forgotten. Now, I had to deal with my own envisagings of what they saw – not quite Zoe's devil with blood dripping from his teeth, but a twisted relic of another time with a hooked nose and the fanatic history of his people in a ripped, evil-smelling sack on his back. Rumpelstiltsinikov.

Did I imagine that the table of Charmian's friends, to whom she introduced me punctiliously, one by one, zealously refused to meet my eye and barely touched my fingertips when I proferred my hand?

'Ha!' did I imagine I heard one of the actors say?

Ha what? Just Ha.

Ha for Hamas.

Did I imagine that I saw paint – swastika paint? – on at least two of the hands that recoiled from mine?

Did I imagine that one of the two women bringing round assorted canapés so angled her plate that I could only reach dates wrapped in bacon. Never mind the bacon, were the dates Palestinian?

Did I imagine that the second woman bringing round the canapés was careful to angle her plate away from me altogether?

Did I imagine that the host directed me to a toilet in the basement when everyone else was shown to one of three on the ground floor?

Did I imagine that a towering, broad-backed, granite-jawed ecclesiastic in a black cassock waylaid me on the basement steps as I was returning with wet hands (I hadn't wanted to defile my host's towel) and asked if I thought we were nearing the end?

The Devil, was he? The Devil sent to fool me, in holy garb, before casting me down into the blackness?

No, he at least turned out to have an existence beyond my fantasies of dread. He was the gay priest who had a secret wife in Charmian's current ITV soap opera and had turned up to the party in full regalia for the mirth of it. Charmian was the wife whose flaming red hair had tempted him out of celibacy. Typecasting.

'The end of the Jews, do you mean?' I asked.

He could have laughed but he didn't. 'No, the fuckin' feudal system. Of course the Jews.'

'Are you drunk?' I wondered.

'No, I am Irish.'

'It's my sense,' I said, trying to manoeuvre him back up the steps, 'that the Irish aren't very keen on the Jews right now.'

'Never have been. "They sinned against the light, and you can see the darkness in their eyes." Do you know who said that? Mr Deasy the schoolteacher. Nasty piece of work. Let me see the darkness in yours.'

'We're in a cellar. Everyone has dark eyes in a cellar.'

' "And that is why they are wanderers on the earth to this day." Do you know who said that?'

'Still Mr Deasy?'

'Right again. *Ulysses*. Do you know who wrote that?'

'Of course I know who wrote that. Everyone knows who wrote that.'

'Great friend of you Jews, you know.'

'From what I hear, Ireland could do with a few more right now.'

'And where would you be hearing that from?'

'It's known.'

'Oh, it's known? And do you know — talking of knowing — who the first and finest man in Ireland is?'

'Leopold Bloom.'

'A Jew. Precisely. So what's your complaint?'

'I don't have one. I am a fanatic admirer. Nelly, I *am* Leopold Bloom — the greatest of all wanderers on the earth to this day.'

'You've mistaken me for someone else, Mr Jew. My name isn't Nelly.'

'Come on, Father, play the game. I've played along with yours. *Nelly, I am Heathcliff.* Catherine's protestation of her undying love for Heathcliff. Thought you'd know it, being a literary man.'

'I don't read cheap romances.'

'*Wuthering Heights*? A cheap romance! Not a patch on *Ulysses*, I grant you, but then it's got no Jews in it. Though I have heard it argued that Heathcliff was originally to be called Henriques after a Sephardic Jew from Lisbon whom Emily Brontë found wandering on the Yorkshire moors and mistook for a gypsy.'

'And who have you heard arguing that?'

'Me.'

He paused to light a cigarette. In this airless dungeon and with all the alcohol in him I feared he'd blow us up. 'Having given what you say due consideration,' he said, 'I can tell you it's bullshite.'

'You don't think unmarried women with wild imaginations go wandering the moors looking for Jews? You clearly haven't been to Yorkshire.'

'No, I bloody haven't. Too many Jews there already. Don't know why you'd go looking on the moors for more.' He laughed, ruffling my hair. 'Just winding you up. As an Irishman I'm an honorary Jew myself. That's what the great God Joyce taught me. Scratch one and you'll find another.'

Though perilously positioned on the basement steps himself, he enfolded me in his arms. 'Let's go upstairs and have another drink on brotherhood,' he said.

Which is how Charmian came to find me half-cut on the couch with a giant whiskey priest from Dublin, smelling of shallots and barley.

'He's bugger of a Jew, this one,' he explained to her, kissing both my cheeks.

She looked alarmed. 'It's all right,' I said. 'Bugger of a Jew is the nicest thing anyone's said to me in months.'

'Don't encourage him,' Charmian pleaded with the priest.

'He doesn't need encouraging. He's the greatest of all wanderers on the face of the earth, he tells me, and I, for one, believe him.'

'Not that he's wandered very far from Streatham,' Charmian retorted. Tartly. Tart was her party mode.

'I've come further than you think,' I said. 'While remaining, I grant you, exactly where I started out.'

'In your wife's bed-warmed rump, I hope,' said the priest, whereupon Charmian saw other friends she wanted to talk to.

And as the Catholic priest fell asleep in my neck I saw through the fumes poor cuckolded Leopold Bloom in the pork butcher's buying non-kosher meat, reading a prospectus for a model farm in Palestine on the lakeshore of Tiberias, and deciding no, measuring this against that, no, no, farming in Palestine was not for him.

A barren land, bare waste. Vulcanic lake, the dead sea: no fish, weedless, sunk deep in the earth. No wind would lift those waves, grey metal, poisonous foggy waters. Brimstone they called it raining down: the cities of the plain: Sodom, Gomorrah, Edom. All dead names. A dead sea in a dead land, grey and old. Old now. It bore the oldest, the first race. A bent hag crossed from Cassidy's clutching a noggin bottle by the neck. The oldest people. Wandered far away over all the earth, captivity to captivity, multiplying, dying, being born everywhere. It lay there now. Now it could bear no more. Dead: an old woman's: the grey sunken cunt of the world.

So was that the problem? Just too old. Too long a-wandering, while our ancient home mouldered without us, the grey sunken cunt of the world?

Our ancient home. *Ours.* Not, though, 'to take from others, but to build the ruins . . . We claim no rights on our past, but on our future.'

So wrote Ben Gurion in 1918.

I did the sums in my swimming head. Four years later, *Ulysses* was published. Just five years after the Balfour Declaration.

How innocent it all sounded, investing in a model farm on the shores of Lake Tiberias, building the ruins.

The priest snored comfortably in my neck. I was of a mind to snore comfortably in his.

I felt protective towards myself. Sleep, Ferdie.

Geh schlafen, as my Mutti's Mutti used to say.

PARADISE LOST

And in his sleep he had a dream.

He and the Uber driver in their model-farm clothes digging up the potatoes together. Amused. No, delighted. Two men enjoying the sun. Laughing. Claiming the future, for them both. *Mindful*. Mindful of each other.

You can smell your own country, Ferdinand thinks. You can recognise the arid tickle of the desert at the back of your throat. But the Arab tastes it too.

Ferdinand pauses and mops his brow. The Arab passes him water. Ferdinand drinks . . .

They sit on a rock. Ferdinand gives the Arab a matzoh sandwich of boiled fish and grated horseradish.

'Ugh,' the Arab says, passing Ferdinand a pitta filled with hummus.

'Yum,' Ferdinand says, 'I could get used to this.'

Not too used, I hope, the Arab thinks.

They talk about their families. The Arab is proud of his sons. Ferdinand isn't proud of his daughter but as this is a dream he pretends he is.

They resume digging. A lovely rhythmic motion, backbreaking but in the synchronicity energising, as though each is doubled by the efforts of the other. Ferdinand remembers having said he likes to be inside himself, but he likes to be inside the Arab too. By 'inside' he means in touch with the music of the Arab's movements. Within the soul of him. It's like dance, Ferdinand who is not a dancer, imagines.

He doesn't know what the Arab imagines.

Perhaps if he had taken more time to find out, the Arab would not abruptly have cast aside the potato fork and walked away.

Ferdinand cannot understand why their partnership is no longer functioning. A moment ago it was working wonderfully. Or so it seemed to him.

Have I pushed too hard, Ferdinand wonders. Have I made assumptions about possession, have I taken more than my fair share of potatoes?

Or has the Arab suddenly woken up to who I am and decided to swallow all the Nazi propaganda sloshing around the Middle East about the Jew who wheedles and connives, the Jew who steals and kills, the Jew who keeps to himself but still manages to infect your women with syphilis, the Jew alongside whom you dare never work the soil?

He returns to the living with a sour taste at the back of his throat, a priest's head in his neck, and a feeling of profound sadness.

You can smell your own country even if you've never been there.

From all dreams there is a bitter awakening.

THE LIMACOLOGIST OF BELSEN

Out of the blue, Margalita rang me to say there were men in my mother's drive with big machine. She couldn't describe the machine. Had she told my mother? Yes. Had she asked my mother who they were? Yes. Mrs had said mind own business.

I was there in forty minutes. My suspicion had been that Banksy's gang was putting up a new and bigger mural, unafraid, now one could spread any old libel about Jews, of being caught. But when I got there I found a van with its tailgate down and two men the size of elves feeding either my mother's papers or my mother in person into the rotating blades of an industrial shredder.

I was relieved to see her in the hall, wanly watching, not unlike the Lady of Shalott at her window.

'What the hell's going on out there?' I asked.

'I finally decided you were right.'

'And I've finally decided I was wrong.'

'I'm doing me a year at a time,' she told me.

'I'll go and stop them,' I said.

'They're paid in advance.'

'That doesn't matter. When did you start?'

'Yesterday.'

'No, I mean *where* did you start. What year.'

'I've just told you. Yesterday. I'm going backwards.'

I was mightily relieved. That meant there'd be time to ensure she wasn't shredding Belsen.

'I thought I'd get to your birthday and then stop,' she said.

'What's the logic of that,' I asked, 'other than sadism?'

'How is it sadism? I'd call it mother love.'

Mother love? Was this Isak's doing? Had my mother's fortress against tenderness become a gingerbread house of sweet talking and kisses now he'd taken up residence? Had he shown her his butterfly tattoo?

'How so?' I asked, dreading the answer.

'Before you there was history. After you there was house-work. On your arrival I became merely human. And no one wants to know about that.' She paused. 'Unless you do.'

'I don't need paperwork relating to my birth, Mutti.'

'Then we're all hunky-dory,' she said.

I laughed at the usage. 'I've never heard you use that expression before.'

Something dark, like the reflection of a large bird on water, crossed her face. 'I am surprised I remember it,' she said. 'Have I told you about Adele? A cheerful English girl who made dolls out of rags. For a few weeks she assisted me in Kramer's kitchen. She didn't know why she was in the camp. She had come over from Manchester to see family and the next thing they'd picked her up off the street. *Name? Adele Rose. Right, komm mit uns.* "It'll be hunky-dory," she used to say, meaning everything from the next meal to the rest of our lives. One afternoon they burst into the kitchen, told her to collect her dolls, and said *Komm mit uns.* "It'll be hunky-dory," she said over her shoulder. "Yes, hunky-dory," I said back. I was a newcomer myself. I still believed in the future. Hunky-dory was an incantatory promise. All would turn out well so long as you kept on smiling.'

'And baking.'

'Don't be insolent, Ferdinand.'

I wasn't being insolent. I was otherwise mentally engaged. All I could think was how wrong it had been of me to bring a shredder into this house. There *was* no detritus. Nothing didn't matter.

'I'm going to send those men away before they destroy any-thing else,' I said.

She didn't argue.

She was in unexpectedly complaisant and confiding spirits. I wondered if she was thinking what I was thinking, that in a world that wanted you not to exist, keeping every scrap of your life was an act of defiance. In which case had she hired those elves to shred her life in order to show she no longer believed it mattered, that defiance was fruitless? Fine, here, take what you want. Lose/keep. Live/die. Who cared?

Was that what had got her through? A supreme indiffer-ence? She'd been accused of evasiveness when writing about her relations with Josef Kramer. Had she tolerated more than she'd admitted? Whatever had happened – as something surely must – had she found a way of not noticing, of pretending it was happening to someone else? She was a child. Well, whatever helped her survive was hunky-dory as far as I was concerned. You did what you had to. But I wished she had passed on some of her supreme indifference to me. Teach me not to care, Mutti.

We sat quietly for a while, not quite looking at each other.

'I gather it's bad out there,' she said at last.

'It?'

'Don't treat me like a child, Ferdinand. There's only ever one "it" that's bad for us.'

'Who's been talking to you?'

'I have ears. I have eyes. You've got paint on your hands again. Do you really think I don't know what you've been doing?'

'How do you know?'

'I look out of my window. By the time you arrive with your paintbrush I've been awake hours. That's if I've slept at all. You can't suppose I sleep.'

'I just thought by now—'

'Which now is this you're talking about? There is no *by now*. The past is now.'

I hardly needed telling that. I raised an apologetic hand. You don't barter time with someone who'd been where my mother had been, whatever bargains she'd struck with survival. You shut up. You keep your 'I just thoughts' to yourself.

'I am amazed,' I said, picking my way through words as though they were a nest of poison spiders.

'Amazed by what?'

'Amazed that you can see through those windows. They mustn't have been cleaned since I lived here.'

'I can see through dirt, Ferdinand.'

'Then why don't you wave when you see me?'

'You look preoccupied. And contented. I've rarely seen you so self-composed. Painting over swastikas evidently suits you. You could have made a career out of it.'

Like playing the donkey.

'I have made a career out of it.'

'I trust they pay you well . . .'

'I do it gratis. But a question. Those swastikas face out. How do you know they're swastikas?'

'What else is anyone going to paint on my walls? Roses? This isn't the first time. Oswald Mosley came in person to paint a swastika on my garden wall. I banged on the window, made a fist, and he cantered off on his horse. I'm surprised, Ferdinand, that you'd think they bother me. Besides, they'll be back. They always come back.'

'Then so will I.'

She laughed. At me or at the world?

'Talking of coming back, where's Isak?' I asked.

'Gone for a run. At least that's what he told me.'

'A run? Doesn't he know that Draxlers don't run?'

'I did when I was little.'

The idea of Mutti little touched me. In my mind's eye I saw her skipping along the Ringstrasse. Happy. Laughing. Like hunky-dory Adele before they took her from the kitchen to the furnace. Like Zoe before she went to university for a brain transplant.

As usual, my mother read my thoughts from my heartbeats. She knew me from the first throbs of my unborn agitations to the highly strung being I became. How long in the womb before a Jew knows he's a Jew, starts fearing for the future and loves his mother too much? The mother in question snapped her fingers. 'Come out of there,' she said.

It was my turn to laugh. If only coming out of there was as easy as the snap of a finger.

'Do you know what the difference is between then and now?' she asked, apropos, or so it seemed, of nothing.

'Then and now?'

'Don't be obtuse, Ferdinand. Between the Josef Kramers and the Hamasniks . . .'

'Just a guess, but did the Josef Kramers like us more?'

'You are on the right track. They feared us more. They believed we had a pact with the Devil. They really did think we ate babies for breakfast. They overestimated us. Kramer called me a little she-devil and marvelled that my hands weren't scaly. He asked me to bend over and show him my tail.'

'Mutti!'

'Be a man, Ferdinand. It's time you faced the fact that your mother has a *toches*.'

And a tail, I thought.

'It's hard to credit they truly believed all that,' I said. 'They read Leibniz and Goethe. They were rationalists at heart . . .'

'We too read Leibniz and Goethe. Which they also knew. That we could be devils and thinkers confused them. We were too haughty for them. They didn't only believe we wanted to control the world, they feared we might succeed. Why else did they build that giant machinery to wipe us out when all they ever needed to do was make us feel bad? The Hamasniks have half the brains of the Nazis but they've worked us out. They know our weak spot. Persuade us we've stolen someone else's land and turned it into a *Scheisshaus*—'

'You've been listening to Isak.'

'I don't need to listen to Isak. I've read books. I've seen photographs.'

'So you too think we've turned someone else's country into a *Scheisshaus*?'

'No. I think we've turned our own country into a *Scheisshaus*, but that's not what's important. Town planning was never our strong point. God took one look at Gomorrah and flattened it. Maybe those who say the kibbutzim were what we did best are right. We are always in too much of a hurry to make beauty. Always harried. Always having to pack up and leave.'

'Vienna was beautiful.'

'Yes, but we didn't build it.'

'Yes, but we inhabited it beautifully.'

'I wouldn't shout that out. "Then go back there," they'll tell us.'

'But isn't that what you think the Hamasniks have been hoping all along? That we'll pack up and go back?'

'What's wrong with that argument is that there is no back. What the Hamasniks do know, however, is that we will always believe the worst of ourselves and ultimately allow whoever has use for us as slaves to lead us quietly away. If you make the Jews victims they rise from the flames. We love surviving a disaster. But the minute a Jew thinks he's won he curls up like a snail.'

'We were victims last October, Mutti. That hasn't worked out too well.'

'Give it time. And anyway, that wasn't an isolated event. It was punishment for a century of winning, was it not? We'd been saving up guilt and worry all that time.'

'*We*. Who today is "we"?'

'The thinking, shrinking Jews like you.'

'Me?'

'Yes, you. The snails.'

I shrank from the comparison. 'Do snails know guilt?' I asked.

'Ferdinand—'

'Shame, then?'

'Let me surprise you. I had a friend in the camp – Stefan – he cleaned the pans and scrubbed the potatoes – a limacologist in his real life. His love was the study of gastropods.'

'Then he must have known whether snails feel guilt or shame.'

'I didn't get the opportunity to ask him. I was more interested in his thesis that they knew love. Intense love. And loyalty.'

'Do they mourn the loss of those they love when the lawn-mowers come through?'

'I didn't get the opportunity to ask him that either. And before I could, they took him away. *Komm mit uns*. He had made a small collection of snails and secretly kept them in a box. He gave them each a name. Gunter. Manfred. Wolfgang. These they found and trod on one by one. He wept as he was led away, listening to the slow crunch of his friends.'

'That's a sad story, Mutti.'

'What isn't? But why did he cry? Because he felt pity for the snails or because he couldn't forgive himself for collecting them and then not concealing their whereabouts?'

I couldn't imagine weeping over a snail myself, but I said, 'Our consciences are too nice.'

'Mine isn't.'

Was she telling the truth?

'You, I suppose,' she went on, 'would have felt sorry for

yourself *and* the snails. You don't have to tell me. You are your father's son. Greedy – both of you. Show you a reason to feel bad about yourself and you grab it with both hands. This is what kept your poor father a diasporist. The whole Palestine business turned his stomach. He was a Jew of everywhere and nowhere. And you know where they end up . . .'

'Streatham,' I said.

'You find it funny, Ferdinand?'

I didn't.

'The Jew, your father thought, should always be a wanderer on the face of the earth. So he never set foot in Israel in case it tempted him to stay. You're the same, I know. This is why you too have never been there. You'd have dropped to your knees in remorse the minute you saw a Bedouin. *God forgive me, I've reduced this poor man to travelling by camel.* And the next thing you'd be offering him your Land Rover.'

'But what's your excuse, Mutti? *You've* never been to Israel either. Even when they invited you.'

'They never stopped inviting me.'

'Then why didn't you go?'

'I'm a European.'

'The country is full of Europeans.'

'I don't like trains.'

'Mutti, trains aren't how you get to Israel.'

How you go to Israel didn't interest her.

'That fruitcake Freud,' she went on, following a logic of her own, 'who wasn't any kind of Jew until he found himself fleeing the Nazis, had a theory that the ancient Hebrews killed their tribal father, Moses (whom he didn't think was any kind of Jew either), and never recovered from the trauma of doing so. Do you want to hear the psychic history of our people, in six words? *They murmured, they murdered, they misgave.* Thereafter, the downside of the patriarchy was that every father would see his son as his assassin and every son would be consumed by misgivings. Which explains—'

I knew what it explained. The guilty secret every Jew carried within him and was forever doomed to expiate. Hurt a Jew and there will eventually come an hour when he will apologise to you for it, the 'it' not being what you did to him – though he'll feel bad about that – but what he did to Moses.

'This, to the eternal hellish credit of its cynical stupidity,' my mother went on, 'Hamas understands better than the Nazis ever did.'

Yes, Mutti. Yes, Mutti.

But I had a question. Was the guilt handed down to us from those ancient fratricides transferable? Did it have to be brewed over centuries in the simmering genes of Jews or could any johnny-come-lately just hop on board the shame train and promiscuously apologise for Jewish delinquency for the sole purpose of bringing it to the world's attention?

No prize for guessing which johnny-come-lately I had in mind.

Not in my name, he declared as he marched through London under a name that wasn't his anyway.

'Not in our name either,' my mother said. 'Only a Jew can say sorry for being a Jew. It's not optional. We can't stop him killing Moses if he wants to, but he must do so as an independent.'

O, noble Mutti.

Had there been any tradition of kissing between us, I'd have kissed her.

'But there are others like him,' I said, 'who *are* Jews in the way he's not but who share his bad faith. How can this be?'

'Don't be a baby, Ferdinand. There always have been bad Jews. Being bad Jews is what Jews do. There's no one better.'

While we were getting on so well I thought she might like to hear about the latest gambit favoured by the Not-in-My-Namers whom Axelberg marched beside.

'It goes like this,' I said. 'Let a Jew so much as allude to Jewish misfortune and he is accused of weaponising it, deploying it to blackmail easily susceptible non-Jews into acquiescence in Jewish crimes. Thus, we weaponised the October Massacre, weaponised the Shoah, weaponised the pogroms, weaponised Dreyfus, weaponised the Inquisition, weaponised the Babylonian Exile, weaponised the Romans, weaponised the Garden of Eden, weaponised Creation itself. We are even charged with weaponising you, Mutti.'

'I should hope so,' she said with one of her almost-laughs. 'But I'm assuming he's a friend of yours, this Shape Shifter . . .'

'Colleague, Mutti.'

'Whatever he is, why don't you bring him here? I'd like to hear him de-weaponise Belsen.'

I relished the encounter in advance, imagining her crushing him under her foot like a snail.

'If you are sure,' I said. 'I have to warn you – he's pretty vile.'

'Ferdinand, have you forgotten the sorts I've met?'

'The Beast of Belsen has nothing on the Slimeball of Strawberry Fields, Mutti.'

'Bring him to me.'

I thrilled to her menace. He would be my gift, son to mother. I would deposit the carcass at her feet, like a cat bringing home a half-dead mouse.

ZIGRAINE

But where was he, this half-dead mouse?

On what he called a sabbatical, arranged months before the massacre he had taken to referring to as the Hamas Hooha – a phrase he put inverted commas around with his fingers, wagging like donkey's ears. Rumours had reached me of his driving a renovated ambulance round the country, distributing pamphlets and providing pensioners with lists of grocery items it would speed up the destruction of the Zionist Entity not to buy. I delighted, I had to say, in his absence, no matter what contribution to the ethnic cleansing of the Holy Land the Swanage Co-op was making.

In order to pre-empt any hostility on his return, I bought him a new yarmulke, kippah, skullcap, whatever he chose to call it, and left it wrapped in tissue in his locker with a card. On the card was an extract from Lennie Bruce's famous routine explaining the differences between Jewish and goyish – I thought the good-natured comedy would heal the wounds – *If you live in New York or any other big city, you are Jewish . . . If you live in Butte, Montana, you're going to be goyish even if you're Jewish . . .*

Welcome back to being Jewish in Streatham.

For the next fortnight Max avoided me. Was my gift gross in some way? I asked Charmian her opinion. I always asked Charmian her opinion. Though it was her impulsiveness that attracted me to her originally, just as it was my staidness – or so she said – that attracted her to me, we cancelled out our extremes to achieve a happy medium of good sense. Call it a marriage of true minds. The actress and the headmaster. The skier and the grammarian. Why, then, we hadn't produced a true-minded daughter I don't know. I suppose the answer is that she was, in her own perfidious mind at least, true to herself. The great illusion of the young. We are who we are. Be someone else, Zoe, I had begged her often enough. But by that she thought I meant go to the synagogue twice a day and wear skirts to your ankles.

'Let her rebel,' Charmian advised.

'You mean let her de-Jew?'

'There isn't strictly speaking that much Jew in her to de-Jew,' Charmian reminded me.

'Matrilineally speaking, maybe not,' I said, 'but do my genes count for nothing?'

'Just let her be,' Charmian repeated, eschewing the great genetic-code debate. 'Playing the Jewish father is not going to help a girl who is already in revolt against the idea of fathers, never mind Jewish ones. It will pass.'

'God willing,' I said.

'If I were you,' Charmian advised, 'I'd leave God out of it too.'

Charmian, anyway, to return to Max Axelberg, put her mind to my question. Did she think my peace offering could have offended him in some way? She took a day to think about it and then said yes. The Lennie Bruce routine might well have struck him as a rebuke. If you live in Butte, Montana, you ain't no Jew, and Max Axelberg né Tony Evans was mayor of Butte, Montana.

I grabbed him when the opportunity presented itself and apologised. His face lit up.

'No, not for Gaza,' I said.

He dismissed the card. Just didn't find Lennie Bruce funny. Another way in which you're goyish, I thought. The real offence – because he had indeed been offended – was the skullcap. I'd sent him a crocheted one. The most elaborately crocheted skullcap money could buy.

Didn't he like it?

It gave him a migraine, he said.

I wondered what on earth there could have been in the yarn. Was this a new way of poisoning Jews?

Turned out it had nothing to do with the yarn. The insult was in the symbolism. Didn't I know that a crocheted yarmulke was the favoured headgear of the ultra-religious Zionists who manned the settlements?

I stared at him. In his distorted features I could see the lightning strike that was Z for Zion forking its way to his brain like a madness.

He would die of this eventually, I thought. Just as I, eventually, would die of him. But he was a hill I was prepared to die on. In the meantime, there was my mother's promise to look forward to. Fetch the weaponising little shit to me, she'd said, if not quite in so many words, and I'll crush his testicles for you the way the guards at Belsen crushed Stefan's pet snails. *Crunch.*

Shouldn't that have been *crunch, crunch*? No. Hitler had only one ball, and I saw no compelling reason to give Max Axelberg two.

He had two names. That was enough.

I had a delicate balancing act to perform. Now he was back, we had business to discuss. I couldn't allow our embittered relations to sour the whole school. On the other hand, I couldn't stomach the thought of his not knowing how profoundly I despised him. To keep tensions simmering without allowing them to boil over, I affected an exaggerated concern about his health, staring deep into his eyes, telling him he looked pale, suggesting he have the rest of the day off. 'Zigraines are not to be taken lightly, Max,' I would add.

'What did you say?'

'I said a Zigraine is no laughing matter.'

For one delicious moment I thought he was going to ask me what a Zigraine was. Then a cloud of all-comprehending contempt for me passed across his face. 'I am glad I amuse you, Headmaster,' he said.

He didn't know that what really amused me was the thought of my mother crunching his ball.

Yes, the war between us did more than attack my reason; it regressed me to early childhood.

How we came to be standing on one leg in the middle of my office, each with a trouser leg rolled, Max Axelberg triumphantly proclaiming Zionism to be the theft of someone else's country, I suffering cramp, but just managing to answer 'That's structural mendacity, and you know it' – takes a little explaining. I had dared him, in the spirit of the Roman general challenging Hillel the Great to teach him the meaning of Judaism in one sentence, while standing on one leg, to do the same vis-à-vis anti-Zionism. We had reached this point in the course of another of our arguments about the legitimacy and longevity of Jewish dreams of return that had seen me quoting 'By the rivers of Babylon, there we sat down, yea, we wept, when we remembered Zion', and Max expressing astonishment that I was prepared to root Jewish rights to Palestine in a Psalm calling for Babylonian children to be dashed against the stones, thereby eliciting from me the reply 'Context, Max, context. Your favourite word', which brought on a second spasm of cramp that I could ease only by hopping around the immovable Axelberg, crying, 'Ow, ow, holy shit!' Which was the sight that confronted my new and inexperienced secretary, Cynthia, when she entered my office with a sheaf of school reports for me to sign.

'Oh!' she cried, dropping the papers.

'It's OK, Cynthia,' I said, 'Mr Axelberg and I are discussing the essentials of the Jewish faith. You can leave the papers. I'll pick them up.'

Whether the spectacle of the headmaster dancing with his deputy in a state of Masonic undress and howling would be sufficient reason for Cynthia to tend her resignation, only time would tell. But for me to lose a second secretary so soon after losing the first was sure to be damaging to my chances of remaining headmaster.

LEILA KHALED HALL LONDON SW16

Zoe, her fine face crumpled in anger, suddenly turned up waving a black, white and green flag in the garden of the house opposite ours.

I say 'suddenly' but what, in the context of Zoe, does that word mean? Time moves differently when you are worrying about a child. I say 'suddenly' but anything she did was so expected it could have happened already. Think of me as a stopwatch and Zoe as the stop/start, pause and reset button.

The effect of this was to steal the future and make memory move in fits. 'When was the last time we heard any good news about Zoe?' I asked Charmian.

'How long is a piece of string?' she answered. 'Given your starting point, what good news about Zoe could there be?'

'The news that she has smashed her idols and burnt her false gods.'

'Just like that? And then would you love her again just as quickly? Don't mistakes have to be learnt? Otherwise, the renunciation is no better than the error.'

You could tell she'd done Shakespeare in her time.

'Christ, Sharm,' I said. 'All right, all right – let her find her way to the light slowly. Does she have to be waving a flag in the same fucking street while she's finding it?'

Charmian called that a fair question. In the whole of London did she have to wind up here, in Number 33, the very house that had marked the slaughter of Jews on the night of the massacre with a party calling for the slaughter of more? In fairness, they'd been nice about it and lowered their voices when I'd told them

Charmian was trying to sleep. 'Gas the Jews' sotto voce had a charm. If one had to be gassed, sotto voce was the pitch to be gassed to. My mother once told me that some of the guards in Belsen had lovely voices and sang as we went into the ovens. In we went to Schubert's *Winterreise*. Witness the advantage of being slaughtered by Europeans.

An Italian academic rabbi friend of Charmian's — if that needs some explaining, he was the son of a friend of her father's — had been endeavouring, at Charmian's behest, to soften my attitude to my daughter's politics and to that of the protesting young in general.

'It just entrenches them in their views to accuse them of anti-Semitism,' he said. 'I know them. They're just children.'

We were in a Chinese restaurant in Soho. Chinese food soothed me. Chinese waiters didn't notice my existence. Eating with chopsticks slowed my heart rate. I'd even put it to Charmian that we should consider running away to China when Streatham finally became unsupportable for Jews which, by my calculations, was any minute now. I'd read that there'd once been a thriving community of Jews in Harbin. Why not again?

Marco put his hand on my sleeve. 'Desperation makes us weak,' he said. Because he had the gentle and almost sanctified face of a Botticelli youth, no matter that youth was long gone from him, I let him take these liberties with my person. In fraught times it can be easeful to be touched. But I wasn't prepared to buy the 'they're just children' argument, no matter that my wife accused me of being one.

'Yes, I was a child once,' I said. 'But even then I didn't wave flags and chant slogans for no other reason than that everybody else my age did. You don't have to be very grown up to know that where the mob goes, you shouldn't. And to be clear, I don't accuse them of anti-Semitism. Not conscious anti-Semitism anyway. Half of them won't know what a Jew is. But there are sins no less grievous than hating Jews. There is hating, full stop. There is a readiness to swallow jargon and accept disinformation. There is defamation. There is being on X. There is knowing nothing. In a word, Marco, there is stupidity.'

'Do you think it helps to call them stupid? Doesn't that just firm up their position?'

'People said that in the Brexit years. Whatever else, we never dared call even the stupidest of Brexiteers stupid. That would just confirm them in their hatred of an elite and make them more obdurate. So we never called them stupid and what happened? We got Brexit.'

'My friend, these protestors are young and passionate. How old is Zoe? Eighteen? You should be proud she is a dissenter.'

'I would be proud if she were a dissenter. But what, right now, is she dissenting from? Every word she utters, every action she performs, is slavishly conformist. She is so a child of her times she could be a robot.'

'A robot wouldn't care so deeply.'

'That would depend on who programs it. "Caring" too can be an expression of orthodoxy.'

'So what's so wrong with an orthodoxy that promotes humanity? If your daughter is programmed to stop cruelty, isn't that better—'

'It's not better than anything.'

'Then what do you do to stop the slaughter?'

I put my hand on his sleeve and smiled. 'I talk to a rabbi.'

He smiled back. 'I only wish that would help.'

I liked him because he knew his limits. And because the lines on his handsome, regular, boyish face were more disfiguring than they would have been on a man who looked his age. It was as though his face were at war with itself – age wanting to punish his beauty for something. Optimism. Naivety.

'What do you have,' I asked, 'against telling them the truth?'

'Nothing. Of course nothing. But do you possess the truth?'

'I possess a smidgeon more of it than they do. We are obliged – every one of us – to be amateur historians of how things come about. The marching young don't want to understand that history operates in time. They think bad things just fall out of a clear blue sky. That way they are easier to demonstrate against. Forgive me, Marco, but I cannot forgive them.'

'Not even your daughter?'

'Especially not my daughter.'

The rabbi smiled the melancholy smile of a quattrocento angel and sighed. 'Have *rachmones*,' he said. 'Show pity.'

The Chinese waitress gracefully unwrapped my chopsticks. I presumed she saw that my hands were shaking. She wore a black and gold dragon-print cheongsam, open at the sides.

'You'd look ravishing in that,' I told Charmian.

I didn't think Zoe was showing us much pity by moving into a Liberation Squat right across the street and waving a flag that was bound to cause us – cause me, anyway – much heartache and then retiring for the night to a tent in the front garden with a Hamasnik.

There were no other empty houses in other streets in other suburbs she could have camped in? Did it have to be across the road? Did it have to be in Streatham? She couldn't have occupied Tooting or Wandsworth?

Charmian found her actions less provocative. 'At least we know where she is,' she said. 'We can keep an eye on her from here. You might think I'm being sentimental but I believe that's why she's done this. It's her way of saying she wants to come home.'

'If she wanted to come home she could have come home,' I said. 'She doesn't have to taunt us with her disaffection in the very street where she was born.'

'You're not a good psychologist,' Charmian said.

'And she's not a good daughter. At the very least it is not tactful of her to plot the Final Solution to the Jewish problem in front of our noses.'

'I doubt she thinks that's what she's doing, Ferdinand.'

Ferdinand, not Ferdie. Ferdinand — my formal *ancien régime* reactionary's name.

'I doubt she thinks, full stop. Right opposite us, Charmian. Right opposite! Don't tell me that's coincidence. And did they have to rename it Leila Khaled Hall? I very much doubt Zoe would have heard of Leila Khaled before yesterday. Now she's a hero. She's probably got Leila Khaled's face tattooed on her *toches*.'

Charmian shrugged her famous Cassandra Clytemnestra shrug. 'I don't know who Leila Khaled is either.'

'A sort of Palestinian Che Guevara. Pockets stuffed with grenades, she hijacked a couple of planes in the 1970s.'

'Were many people killed?'

'I don't think so. Maybe a fellow terrorist. But that's not the point. There might have been. And she's the reason it takes so long to get through airport security. She took the fun out of air travel, Charmian.'

'Not funny, Ferdinand.'

Ferdinand — my not very funny person's name.

'I remember the last time we went abroad with Zoe,' I went on, 'she was the first to complain that they confiscated a bottle of her perfume . . .'

'Still not funny, Ferdinand.' Soon she'd be calling me Ferdinand Draxler MBE.

'. . . now she glorifies her.'

'There are worse women she might have glorified.'

'Name one.'

'I don't have a list of bad women at my fingertips. I'm not you.'

'What does that mean?'

'Ferdie, when we first met, you knew the name of every woman who worked as a guard in Belsen.'

'And Auschwitz.'

'There then. You collected them. Like autographs.'

'Better to be morbid than in denial. It wouldn't surprise me if Zoe and her blood-crazed chums think the Jews invented Auschwitz to justify turning the Al Aqsa Mosque into an apartment block.'

'What do you know about her friends?'

'I know what they tell me. They don't exactly keep their thoughts to themselves. Look for yourself. Charmian, a giant full-colour photograph of a Middle Eastern terrorist willing to blow up a plane does not belong on Strawberry Fields, Streatham. Even a freedom fighter should respect the built environment. What if they've got weapons over there? We are in their direct line of fire.'

'I know my daughter. They won't have weapons.'

'They have eyeliners. Where does this end, Charmian?'

'When the kids get bored.'

'*If* the kids get bored.'

'Or grow up.'

'What if they don't grow up? What if it's too much fun glamping in the suburbs and calling it the Occupation? What if their next move is to take over Streatham Common? What if they won't let us cross unless we recite a poem by a Palestinian poet and observe a minute's silence?'

'What if we don't know a poem by a Palestinian poet?'

'Then you should be ashamed of yourself. But I'm sure they'll have some to hand out. That will be one of Zoe's tasks. We taught her to love literature.'

'Who told you she does that?'

'No one. It's an inspired guess. Don't underestimate them,

Charmian. They've covered every eventuality. You think we've been here before but we haven't. This isn't Vietnam all over again. This is younger and more hysterical. This is Vietnam with fewer words, more sinister packaged opinions and TikTok. Social media loves the youthfulness of it. It has an interest in preventing anyone getting bored or growing up. There's an entire restructuring of history for young minds going on out there and our little Zoe is part-instrumental in it. Killers become saviours. Bad becomes good. False becomes true. How long before the great unravelling takes us all the way back until Creation returns to Chaos – light become darkness again, the earth become the sea.'

'This is a gloomy thesis to build, Ferdie, on the evidence of a poster of a forgotten Palestinian hijacker flapping about in a garden across the road.'

'She isn't forgotten.'

'She will be tomorrow.'

'If there is a tomorrow. Get real, Charmian. The world will end somewhere, sometime. Why not Strawberry Fields next week? Apocalyptics have always prophesied that it will come down at last to the Jews versus everybody else. Well, here we are. Nicely lined up. You and I—'

'I'm not Jewish. Or have you forgotten?"

'You could have been. You could have taken lessons. Bought a wig.'

'I thought I'd leave the Jew to you. You do it so conscientiously.'

'All the better. I alone on this side of the street, those who would blow me out of the sky on the other.'

'Oh, Ferdie, Ferdie.'

'Oh, Ferdie, Ferdie, what?'

'Sometimes I fear you are being serious.'

QUE SAIS-JE?

'Fuck it,' I said that night, 'we're going in.'

'We?'

'It's a manner of speaking.'

'In another manner of speaking, you're not going in. Dressed like that, you're not going anywhere.'

I had covered my head with a tea towel and carried a bread knife. I looked, I thought, like Valentino in *The Sheik*. Charmian thought I looked like Wilson and Keppel costumed for their famous Egyptian sand dance.

'Are you telling me I look the part?'

'Have you been drinking?'

'Bottles and bottles.'

'Don't even think about it, Ferdie. You go in, I go out and don't come back.'

'You can't stop me,' I said. 'I'm over eighteen.'

'I question that.'

'Do you want to see my driving licence?'

'Ferdie – tell me what you intend to do when you get there.'

'Climb the wall. Slash the poster. Pull down the tents. See if I can find the original house sign and rehang it. *Holly Lodge* – I always liked that. And rescue Zoe.'

'Don't do it,' Charmian said.

'Why not?'

'You'll make a fool of yourself. You'll trip over the wall. You'll fall on your bread knife. You'll grab a girl who isn't Zoe. You'll get your nose bloodied. Don't turn their circus into yours. Have some pride, for God's sake.'

'And opera buffa? What was it you told me about the Greeks?'

'A great buffon knows when to play down the buffoonery.'

'So first you worry that I'm too serious, then you worry I'm not serious enough.'

'Yes. But of the two I prefer you serious.'

She remembered what her father had told her about Jews. That they'd been demoralised. That they had forgotten how to be in earnest about themselves. Life as a Jew was either a catastrophe or a witticism. Her husband was not a light or comic person. His passion, when she met him, had been English grammar. Later he became the headmaster of a well-regarded primary school. He gave seriousness a bad name. Get him on the subject of education and you'd wish you'd never been born. Yet the minute he was called upon to be a Jew he hyperbolised himself, taking shelter in the absurdities of *commedia dell'arte* one minute and the agonies of high tragedy the next. Why couldn't the Jew in him stay still?

'What is it in yourself you fear finding?' she asked me.

'Ask me, rather, *who* is it in myself I fear finding.'

'Go on. Who?'

'The primitive, suckled in a creed outworn. Now ask me who else I fear finding in myself.'

'Tell me.'

'The parvenu, suckled in no creed at all.'

'You are hard to please.'

'I think it's more that I am easy to be distracted. There are so many ways of not doing Jewish well. Every day I am less the Jew than I might have been.'

'Who told you there was a Jew you might have been? Who burdened you with that – your mother?'

'Good God, no. My mother didn't think there was a good Jew in me to let down. There's no measuring up to Belsen. I am like a million other Jews. All second- or third-generation survivors, all dwarfed by our own history. The mystery is that so many non-Jews wish they were us. They begrudge us our dwarfing. They resent our being gassed when they weren't. They think that gives us an unfair advantage over them. The fucking Chosen Ones. Understand their envy and nothing will surprise you again. But you never will understand it. The role of the Jew is to make life inexplicable.'

She put her arms around me and kissed me tenderly. Of late she seemed to be putting her arms around me every day. Did she know something I didn't? Did she know I was in danger? Did she know my heart was giving out? Did she know the blood would soon be guggling out through my ears? Had our daughter told her there was a price on my head?

She divested me of my tea towel. Took back the bread knife. Kissed my nose.

'Let me save you from your mother,' she said.

To the surprise of both of us, we wept a little in each other's arms.

Zoe's squat vanished almost as soon as it appeared. After four days of repetitive drumbeats and droning it was gone. Not my doing, though I'd tried. I'd rung the police to report incitement to racial hatred but when I quoted *From the River to the Sea* the woman on the other end of the phone couldn't hear anything offensive. The words called for nothing less than an annihilation of an entire nation I told her. I gave her the dimension of the territory – this the river, this the sea, there the Jews at the bottom of it.

'Sounds beautiful there,' she said.

'Don't tell me *you* want it now.'

'Only to visit. I've always fancied floating on my back in the Red Sea.'

148

'Dead Sea.'

She sighed. There I went again. Death death death. She thought I should lighten up. What I described was just young people having fun. I told her I was a headmaster and knew the difference between fun and murder.

'Like I say,' she said and that was that.

In the end it was a mother of triplets complaining about the parties after midnight that got the jamboree shut down.

'See,' Charmian said. 'You aim too high. The destruction of the Jewish people is not going to cut it with the Metropolitan Police. You're better off seeking a noise-abatement order.'

According to gossip in the street, the protestors left bottles, needles, used condoms and other items denoting debauch on the lawn of the appropriated house.

'Now how do you feel about our precious Zoe?' I asked Charmian.

'I suppose it depends on what those other items denoting misbehaviour were,' Charmian said. 'I don't mind if she had a drink – and who are you to talk? – and I'm pleased she's being sensible and practising safe sex. You?'

I? The question put me on the spot. I too didn't begrudge Zoe a drink and accepted Charmian's view on safe sex while not wanting to put my mind to the conjunction of daughter and condom. Zoe might not have been a Jewish daughter but I was still a Jewish father.

More troubling to me was the idea that bashing the Children of Israel could be the pretext for a party. I feared and hated the extremism of the young, but I hated just as much the thought that they couldn't give their undivided attention to it. Wasn't the destruction of my people deserving of a little more respect?

'She's a flibbertigibbet,' I told Charmian.

'Well isn't that better than being a zealot?'

'She's both.'

'Give the poor girl a break,' Charmian said, putting the bread knife back in the drawer.

Poor girl! God almighty!

A RAT CALLED JEW

It seemed to be spring. Don't ask me in which year. 'How has that happened?' I asked Charmian.

'It follows winter, Ferdinand.'

'Nothing follows the winter we've just had.'

'Well, here's spring.'

'It must be a false spring.'

'Just welcome it.'

'And how do you propose I do that?'

'Take me to the country.'

'Shar, I have a school to run.'

'Take your school to the country.'

I thought about it. The country was a bit far but the Common wasn't a bad idea. While I was pondering who to take – because dragging the whole school round Streatham Common was out of the question – a delegation of anxious Jewish ten-year-olds appeared in my office, wanting to know if there was any truth in the assertion made in a poster which had suddenly appeared all over Streatham and been put onto TikTok that Jews were descended from pigs, which was why Jews weren't allowed to eat them. The poster showed a pig eating a sandwich with a Jewish banker in it.

I gathered them into my arms and kissed them one by one. 'You are all descended from angels,' I told them.

'Even the rich ones?' one of the children asked.

'Rich or poor, we are all the children of God,' I said.

I didn't doubt there'd be a backlash from socialist Jewish

parents and non-Jewish parents in general. But what the hell? It was spring.

Remembering the innocent good times when sweet little unaffiliated Zoe, Charmian and I had joined an effort to remove rubbish from a scraggy bit of mudflat on the River Thames, I hit upon the idea of equipping my sad gang of petitioners with hooded overalls, paintbrushes and small cans of Agreeable Gray and getting them to accompany me around the neighbourhood, in and out of the Common, painting over any sign, symbol, epigram or cartoon that intended to demean or distress us. Children love a task. Much as I didn't look like Snow White, my assistants resembled the Seven Dwarfs and we sang 'Whistle While You Work' as we went about cleaning up the city.

When hearts are high, the time will fly, so whistle while you work

To be certain they didn't paint over Hazchem signs or some sub-Banksy but still priceless graffitist, they had to report to me anything about which they had serious doubts. Blood-red hands had to go, of course. As did the inverted red triangle of Hamas resistance. Stars of David without any comment were problematic, but Simon said they were there to show terrorists which building to blow up, so those we painted over. What about Stars of David inside a swastika? Some thought we should just delete the swastika. Others argued that we shouldn't keep the remaining Star of David because it had been contaminated. I was with the others. A Star of David inside a swastika was like a Jew who marched for Hamas. Damaged goods. After a show of hands, we slapped on the paint, leaving Emanuel to worry whether it could ever be permissible, whatever the circumstances, for a Jew to do that to a Star of David. I put my arm around his shoulder and told him I admired him for his scruples. The next Star of David we encountered in a swastika he could make his own decision about. Ten minutes later he asked what he should do about a Star of David hanging from a noose. 'Cut it down,' was the consensus.

As for the rich Jew pig-sandwich, not a one was to be found by the time we got to the Common. Had someone made it up? Or had the Pig Marketing Board stepped in?

And so time flew.

Sara found a rat with the word Jew written on its back. Because she had a pet rat, she wanted to save this one. We had a show of hands. Yes, all right, but only if we painted out the word Jew. Mark suggested changing Jew to Gazan. No, said Aaron, we weren't in a fight with the Gazan people. So we painted over the rat. 'Sorry,' I heard Sara saying under her breath.

Slogans, as opposed to symbols, were submitted to my adjudication before being cleaned up. *Jews Did 9-11*? Paint over. *Zionism is Nazism*? Paint over. *Free Palestine*? I hummed and hawed. Leave, no, paint over. No, leave. What about changing it to *Free Palestine from Hamas*? OK, yes. *Jew-Free Zone*? Paint over. *Zionazis*? Paint over. *Kill Jews, Gas Jews, Drown Jews* – paint, paint, paint. 'What about *Fuck the Jews*?' Martin asked, pulling Sara's hair. 'That's enough of that, Martin,' I said. But that set off a round of doing something dirty to the Jews. 'What about *Shag the Jews*?' 'You've made that up, Barry,' I said. 'Sir, sir, sir – what about *Cunt the Jews*?' whereupon I proposed we break for biscuits.

'See, children,' I said when we got back to school, 'we have it in our own hands to remove whatever they say about us.'

But Sara, who was still mourning the rat, wondered if that meant they would have to go around with paintbrushes for the rest of their lives.

Her small, anxious voice was as a cry from an already desolated future.

'Very good question, Sara,' I said.

'But what's the answer, sir?'

I had to tell her I didn't know.

'How was that?' Charmian asked when I got home.

'Rather lovely. Touching. I don't know. Upsetting.'

'Did you see the bluebells?'

I hung my head. I was my mother's child. I hadn't seen any bluebells. What did bluebells look like? 'No,' I said. 'Only rats.'

'IF I AM OUT OF MY MIND, IT'S ALL RIGHT WITH ME...'

Once word spread of the lovely time we'd had painting over Rats Called Jew and Jews Called Rat, even our non-Jewish children wanted to join in. I explained that this wasn't going to be a regular occurrence, that the curriculum didn't make provision for the daily removal of moral effluence from the capital, but the clamour for it grew. Among the staff, only Max Axelberg, the would-be Jew who wasn't, and Gillian Wallenstein, the Jew who wished she wasn't but was, spoke out against it. What sort of example of tolerance was this to be giving our pupils?

I meant to guffaw but I fear I spluttered. Charmian had told me I was spluttering in my sleep. I called the rebels into my office. 'You'll be telling me next,' I said, 'that painting over expressions of anti-Semitism was an attack on the free speech of anti-Semites?'

They were pleased I understood their position. 'Precisely, Headmaster,' Max said.

Gillian towered up at me. 'I'm glad you see it that way,' she said.

I slapped the side of my head and told them to get out of my office.

I had not the slightest doubt that word would get around the school that I was self-harming.

It wasn't in deference to Max or Gillian that I finally said no to another clean-up. I knew from the experience of trying to keep my mother's gate free of bile that graffiti could not abide a vacuum and mutated the minute one's back was turned. I'd read that come the end of the world – and by my reckoning that meant any time soon – only tardigrades would remain alive. Wrong. Graffiti, too, was indestructible. Could the world really end without the moving finger writing Death to Jews on a nuclear shelter wall?

Best to let my pupils learn about the indestructibility of animus in their own time.

It should have been possible to laugh all this off. It was not the work of wise men and women. It was not even the work of the victimised or grief-stricken. When you are nearly touched by catastrophe you don't seek relief by vilifying Jews. Graffiti is the work of those who hate vicariously, the second-hand salesmen of grievance, piggybacking on the wrongs suffered by someone else. So why didn't I laugh it off? Could it have been that I too wanted something I had no right to, or at least had *less* right to than I let myself believe? Was I drawing sustenance from the cacophony? Did I recognise myself now only in the rage it engendered?

And the marches? Were they the work of wise men and women?

You'd think I'd have got used to them by now, like London marathons, half-marathons, quarter-marathons. But they were getting louder. I had started to hear them from my garden. First the helicopter overhead, then the drums, then the chants. From my greenhouse in Streatham I could catch snatches of conversation.

'I just picked out Zoe's voice,' I told Charmian.

'No, you didn't.'

Peace marches, they were said to be. 'I don't hear anyone saying they want to kiss a Jew,' I remarked to Charmian.

'You don't hear anyone saying anything,' she answered. 'We're six miles from those marches.'

'Measured terrestrially, maybe. Cosmically, they're at the corner of the street.'

'Then go inside, Ferdie,' she said. 'And shut the windows.'

I told her I was not an ostrich. I didn't think that what I couldn't see or hear had disappeared. Locked inside the house I would still know that ancient calumnies and defamations were being voiced today, in the twenty-first century, right here, this very hour, on the streets of London. 'You would think,' I said, 'that people would smell a rat, think twice before accusing me of the very crimes they accused me of in the thirteenth century.'

She made me lemongrass tea and suggested a lie-down. But I wasn't much better lying down.

'You're a nightmare to share a bedroom with at the moment,' Charmian said.

'Am I snoring again?'

'Snoring, shouting, swearing, cursing, screaming.'

'Do you remember anything I shout?'

'Yes. It never varies. *How fucking dare you!*'

'Do you know whom I'm shouting at?'

'At a guess, I'd say the world. And, of course, people who confuse "who" and "whom".'

'Anyone listening?'

'One person.'

'Whom?'

'Ferdie, your jokes aren't funny.'

'Says whom?'

'Say I. I can't speak for the inside of your sleep, but on the outside I'm your only audience.'

'And you're sure I'm sleeping? *How fucking dare you* is my default position when I'm awake too.'

As though she didn't know that.

'It's getting harder and harder,' I went on, 'to distinguish dream from nightmare, sleep from waking, today from yesterday . . .'

As though she didn't know *that*.

The following week, she told me I was stimming.

Stimming was not a word I knew.

Self-stimulating. Biting my nails, pulling my hair out, punching the side of my face, cracking my fingers, banging my elbows on my desk, jiggling my legs, grinding my teeth, making threatening gestures with my napkin.

I denied the napkin.

'You don't know you're doing it,' Charmian said. 'You twist and knot it under the table until it resembles – I don't know what, a mace and chain, one of those weapons slaves fought one another with in the Roman Colosseum – and then you thump the table with it.'

'This is a first. I've been accused of arming every event in Jewish history, but never, until today, my grandmother's Viennese table linen.'

'I'm not accusing you, Ferdie. With your mother it wouldn't be surprising if you militarised a matchstick – which, by the way, I think you should stop using as a toothpick in public.'

'I have stuff between my teeth.'

She didn't answer.

She was right about the napkin, though.

The next time we went out to dinner I scrupulously avoided playing with it, but the minute the conversation turned to Jews I began knotting it and hitting the table.

'Who are you attacking, Ferdie?' an old school pal of Charmian's asked.

Charmian answered for me. 'The world,' she said.

The two women exchanged knowing looks. They could have been mental health clinicians enjoying a night out. Did I see Charmian mouth the word 'autistic'? Did I see her friend mouth 'neurodivergent'?

Because I didn't want to spoil the meal I didn't shout how fucking dare you. How fucking dare you equate a Jew with a neurological disorder. But I didn't stop whipping the table.

No, I told Charmian the next day, I wouldn't see a doctor. Two and two didn't equal five. Jew and Jew didn't equal genocide. I wasn't to blame for those who thought they did.

'Let's say you're right,' Charmian said. 'How does that help you?'

'Help me to do what?'

'Stay sane.'

'If madness is the price of telling the truth, Charmian . . .'

A wild eyebrow display from Charmian.

I knew what she was thinking. King Lear? Not Jewish enough. Hamlet? Neh. Shylock, then? Maddened, but not mad. Kafka's Gregor Samsa was more like. Bellow's Herzog? Too literary. My very own antic disposition – the Chlodnik my mother had seen in me, the country bumpkin who could run rings round a Cossack? Too obscure.

And I knew what she feared. That if madness was the price of telling the truth, I would choose madness.

PART 2

UNDER THE GHARQAD TREE

If you could lick my heart, it would poison you.

Yitzhak Zuckerman, hero of Jewish resistance to the Nazis

TWO STATE SOLUTION

After the delegation of anxious pupils, a delegation of fraught parents. What had I done to their children? Sara hadn't talked for days, was refusing to eat, and had released her pet rats into the wild. The wild? Streatham Common. Aaron could only get to sleep after counting imaginary swastikas. Emanuel had drawn Stars of David hanging from nooses on his bedroom wall. Didn't I think I should have asked their parents' permission before enlisting ten-year-olds into my dwarf army of fumigators? I apologised. I had thought they were enjoying themselves. We had whistled while we worked. But, yes, I should have thought harder about the long-term effects of exposing them to the sign language of their would-be murderers.

Then again, would the children have been quite so anxious in the first place had their mothers and fathers not allowed them to access TikTok on their smartphones any time of the day or night? Might I suggest a little more parental invigilation?

Was I telling Mark and Stella Davidoff how to bring up their children?

Almost, I was. Though to me it felt more like telling the Davidoffs how to bring up themselves. If our enemies were able to walk all over us, was it not because we had forgotten the great lessons of self-preservation we'd been taught in the days we listened to our God? We were once a fastidious people. We knew to keep our distance from those who didn't divide holy from profane or milk from meat. The wilderness teemed with wild beasts who had no regard for us and the desert thronged with tribes who had even less. In separation lay the secret of our refined ethic. This was not that. That was not this. Glastonbury was not Jerusalem.

We were not them.

And don't tell me this is apartheid. I want to deprive no one of their civic rights. If anything, it's more about depriving ourselves of the joys of societal togetherness, in the manner of monks or any other contemplative order of monastics. Choosing separation for oneself is about devotion to an idea that isn't universally shared. Whoever calls this apartheid is not a person with whom I want to share anything.

So did I think we should be hiding ourselves away again? In a ghetto, say. Almost. But I also almost didn't.

Almost had become my modus operandi.

I almost told the exquisitely scented Dr Magdy what I thought of the way he, too, was bringing up his children. Almost, almost. Because the public discourse had turned so violent we had to be doubly careful how we talked to one another face to face. We kept up a pretence of cordial relations and good manners – he shook my hand warmly when we met, 'Arab to Jew,' he said, 'chosen by each other for endless struggle'; 'A long struggle indeed,' I answered – but we were careful not to specify. He didn't accuse me of planning the extinction of his people and I didn't accuse him of planning the extinction of mine, though I didn't accept that his son was using the word jihad in the sense of striving to attain spiritual righteousness when he spray-painted it on the pavement outside the school.

Dr Magdy was here to express sorrow that his two sons had not been invited to join us on our hate hunt, not only for their sakes, in that they felt passed over, but so that the Jewish kids could hear the other side of the story. I told him that we'd heard enough of the other side of the story. That we'd heard, for many years now, almost nothing else.

He leaned forward on my desk and slowly put his fingers

together. This had the surprising effect of getting me to do the same, though I wore only a single wedding ring and his hands were ornamented with all the jewels of Arabia. He could have been a travelling salesman in gold. The closer he leaned into me, the closer I leaned into him. The longer he kept his fingers together, the longer I kept mine. There was something dream-like and sensual about this encounter, though encounter was not the word for it. We affiliated, we coalesced. Many more minutes of this and I'd be telling him I loved him.

'You are a wise and I imagine learned man,' he said, and waited. I too waited. Yes, I was falling in love with him all right. First Zoe, now me – what the hell was wrong with my family? By my family I didn't just mean the Draxlers. I meant Jews in general, marching side by side in love with people who wanted to kill them. Did Dr Magdy want to kill me? Oh, the thrill of it.

'So I must assume,' he continued, 'that you are familiar with the Hadith – that is Arabic for story or lesson – of the gharqad tree.'

I was familiar with the meaning of Hadith, I told him. But had to admit ignorance of the gharqad tree.

He opened his fingers slightly, as though to let forgiveness through.

I opened mine to show I was both grateful and respectful. I shifted in my chair so he could see the Koran on the book-shelf behind my head, alongside the twenty-nine volumes of the Babylonian Talmud.

'I'm surprised,' he said, 'since the gharqad is considered a Jewish tree. And, what is more, I see' – here he nodded in the direction of a print of a William Morris honeysuckle painting on my wall – 'that you are a lover of nature.'

I laughed. 'That I know of,' I replied, 'there is no such thing as a Jewish tree. And as for my being a lover of nature, just about the only living thing I know is honeysuckle and I only know that courtesy of the grammarian Ronald Ridout who found in the very word the quintessence of Englishness.'

Not twenty yards from the window runs a honeysuckle hedge, and close to the top a pair of linnets had with great cunning built their nest and hatched their little brood.

The Arab smiled his scented smile. 'Ronald Ridout's books I remember from school in Damascus,' he said. 'If my English is passable I believe I have your Mr Ridout to thank for it.'

No wonder I felt a bond with him. What grammar has joined together let no jihadist put asunder.

In answer to my asking what made the gharqad tree Jewish, he put his fingers together again. 'According to the aforementioned Hadith,' he said, 'the End of Days will come when we fight our final war with the Jews.'

'How will you know it's the final battle?'

'Because the Jews will be running away . . .' He separated his fingers and made running movements with them on my desk. Run, run, run . . . 'But there will be nowhere for them to hide because even the rocks and stones will open their mouths and call out, O, Muslim, there is a Jew hiding behind me or in my shadow. Come and kill him. Only the gharqad tree refuses to take part in the slaughter of the Jews and says nothing. But because Jews seek safety behind gharqad trees we know where to find them . . .'

'And do what?'

'Exterminate them.'

I sat back in my chair. A rat called Jew.

'Please don't think I subscribe to this teaching,' he said.

I had by this time – by the way – fallen out of love with him. 'So why do you tell it?' I asked.

'Out of friendship. I think you should know what you are up

against. Though versions of this Hadith date back to early Islam, this one appears in the charter of Hamas. It's a problem—'

'It is indeed,' I said. 'I hadn't realised Hamas was quite so spiritual.'

'Well, theirs is a reading of Islam not all Islamic scholars agree with. Extermination of the Jews might or might not expedite the End of Days. Myself, I think some other solution can be found. Hamas do not. In short, I think removing a few posters won't deflect them from their course.'

'Then why did you object to it?'

He smiled. 'Have I not said? Because my sons felt left out of an adventure. And to get your attention, I suppose.'

'And now you have it?'

He rose and put my hands in his. 'To wish you luck. This is a good school and you, I believe, are a conscientious headmaster. I pray for all good things for you.'

I couldn't let him go without wondering if, by the side of the story of the stones and the tree, all other expressions of Jew hatred didn't pale into insignificance. He seemed annoyed that I called it Jew hatred. Arabs weren't racists, he said.

Maybe not, but they were anxious to see the back of Jews.

He smiled at me. 'Wouldn't you be?'

'If . . .'

'They kept killing your people.'

Kept killing. I reached beneath my desk for a napkin to twist. *Kept killing . . .*

'Look,' I said, 'you could always make a decision to moderate your melodrama and think peace. Losing doesn't have to be so hurtful. If you weren't a shame-people you'd accept defeat and stop looking forward to the next war. Yes, one day you will win. The odds favour it. And at last your shame will be redeemed. But ask yourself at what cost in human life. In the meantime, reconcile yourself to defeat.'

Was that the most insulting thing I could say to someone for whom every letter of the word defeat was as a dagger to the heart?

I hoped so.

He paused and moved his face closer to mine. Was I frightened of him?

He hoped so.

Finally he said, 'I will ask the same of you. One day we will win, I agree with you, not because we're stronger but because you're weaker. We can't bear to lose but you, my dear friend, can't bear to win. You are melting before our eyes. Something in your faith makes you faint-hearted. Good socialists but poor warriors. You had your brief hour as soldiers, felt bad about it, and now your spines are broken by guilt. A moral degradation is spreading throughout the Jewish armies. You have lost your moral compass. The best of you are full of remorse, the worst of you are grown cruel and mindless. We are witnessing the beginning of your end.'

'You say that with satisfaction.'

'I do.'

'You want the Jews gone?'

'From my part of the world, yes. And if that means from the world altogether, then so be it. I won't weep.'

'Bring on the End of Days . . .'

'Yes. Bring it on.'

'You speak as though you are no more than a witness to this. Whereas you are, in part, its architect.'

He opened his arms to me. Brothers.

'I?' he wondered. 'How?'

'What your endless wars have failed to achieve militarily, they have achieved psychologically. As you say so eloquently, you face a near broken enemy. Jews today have more to fear from themselves than from you. They fill themselves with more distaste than they fill even you. For this you can congratulate yourselves. You've done what even Christianity couldn't do. You've mounted a relentlessly sentimental propaganda campaign that's convinced half the world – and that's the half that has Jews in it – that the Blood Libel was no libel after all. Not every citizen of the medieval world believed the Jews were in league with the Devil. Today everybody does. Even my daughter. *Even*, on a bad day, me. Your doing.'

'Are you suddenly not responsible for your own actions?'

'And have you not been responsible for yours? You have waged endless wars and complained when you did not win them. I'll split the difference with you – call it a Two State Solution – we are each the other's creature. And each the other's curse.'

'But you have the land.'

'The land! Our few miserable acres can hardly be said to constitute "the land", Dr Magdy, when you consider the millions of hectares that make up Arabia. But all right – if you cannot tolerate the idea of a single Jew on a pinprick of Arab territory – we have the land. But it's only temporary. And in the meantime you go on your way weakening our wills and poisoning our souls. I congratulate you. Allow that you have sacrificed thousands of your own people to achieve this, and I will allow that yours is the most successful act of demoralisation ever carried out by one people against another.'

'The Jew is his own making.'

'And so is the Arab his.'

We paused, smiling into each other's faces. Did we get a kick out of this? He rose. I rose. We embraced, like brothers.

Suddenly I had brothers coming out of my ears.

WHEN WILL WE KNOW IT'S
TIME TO LEAVE?

I didn't doubt I would be fired when word of this conversation reached the school governors. I had crossed a line. I had crossed several lines. I had called a blood-curdling piece of Muslim prophecy a blood-curdling piece of Muslim prophecy and that, in the first quarter of the twenty-first century, walked and quacked like Islamophobia.

Yes, we'd embraced, but a headmaster is not meant to say such things to anyone, let alone the father of a pupil. I knew I would not remember why I said what I said, any more than I would remember to whom I said it. What did he look like, this Arab gentleman? Did he have a beard? Was his head covered? Did he wear a Savile Row suit? All I remembered was the coruscation of his fingers. I hadn't looked at him and even had I looked I wouldn't have seen him. I'd been staring into the hurricane, calling on the Lord of wind and fire to give me courage.

Furthermore, I had told a number of Jewish pupils that they were the children of angels – a distinction they hadn't hesitated to boast about in the playground, thereby upsetting non-Jewish pupils who reported it in turn to their parents who would surely have interpreted it as further proof of the theological apartheid practised by The Chosen.

And thirdly, I had lost, or was any day about to lose, my second secretary in six months. The reason? She had discovered me *in flagrante delecto*, partially undressed and standing on one leg in the presence of my deputy – who was surely a reluctant party – declaiming cries and oaths which, by my own admission, were incomprehensible to anyone not of the Jewish faith.

'So when?' Miles and Helen Graverman asked, bursting into my office with far less regard for the niceties of protocol than Dr Magdy had shown. Yes, Magdy had turned up with my death warrant, but he had manners.

When what? When would I be told to clear out my belongings? Surely word of what had been said one minute ago could not have got out already?

'When will we know?' the Gravermans went on, seeing my confusion. I thought they were going to bang my table with their fists. 'When?'

'When will you know what?'

'That it's time to leave.'

'Leave where?'

'Where do you think? Here. This country.'

I suddenly felt very weak. How was I expected to know? I was a teacher not a prophet.

I had been sitting here for five solid days, taking questions and answering complaints, changing the books most evident on my library shelves to suit the religious disposition of whoever was booked in to see me. I have said I had the Koran with Arabic-English word-for-word translation on the shelf behind my head – a gift from the Streatham Islamic Society in the days when a Jew was not an anathema and could be rewarded for his contribution to interfaith understanding – and twenty-nine volumes of the Babylonian Talmud. I even went so far as to have *The God Delusion* by Richard Dawkins visible but not prominent in case some furious non-believer burst in, wanting to know why atheist hymns weren't sung at morning assembly. Though in point of fact nothing was now sung at morning assembly. Dawkins was wrong. God wasn't a delusion; He was a flashpoint.

It wasn't easy, sitting in the centre of this storm without a napkin to twist under the desk. Now I knew what stimming was, I'd gone to extreme lengths to avoid it. I made fists of my hands so I couldn't crack my knuckles or pull my hair out. I yawned a lot so as not to grind my teeth. I interlocked my ankles to stop my legs jiggling. I wished Charmian would pop in with a sandwich so I could ask if I looked mentally healthy enough for her. But I wasn't sure I could deal with *when will we know it's time to leave* without gouging my eyes out.

When will we know it's time was the party-question from hell that all Jews asked at some time or other no matter which country they were in or how safe they felt there. Jewish couples with children in particular asked it with urgency. Had we been living in Berlin in the 1930s – the question went – when would we have realised we had to run? What year? And where would we have run to?

Where to was a question finally settled, for all but the most anxious of Jews, with our repatriation into the land of our forefathers, the land flowing with milk and honey. Milk, honey and security. And to be secure we didn't have to go there in body. Henceforth, we could avail ourselves of sanctuary long-distance. They couldn't touch us now. We had what others had. But we forgot that we were not permitted to have what others had, that the very idea turned the minds of those for whom the Jew was by definition – by necessity even – a vagrant.

Hence the joy unleashed when a pogrom like the European pogroms of old, with some new folderols of Middle Eastern savagery thrown in, shocked Jews out of their complacency. Where do you think you're staying, oh Jews?

And where did that leave to run to?

My sometime alter ego, Chlodnik, always one for a bad, black joke, whispered in my ear. 'Berlin.'

That I hadn't yet played the *when will we know* game with

Charmian didn't mean the question hadn't occurred to me. My reluctance to discuss it was a consequence only of her not being Jewish. She didn't have to worry. As she wasn't in any danger, she didn't have to leave. Unless, that is, some new segregation law were to be passed that drew no distinction between Jews and their spouses.

'Don't worry,' I told Charmian. 'Should that happen, we'll get divorced in good time.'

'But how will we know when that is?' she asked.

'Good joke,' I said, kissing the top of her head.

'Who's joking?'

I kissed her head again. We could have gone on like this all night.

Being a husband was one thing, being a headmaster was another. I couldn't take responsibility for the safety of Emanuel's parents. 'Who knows?' I answered. 'Who ever knows? All we can do is work on the assumption that nowhere's safe for long. Keep a cabin trunk packed under the bed.'

They already did.

'Be sure your travel documents are up to date.'

They already were.

'And say goodbye to your children in good time.'

They already had.

BROTHERS IN ARMS

I waited, in an orgy of stimming, for the letter informing me of my dismissal. The governors couldn't have been in two minds. There was only one explanation for the delay: discussions must have been ongoing about my punishment. Dismissal was not enough. Not impossibly they were looking for a talking tree to hang me from.

Axelberg, as my deputy and unwilling partner in weird erotic practice, must surely have been in on the conversation. Had he noted any extreme changes in my behaviour? Ha! How long did they have? Whatever the explanation, I'd never seen him so animated, waving his little hands about so violently that he was knocking off his own yarmulke, warmly greeting members of staff he must have known were beginning to go off him and pestering me as to when would be a good time for him to visit my mother. Ever since I'd told him she would like to meet him – it was a measure of his vanity that he never wondered why – he had been like a child promised a trip to the seaside. Every other day he would check the date of the proposed visit. He was preparing himself for meeting her, he informed me a dozen times, by reading her memoir. He had been very moved by it, he said.

I brooded over his ill disposition towards me, sure that he knew my fate and couldn't wait to divulge news of it to my mother. 'Your precious son has had the boot, ma'am, for insulting Muslims.'

I consoled myself with the thought that if he supposed my mother would give two hoots whether or not I'd been sacked by

Strawberry Fields Primary School for insulting Muslims or for any other reason come to that, he hadn't read her very closely.

I checked with my mother to see if she could see him sooner than arranged. Whenever, she said. And Max? The day after tomorrow? If I wasn't mistaken, he was quivering like a cat in love.

'No time like the present,' I said.

I too was on heat.

I drove us to her house and parked outside. I hoped there'd been a renewal of Yid-curdling street-art on my mother's door for Max to see, but all was blank. Just a question: but could that have been because the man responsible for it was in the car beside me? I didn't truly believe that to be the case but once you start suspecting you end up suspecting everyone.

Max closed his eyes as I rang the bell, adjusted his yarmulke and recited a prayer from a siddur which he kissed before closing it. He also put his finger to the mezuzah and kissed that.

'This is such an honour,' he said. 'I am so nervous.'

'Perhaps if you stopped kissing things . . .' I ventured. Then added, 'And whatever you do, don't try kissing my mother.'

She opened the door to us herself. She wanted, I assumed, to show her strength. Axelberg gave her an Old World bow. He was in Vienna, *circa* 1927, keeping up the pretences of civilisation before the hellish gates of history opened. Maximilian Axelberg, Jew of Yesterday, Today and Tomorrow. Mutti nodded her head to him.

'I have read so much about you and by you,' he said, 'that meeting you in the flesh feels unreal to me.'

He seemed about to apologise to her on behalf of all Christians, before remembering that he was no longer a Christian and now had to apologise for Jews.

'I am all too real,' my mother said.

There was tea waiting on a discoloured silver tray. The best Viennese china was out. To impress Axelberg? Why, for God's sake? What was wrong with a dog bowl?

He sat on the edge of a velvet chair. I offered to pour. 'No,' my mother said, 'you go into the kitchen. Isak's there. Mr Axelberg – do I have the name right? – are you comfortable here?'

Evans, I muttered under my breath. Call the cunt Evans.

She smiled on him. Was she flirting? Would she be asking him to call her Mutti next?

I lingered, just in case. If he called her Mutti I would challenge him to a fist fight. No – I would challenge *her* to a fist fight.

'Go!' she said to me.

It felt like the end of Act 1 of a melodrama when the heroine is asked to choose between two suitors and chooses the wrong one.

I won't describe the kitchen. I have already described the living room and the kitchen was no different. Boxes of letters on the kitchen table. Books, covered in dust, on what were once work surfaces. Folders containing talks and lectures. Torn-out pages from magazines. Unsorted photographs. How my mother ever found a kettle to boil water in I had no idea. On a high kitchen stool sat Isak, looking into space and twirling his hair. Missing his ringlets, I guessed.

We hadn't seen much of each other over the last month or so. Every time I popped by, he was running. I took that to be a euphemism but I had no idea for what. Had he secretly taken up going to the synagogue again?

I asked him if he was feeling better.

'Better than what?'

'Better than you were.'

'Better than I was when?'

'Is this you being playful, Isak?'

'Why do you keep calling me Isak? I don't call you Ferdinand. I'm Ike. Easy to remember. Ike the Kike.'

He slid off the stool, crouched, folded his arms and did a Slovak dance. The Kazatsky Kike.

I could see why Charmian rolled her eyes in a dozen directions when I spoke of the Jewish genius for comedy. Yes, Jews were funny except when they weren't. And, when they weren't, they weren't on a grand scale. Why weren't Isak and I able to leave it at that? Accept our fate. We were of the Brotherhood of Non-entertaining Jews.

All right, of Isak I had no right to speak. He was in the process of reinventing himself. Maybe he'd be wildly amusing company when the reinvention was complete. I held out no such hope for myself. I had no lightness. I was bread dough that didn't, wouldn't, couldn't rise.

From the next room I heard a sound that might have been my mother's laughter. I only say *might have been*. I wasn't in a position to be any more certain than that. I was her son. Mothers such as mine don't laugh much with their sons. The burden of gravity they must pass on inhibits laughter. But I found it impossible to believe that Axelberg had said something amusing. So if she was laughing, there could be only one explanation: it was a relief to her to be with someone who wasn't a son.

Isak seemed to hear it too. He smiled at me. Was it possible that he knew what I was thinking and maybe even thought the same?

And now the mother we had to thank for who we were was laughing like a girl?

I shifted in my seat. 'So how's your love life?' something made me ask him. Probably the feeling that, when all was said and done, love – love of the stolid faithful sort – was all I was good at.

'I don't have a love life. I've told you, I am not like you. I wish I were. Not in any other way. Just the doting Jewish husband part.'

'Don't forget the doting father.'

I knew he carried a torch for Zoe without knowing her. They were fellow rebels. They were both tattooed.

'Let me tell you where I stand on Jewish fathers,' he said. 'It's not a job for a Jewish man.'

'Our Jewish father was all right.'

'Can you remember him?'

'No.'

'There you are. The fathers we remember are the tyrants. The ones whose only mode is that of a jealous Yahweh demanding unconditional love. *Thou shalt have no other Father before me.* And if that's hard on the sons it's even harder on the daughters. I wish you'd let me stepfather Zoe for you.'

'What makes you think you'd like her?'

He paused. 'I like what I hear.'

'You mean you like what she calls me.'

'What does she call you?'

'A child-murdering Zio-pig . . .'

'Yes. I think she has a way with words.'

'And what makes you think she'd like you?'

He paused again. 'I'm her uncle. I wouldn't demand unconditional love.'

'That's because you don't know what love is – your description of yourself.'

'Do you know what the Christians got right, bro? They said Jesus loves you. It isn't necessary that you love him back.'

'So was that how you spent your time in that madhouse in Mea Shearim, rocking backwards and forwards while reading Matthew, Mark, Luke and John? Did the warders know?'

'Why do you want to be rude to me?'

'Jealousy. I want Mutti to love only me.'

'You're safe there, little Ferdie. I was never her favourite.'

'She didn't have a favourite.'

'Oh yes she did. You. You were her Number One Son.'

'Say that again, Isak.'

'If you like hearing it. You were her Number One Son.'

I went still.

Number One Son.

Number One Yid.

Christ!

I put my hands to my head. 'Isak, was it you?'

'Was what me?'

'You know.'

'I don't know.'

'The number plate.'

I advanced on him, got closer to his face than I'd ever been. Saw the sulphur in his eyes. Saw the ghastly unusedness of his pallor. Smelt the devils, unless they were the dying saints, on his breath.

So much for the shirt-drawer exorcism.

'You didn't get rid of them after all,' I said.

He looked bemused.

'Your demons.'

He still looked bemused. God forgive me – in my mother's kitchen I reached for my groin and made the gesture of Onan, beloved of halfwits the world over.

Was that a grin he threw me? The glad-to-be-found-out-at-last smirk?

'You meshuggener,' I said. 'You fucking meshuggener.'

He laughed. 'Of course I'm a meshuggener. One of us had to be. I did it for you. I sucked the madness out of the house so you could go on and be a headmaster and get a knighthood. It's time you thanked me.'

179

'I don't have a knighthood.'

'That's the thanks you get. You should thank me anyway. I tried.'

'You were responsible for the graffiti!'

'Maybe.'

'You turned my car into a coffin!'

'Might have.'

'You dust-bombed my garden!'

'Don't remember that but I wouldn't put it past me.'

'Isak, this was your house. You were born here. You grew up here. How could you defile the scene of your earliest memories? It's an act of sacrilege against yourself. It's like putting a knife into your own heart.'

'That's right. That's a good description.'

He mimed the action – knife, heart, die . . .

'For what? For why?'

'For why not. Not everything has to have a reason. No reason's good. Fucking insanity's even better. Let me tell you, in none of the 613 mitzvot does it say you can't spray swastikas and shit on your mother's gateposts.'

'Where does it say you can?'

'Ferdie – Judaism isn't just a religion of dos and do nots. We are allowed to be various sometimes. We have free will. We are encouraged to make up our own minds on stuff . . .'

'Stuff? Is this what a lifetime studying the Torah does for you? Stuff! What stuff, you lunatic?'

'All sorts of stuff.'

'Such as fouling your own nest?'

'You call it what you like – I call it breaking free of our fucking endless partisanship. Us us us. Always in the right . . .'

I shook my head and took several steps back from him as though I needed to see the full man. Top to toe. The *gantser gesheft*. The whole crazy broken-down malfunctioning works . . .

'Tell me something, Isak.'

'Ike.'

'Tell me. Must the opposite to endless fucking partisanship always be endless fucking betrayal? Can't you just take a holiday from your crazy education? Must you blow up everything you were taught? Don't you see that all you're doing is swapping one extremism for another?'

'It's your daughter that became a jihadist, Ferdie boy, while you were taking a holiday from your crazy education.'

'I didn't have a crazy education.'

'You had Mutti. Never Again Mutti.'

'So was that why you spray-painted her door? Does Mutti belong in the trash for you?'

'I didn't do that.'

'Then who did?'

'It doesn't matter. And I bet she never saw it.'

'Then what was the point of it?'

'What belongs in trash, bro, is not Mutti but the self-pitying Never Againers. Who else demands a guarantee like that? *Never Again . . .*'

'It's not a guarantee. It's an entitlement . . .'

'Exactly, exactly.' He jumped up and down like the mad thing he was. 'There it is. That's why they hate us. *Entitlement.* I bin your entitlement, brother. And that doesn't mean I've left one club to join another. I'll march with whoever will have me. I'm the Jew of the future, Ferdie boy. The Unentitled Jew of Tomorrow. Join me . . .'

'Go home, Isak,' I said.

'Only if you call me Ike.'

'Go home, Ike.'

'This is my home.'

He surprised me. 'I'd have put money on your saying you have no home.'

'Same thing. I am the archetypal everywhere and nowhere Jew. Just like Vati. I want you to try it. You look stressed, bro. You have the mark. You're too much one thing and not enough of another. That's why your daughter pissed off. She wanted to experience the world, not a ghetto. Let me get her back for you.'

'And how do you think a *isedrater* like you is going to accomplish that?'

'Charm, bro.'

'You aren't carrying an AK-47. That's what charms girls like her.'

'I'm carrying more than that.'

I pulled a disgusted face.

Whereupon he enfolded me in his arms, kissed me, and told me he loved me.

I closed my eyes and tried not to imagine I was Zoe.

But answer me this: why were men suddenly kissing me? Sundry men. Old friends, old enemies, brothers, Arabs . . . Kiss, kiss, kiss, kiss. Could they smell defeat on me as soldiers smell it on their generals? So many Enobarbuses to my Antony? *Sir, thou art so leaky that we must leave thee to thy sinking . . .*

Did they know my days were numbered?

AXELBERG IN BELSEN

Had my mother been listening to her sons debate their heritage? Or did she just have uncanny instincts? At that very moment, anyway, she called us into her presence.

Axelberg was on the edge of a worn velvet dining chair, as I guessed he'd been since we arrived, eager to keep up with her as she led him down, lower and still lower, into her experience of the infernal. I could tell she'd turned it on for him, the full Belsen *gesheft. Komm mit mir, Herr Axelberg. Taste my chlodnik soup.* And down he'd gone, with his tongue hanging out – the blood-sucking, vicariously vampiric spiritual ghoul he was.

So far so predictable. He was not just any old Jew now. He was the whole, fully paid-up, kit-and-caboodle Shoah-maven. 'Remember to buy him striped pyjamas for his next birthday,' I told myself. 'And a striped yarmulke.'

What kind of madhouse was this? Ike the Kike who couldn't wait to leave at one end of the room, Axelberg the *toches lecher* who couldn't wait to join at the other, and I, searching for the right killing word, the perfect damning joke, in the middle. While my Mutti, older than Mother Methuselah, sat in the middle of her sticky web, pulling at the filaments that bound us to her and her irreparable history.

I waited for the great unravelling. *I, Max Axelberg, once Tony Evans, the temporary eternal Jew, more sinning than sinned against, want to say sorry on behalf of the Jewish people . . .* Whereupon my mother was to crush his balls like snails. So what had happened? Why wasn't he curled up foetally on her threadbare rug, howling, with his hands between his legs?

What had happened to her promise? Had she forgotten? Or had he won her round to his disgusting theology of disloyalty?

She introduced the brother I didn't like to the colleague I liked even less. 'I think you two will get along,' she said.

'I don't,' I said beneath my breath, lest she meant they were both pleasant men with pleasant views. But then it crossed my mind that she meant they were both unpleasant men with unpleasant views, in which case, yes, they would get along famously.

They shook hands, anyway – each a little too keen to do so, I thought – Axelberg rising from his chair alacritously, as though in a hurry to show he preferred any brother of mine to me on first sight, Isak demonstrating that for all the changes he'd undergone he could still be affable to a man in a yarmulke the size of a pizza.

My mother caught my expression of bottomless distaste – a look acquired from her, let it be said – and signalled me to push aside a box squirting papers, sit on the settee and behave.

'So,' she said, looking around, 'all my sad captains.'

'Are you proposing one more gaudy night, Mutti?' I asked.

No wonder people hated us. Smart, quick-witted, allusive shits that we were.

All Shakespearean clowns were Jewish, I'd written when I was at university. In some moods I thought everyone in Shakespeare was Jewish, they spoke so well and knew such sadness. And everyone Jewish, like Mutti and me, was Shakespearean.

'I am not sad,' Axelberg said. The complacent never are. For all that he'd reviewed a play for the *Jewish Chronicle* and offered me the part of Donkey in his dramatisation of the Gospel of St Matthew, he seemed not to recognise the words of Shakespeare's Antony. 'I am enthralled,' he went on, gazing into my mother's face, which had a softer cast than usual. 'This is a rare occasion for me. I could listen to you all day.'

'He is in high spirits,' I whispered to my mother, 'because he has sucked you dry.'

'I have given my time freely,' she said.

'It's not your time he's after, it's your soul.'

'I've given of that freely too.'

'Then it's time you thought of charging, Mutti.'

'Don't Mutti me,' she said.

Did I catch her exchanging looks with Axelberg? Was Maxie/Waxie now her little baby boy?

'Plus,' I said in a louder voice. '*Plus*, he is delighted that I am going to be sacked for Islamophobia.'

He shook his head. 'This is the first I've heard of it,' he said.

'Islamophobia—' my mother began, but Max cut her off.

'I know what Islamophobia is,' he said. 'I meant this is the first I've heard of Ferdinand being sacked for expressing it.'

'Since Islam is an anti-Jewish faith,' my mother continued as though she hadn't been interrupted, 'don't you think a Jew should be forgiven an occasional lapse . . .'

'Into what?' Max cried. His eyes popped. He gasped for air.

'Into whatever he wants. Hating Jews is not a hanging offence. Everybody does a bit of it from time to time. Even Ferdinand here. I've read somewhere that in moderation it's good for you, like red wine. But I've never heard it said that a little Islamophobia bucks you up. Don't you think' – this to the frothing Axelberg – 'that we're all a bit oversensitive to the feelings of Muslims? Is that because we are frightened of them, do you think?'

I watched my deputy die a thousand deaths, not wanting to cross my mother but unable to accede to the cruel bigotry of her remarks. 'I think you'll find my mother's joking,' I said. Why? Why did I let him off? Could it be that I had a place in my mushy heart for him, after all? Treat the stranger well, the Book of Leviticus taught. Wasn't Tony a stranger in this house?

But I couldn't leave it at that. After all was said and done, I wanted him to remain a stranger in this house. 'I'm surprised that with your sensitivities you never tried converting to Islam, Max. Perhaps one day you will.'

'If you mean that to be funny—' he said.

'We aren't a funny family,' my brother Isak intervened. 'We were brought up to believe life was a serious business.' He'd been standing looking out of the dirty windows. Seeing and I thought hearing nothing. What made him find his voice now I didn't know. But I could tell it was only temporary. He drifted in and out of the conversation, like a spirit that lacked the confidence to haunt. 'We grew up very conscious of the need to strike back at our enemies,' he went on. 'We didn't have the luxury of thinking about their agonies. They enjoyed ours too much.'

'Who did you ever strike back at, Isak?' my mother asked. 'You grew a beard and went mad.'

'See?' Isak said, showing his open palms to Axelberg. 'See what it was like growing up in Belsen?'

'You stop that,' my mother said, turning her blazing face on him. 'You stop that right now.'

Before our eyes, Isak regressed half a century, shrinking into himself and putting his hands up to his face. Like the Isak of old, Isak with his beard and ringlets, Isak in his little black rabbinic suit, Isak with no tattoo of a butterfly quitting the chrysalis, he fled the room.

Max Axelberg lowered his head. 'Shouldn't you go to him, Ferdinand?' he said.

Go to him!

Phony Tony in phony empathetic heaven . . . Oh, how he loved it. The spectacle of a Jewish family coming apart at the seams because it was the wrong sort of Jewish family.

I surreptitiously touched his yarmulke. As I suspected, it was hot.

It behoved me, I thought, to remind my mother why I'd brought him to meet her. 'Max thinks we have turned the Holocaust into a tool of blackmail, Mutti,' I said, hoping this would wake her to her promise to crush his testicles like snails. 'He thinks we use it to justify stealing a falafel on pitta from an Arab street trader.'

'I won't even bother . . .' he began, but my mother had started to push her chair back.

She danced her eyes. I'd forgotten she could do that. 'Well, we all have our views,' she said and, declaring herself fatigued by all the social excitement, announced her intention to retire. To me she nodded a brief goodbye, but to Axelberg she was positively courtly, showing him the door with solemn ceremony, accepting his elaborate bow with a shorter one of her own and taking his hands in hers.

I watched him move to kiss her.

Now! Mutti, I thought, now's the moment to bring up your knee.

Instead, she offered him her cheek.

How did I not faint?

Although I was furious with my mother for not doing to Max Axelberg all she'd promised, at the same time I felt a great rush of tenderness and even pity for her. It appeared she was hungry for company. Not *his* company; *any* company. Yes, she had her sons, but we were not a change or a rest from her own self. We were just more of her. We couldn't bring the outside world into her presence. We could tell her she was remembered and respected still but we couldn't usher the living proof of that and lay it at her feet. By virtue of being her sons that was the one task we weren't equipped to perform. We couldn't recreate the smell of esteem. We weren't dispassionate enough. I should have known that the indifference to report she boasted of could only ever have been a pretence. We go on wanting to live in the world's embrace until we have no more flesh or faculty to be embraced. It was a miracle she was alive, and a miracle she had survived so well, every part of her alive yet. How could she not crave admiration for that? Whatever I thought of Max Axelberg, for my mother his deference was the living proof she still mattered out there, and that meant was still loved. She surely knew he was a fraud, as many a lover, brought back from waiting tables in Corfu or cleaning shoes in Casablanca, is known by the gullible spinster or wealthy widow to be a fraud. It didn't matter. He was company. He was better than no one. And that he should even put time into deceiving her was a species of flattery.

My poor Mutti. She had tried harder than most people to be above the common. But it was bound to be a losing battle. The prouder we are, I thought, the easier we are humbled.

I needed to walk off the sadness of it. I thought about gathering the paint and paintbrushes from the boot of my car but decided that if I saw a swastika on anybody's gatepost I'd leave it there. Hateful as the symbol was, what if it conferred a perverse dignity, showing you had the wherewithal to be hated? Was there some point in the graph of racism when being a victim was a warrant of one's importance? Had I been vicariously high on it myself for the last six months? Were the Hamasniks to lay down their weapons tomorrow and their apologists to apologise for the hateful slanders they'd spewed out, day after day, would I any longer know what to with myself?

I wasn't sure what this had to do with my mother and Axelberg but I felt I had no dispensation to judge her for putting up with him. No person has the right to tell another – not even a son a mother – what is and what isn't an allowable reprieve from life's tedium.

WHOO!

Walking back, I heard the noise of struggle coming from the communal garden opposite my mother's house. I pushed open the gate and found Isak sitting on Max Axelberg's chest among the rhododendrons. Plainly, he was after the yarmulke which Axelberg was holding on to as though his credibility as a pukka Jew depended on it.

'Wouldn't your life be easier, Max?' I shouted across, 'if you just stopped wearing that? At a rough count I can think of twenty times I've seen someone try to knock it off. Add to those the hundred attempts I've made and I'd say it's entered its final days. Time to say a prayer for it. Couldn't you find a religion that allows you to keep your head bare? Hare Krishna, maybe.'

'Get your brother off me and then we can discuss it,' he answered.

Seemed fair. I could do that. I was a headmaster. I'd settled many a kippah fight.

But fairness had fled my being. 'Hit him with your little fists,' I called.

'That's nice,' Isak said, 'telling someone to hit your brother.'

'Then leave him alone,' I said. 'What do you want with his yarmulke anyway?'

'I don't want it. I dispute his right to wear it, that's all.'

'We all dispute his right to wear it, but that isn't really the point. What if he disputed your right to wear a Rolling Stones T-shirt?'

'I'd listen to his argument.'

'Then why don't you listen to his argument for wearing his kippah?'

'I have. It's bullshit. The fucking yarmulke will be the death of us. Like the fucking tzitzit and the fucking tefillin. We've mistaken ritual for virtue, bro. We think we're the living word of God on earth because we wear shmattes.'

How long this would have continued I didn't know. What brought it to a close was the appearance of a beautiful woman, already known — it appeared from the way she gazed at him — to Isak. She wore a long, almost seraphic gown, and a white headscarf draped loosely in the way a non-Muslim would wear it for a brief visit to a mosque. Her figure was so light that you could imagine her entering a place of worship and never being seen again. Her features, though, were heavy — her mouth full and sensual, her lips bruised, her nose fleshy, her eyes burdened. Such a face as would have delighted a Pre-Raphaelite painter who would have called her Miriam or Rebecca and would now be charged with the aesthetic crime of orientalism.

She didn't speak but didn't strike me as alarmed or even surprised by the spectacle of her lover — if such he were — sitting on another man's chest. Not impossibly, this was a regular occurrence. Wherever there was a kippah , there was Isak trying to knock it off. One way or another, her presence made no difference to Isak who neither looked at her nor loosened his grip on Axelberg.

The tussle between the two men had turned silent. Buster Keaton and Harold Lloyd. Miriam, or was it Rebecca, had found a nearby bench and sat in silence. I hadn't at first noticed she'd been carrying a sketchbook. From her silken bag she took a pencil. Slowly, absently, as though in obedience to a higher power guiding its movements, she allowed her hand to skim across the paper. The air about her fell still. It seemed that her presence alone was enough to slow down the normally frenzied business of humanity.

Had a stranger walked into the garden he might have thought it was 1913 or the entire world's sound system had been turned off.

Why I didn't walk away and leave these mute combatants to it I can't say. Quite possibly it was because I wanted to make voluble contact with their mute spectator. Had I, in the immediacy of seeing her, fallen a tiny bit in love? I was an obsessively faithful husband. I hadn't looked at another woman since Charmian came flying out of the sky on skis and broke her ankle as I gazed with rapture upon her. Explain, then, what I was feeling – what I was doing *having* feelings – for Miriam or was it Rebecca. Beyond saying there was a surge within my breast of what could only be called ancestral longing, I couldn't account for what I felt.

I needed to press my lips one final time to those of a woman of the same doomed persuasion. One last exchange of vital fluids before the next bloodbath . . . Will that do as an explanation? No. It didn't do me, either.

If it were true, as Isak had attested, that she was more than a tiny bit in love with him and suffered his not being at all in love with her, her confident, beauteous demeanour gave a false clue to her character. But I felt I needed to speak to her to find out.

I went over to her bench and introduced myself. I didn't offer her a hand. Or dare look at what she was drawing. A fleshly contact, or mere curiosity, would have broken the spell. 'Isak's brother,' I said softly. 'Ferdinand . . . Ferdie.' She seemed not to care. Was she deaf perhaps? That would have explained her strange aura of immobility and unresponsiveness. Tragedy even. So much beauty locked away. And would have explained how she might have fallen in love with my brother. She had not heard a word of the idiocy he spoke.

How would I get on with a woman who could not hear me? I had an MBE for words. Did I have any means but words to find a way into her heart?

Silent prayer, I wondered. She seemed made to silently pray beside.

Baruch atah Adonai, Eloheinu Melech ha'olam,
Shehecheyanu vekiymanu vehigi'anu lazman hazeh.

The prayer to celebrate the new: a new act of benevolence, the wearing of new clothes, sitting silently beside a new woman. True, she wouldn't hear the words, but she would know them already and thrill to their familiar vibration. I had read somewhere that the loss of one faculty can heighten the others, and I imagined our wearing our eyes out with looking and our fingertips with touching. Above all, it was the burden in her eyes I imagined relieving and the bruises on her soft mouth I wanted to kiss away, though the kisses I gave her would be lighter than thistledown, to be blown rather than planted.

Stop this! What the hell was I thinking?

Must I say it? She was a woman of my faith, no matter that I had no faith, only rage masquerading as belief, but then all that would change as I charged myself with having to assuage the pains of being Jewish for her. Love in mute sorrow was what I envisaged, love buffon-free, love which you have had to go through the fires together to delight in.

Dared I touch her yet? I thought not. Dared I look at her? Dared I ask to see her work? This, too, I denied myself. In good time, Ferdie, all in good time.

The wrestling, meanwhile, was reaching its climax, Isak finally succeeding in removing Max's kippah, clambering to his feet, and going on a wild triumphant run around the garden, like a giant from Goya waving his victim's head.

'Whoo!' the mysterious silent woman rose from the bench rose and shouted. She waved her sketchbook in the air. 'Way to go, Ikey.'

★

I found Axelberg sitting in the front seat of my car which, in my earlier hurry to get him out of it and into my mother's hands, I must have forgotten to lock.

'Interesting day meeting my family,' I noted.

'Fascinating,' he said.

'You seemed to hit it off with my brother.'

'You call that hitting it off?'

'I do. Nothing betrays love between one and a half Jewish men more than a wrestle for possession of a yarmulke.'

'Will your jeering never stop?'

'It's all good clean fun, Max.'

He swung around in the car seat, watery-eyed and angry. 'Just what is it you fear I am going to steal from you, Ferdinand? Your secrets?'

'*The Secrets of the Jews* – isn't that all a bit medieval? I have no secrets.'

'You are a family of secrets. Your mother is a Sphinx.'

'I thought you were getting on with my mother.'

'I was. I admire her. But she is an enigma.'

'Mutti? She's an open book. She's been telling her story to whoever is willing to listen for more than half a century.'

'Her *version* of her story . . .'

'Whose version should she be telling?'

'Have you ever done the sums? Have you ever asked yourself how old she must have been when she first entered Belsen?'

'Your point being what, Max? That she made herself up the way you made yourself up? That she spent the war years in a kindergarten in Bognor Regis? Was that why you were so anxious to meet her? To mark her arithmetic?'

'Ferdinand – you must know that not everything even the most truthful people tell you is true. Mistakes are made. Embellishments are inevitable.'

What I knew was that I didn't want to hear him questioning

my mother's young age when she started working for Josef Kramer and her old age when she gave birth to me. Who cared? 'This is just clambering over Auschwitz with a set square and calipers all over again,' I said. 'This is denial-by-birthday.'

For a moment he was too hurt to form words. Did I dare call him a denier – he who had attended David Irving's trial in Austria in 2006 and spat on him! An event – he believed – that subterraneanly contributed to his eventual decision to become a Jew.

'I thought you woke from a coma in Manhattan's best Jewish hospital.'

'That was later. Irving's trial prepared my spirit for what I was when I woke.'

'Don't tempt me, Max.'

'Meaning?'

'You say you spat at Irving. Did you get him?'

'Yes.'

'Max,' I lied, 'I have been to the court where Irving was tried and convicted and I have measured the distance between the public gallery and the defendant's stand. That distance would have been too great even for your prodigious spit to have reached him.'

'You measured before you knew my story?'

'I measured in anticipation of your story. What I'm saying is that dimensions are unreliable data. Data is unreliable data. I could be wrong about the Austrian courtroom. Quite possibly, it's been redesigned since you spat in it. Maybe it has been redesigned precisely *because* you spat in it.'

'So are you explaining away the discrepancies in your mother's Belsen story by saying that time has been redesigned since then?'

'I couldn't express it better. Time is always redesigning itself. You cannot make dates the arbiters of biographical truth, for the reason that there is no biographical truth.'

'That's a convenient way of covering up falsehood.'

'Let me ask you a question, Max. Why does it matter if my mother's story does or does not hold up? What's at issue here? A year? Six months? An old woman's memory? The veracity of the Holocaust itself? Will the whole schmear be proved invalid if you catch my mother out in an inaccuracy?'

'How many times must I say I don't for a second doubt the veracity of your mother's experience? The Holocaust happened. Humanity must live with that.'

'Humanity? Humanity cannot wait to hear the end of it. Humanity cannot acknowledge abomination. We're back with your Hamas Whatsit. Yes, yes, something happened. But if we can find the smallest variation in the story we can make it all go away or, better still, invert it. A tear in the sheet and the entire sheet's ruined – that's profligate moral economy. Honest people mend the sheet, Max. The sheet is still serviceable. The Hamas Bloodletting the same. It happened, however hard those who want it to go away try to discredit those it happened to. Question the honour of the innocent and you corrupt the case against the guilty. Question it often enough and eventually the murdered becomes the murderer.' It was my turn to be upset. I banged the steering wheel. 'Christ, Max,' I said, touching his arm, tenderly, as though we were friends about to be parted forever. 'If you really knew anything about being a Jew, you'd know that it's our historic role never to be believed. Not even by ourselves.'

He opened the car and let himself out. I watched him walk away rubbing his eyes and then turn to raise a placatory hand to me. Perhaps I read more into the gesture than was there; but it struck me with the force of a regret between estranged lovers, something more than an apology, an expression of sorrow that we would never sort out our differences but . . . I didn't know . . . but we were both men with hearts and therefore both susceptible to pain. It also expressed the transitoriness of this moment. Next time we met we would be hating each other as before.

I should have been more understanding of the knot of complications in which he'd entangled himself. In times like no others, people acted unfathomably. My mother had been a precocious young woman, barely out of puberty when Kramer employed her in his kitchens. How young? Maybe no more than twelve. Which would have made her fifteen when she cooked Kramer his last chlodnik on God's earth. Which would have put her in her early forties when she had me. Ripe and luscious at twelve, ripe and luscious at forty-five, ripe and luscious at ninety-four.

Be kinder to him, Ferdinand. He had an innocent, choirboy's mind when he walked in front of a yellow cab on Fifth Avenue, and still had an innocent choirboy's mind when he woke from the coma speaking Hebrew in a yarmulke the size of a Pontifical Hat. Were 'ripe' and 'luscious' words he'd even heard before? What chance he would ever penetrate the hot mysteries of Hebraic eroticism?

I am black, but comely, O ye daughters of Jerusalem, as the tents of Kedar, as the curtains of Solomon . . .

Curtains that Tony Evans had never drawn . . .

A bundle of myrrh is my well-beloved unto me; he shall lie all night betwixt my breasts . . .

Breasts whose dove-like softness Max Axelberg would never lie between . . .

It should be evident that, however graciously – by our standards – we'd parted, my mind was somewhere else. Across the road, in a communal garden, a woman of surpassing spiritual beauty was calling *Whoo!* to me. Sorry, Maxie boy, was the best I could do for him.

Besides which, I was sick of Holocaust talk. The word was wearing thin. We needed another catastrophe.

NOT ANNE FRANK

I couldn't get her out of my head.

'Who?'

There was an old music-hall routine about a Chinaman called Who. 'Who's Who?' the sketch begins.

Whoo was the diaphanous woman I'd encountered in the communal garden opposite my mother's house. My brother's girlfriend. The Brondesbury Beatrice. Whoo, because that was the first word I heard her utter.

I say I couldn't get her out of my head but that wasn't for want of trying. I loved Charmian. My head was hers. And Whoo would not have lodged there for more than half an hour had I not met her again, in company with Isak, at the premiere of a documentary about the massacre of young Israelis at the Nova Music Festival. It was Isak who had bought the seats, so we were sitting together, Whoo in the middle. No Charmian. She was working. She had advised me not to go as well. 'What more do you need to know?' she asked. 'It will only depress you.' I told her I had a duty. 'A duty to who?' Which would have been a good joke had she known she was making it.

'A duty to sup full with horrors,' I answered.

'That's not a duty. It's an indulgence.'

'We will have to disagree,' I said. And the next minute I'm sitting next to YouknowWhoo watching young Israelis being butchered.

I thought how easily this could have befallen Zoe – a music festival-goer herself – the irony being that she didn't accept any of it had befallen anyone. Zionist propaganda, the lot of it. I shed three-way tears – for the women raped and dismembered, for Zoe who wasn't but might have been, and for her refusal to believe whatever did not accord with what she needed to believe. Next to me, Whoo sobbed gently. Next to her, Isak the same. They had more reason than I did. Isak had told me they had friends who had lost children to the murderers. Israel was a small country. Everyone knew, or knew of, someone killed. Of no population was it truer to say that man was not an island. But we all had reason to weep. Wherever we were hanging out or hiding, Jews were a small country with a long memory. Every killing tolled a bell that reverberated through the present and the past.

I thought of putting a consoling arm round Whoo but didn't. We didn't look at each other during the film but I felt her slender thigh warm against mine. We didn't look at each other after the film either. She and Isak had to run. Run? Not the best word to use in the circumstances. Isak heard it and laughed uncomfortably. Though we still didn't exchange words or glances as we left our seats, Whoo silently took my hands and unlaced my contorted fingers.

I walked part of the way home, going over and over what I'd seen and imagining what I hadn't. Dead women, live women. The victims and the not, by grace of God. Zoe, Charmian, my mother, Whoo . . .

Whoo, I knew, had no business being there. She had no place in my heart. But we'd sat together, thigh to thigh, as horror was piled on horror and so she was fatally entwined in it all now, like the fair Ophelia dragged down by pond weed into the weeping brook where, because I was a sick fuck, I confused desire with sorrow.

Isak rang my mobile as I was walking back to ask why I hadn't spoken to her? I told him I'd been consumed by the film. I'd been in no temper to talk to anybody. He said he'd told her that was probably the case. But she'd wondered if I'd kept my distance because I disapproved of her engagement. *Engagement?* To whom? To me, you schmuck, who do you think? I told him I didn't know things had got that far. He said he'd told her the same thing. For the moment, their affair was secret. In that case, she said, I'll have an affair with your brother.

'Were those her exact words?'

'She was more graphic, if that's what you want to hear.'

Jesus, my family!

But I'd asked, hadn't I? I'd asked him to tell me her exact words instead of telling him to drop dead.

'Are you two getting off on this?' I asked. 'Are my wishes to be consulted on this at all?'

Isak guffawed. What man wouldn't welcome an affair with . . .

Gloria!

'If you don't like her name she'll change it for you, bro. She's all things to all men. When I met her she was working in a psycho-sex-club for ultra-religious schizophrenic Jews in Jerusalem. She was much in demand. If they wanted Salome, she could be Salome. If they wanted Judith beheading Holofernes, she'd be Judith. Didn't you have a print of that over your bed, you weird fucker? Anyone would think you wanted to be a butcher when you grew up. But let's not go there. Some, even weirder than you, asked for the Virgin Mary. Figure that. Orthodox Jews. She was official war artist for the IDF, after that. She could do anybody's style. Ask her to be Picasso and she was Picasso. Ask her to be Damien Hirst and she'd be Damien Hirst . . .'

Either I'd stopped listening or I was listening so hard my ear burned. Gloria! Was he telling me her name was Gloria?

Gloria for Christ's sake! Wasn't that the signature at the bottom of the street-sweeper stencil? *Gloria In Excelsis.*

Ask her to be Banksy and she'd be Banksy . . .

'Isak,' I said, 'what the fuck have you two been playing at? When I asked you if you'd had anything to do with the Banksy you said categorically no. Now you tell me your artist girl-friend is called Gloria. *Gloria In Excelsis.* A coincidence? I don't think so.'

'A bit of fun, Ferdie, that's all.'

'What kind of fun was that, you lunatic?'

'Get a life, Ferdie. And if it's too late for that, at least get a joke.'

'The joke being what, Isak? That Mutti would have had a heart attack had she seen it?'

'Mutti has no heart, bro.'

'I then?'

'Yeah, yeah, you always were all heart. We were messing about, Ferdie boy. I thought you'd see right through it. If we didn't want you to know, do you think she'd have signed it? Didn't you even notice that the street-sweeper was Jewish?'

'Because he had a big nose? What was that meant to satirise, Isak? Jewish self-hate?'

'You.'

'Me?'

'Yes, you and your tremors and terrors.'

'I don't go in terror of being swept into the rubbish.'

'Yes, you do Ferdie. That's exactly what you go in terror of. That's why you were tearing across London with a little tin of paint, chasing anti-Semites. But there were no anti-Semites in Brondesbury. Not with artistic talent anyway. That was where we came in. Just Semites playing games with you.'

'For what fucking purpose?'

'To make you lighten up.'

'Jesus Christ, there'd been a massacre, Isak. We've just watched a film of it.'

'Oh Jews, Jews! There's always a massacre of Jews somewhere.'

'You don't think that.'

'No, I don't think that.'

'Then why do you say it?'

'Because I'm a meshuggener like you. Just a different sort of meshuggener. Anyway, we've never really discussed it – what did you think of Gloria's pastiche? Good, wasn't it?'

I put the phone down.

Ten minutes later he rang back.

'Gloria says sorry,' he said.

'And you?'

'Ditto. Gloria also says sorry for ignoring you in the garden the other week too. She thought you'd like that. She's an astute reader of character.'

'She'd never met me.'

'I'd described you to her and from that description she fashioned herself in the image of your desires. Good, isn't she?'

'I have no desires that Gloria could satisfy,' I lied.

'Of course you don't. You go among the Gentiles when you want a shtup.'

'Leave my head alone. You've got Max's yarmulke, call it a day at that.'

'You're my brother. I want you to have the whole Jewish experience you've missed.'

'I've missed nothing, Isak.'

'Liar. I've met your wife, remember. Beautiful woman. Loved the red hair. Has she still got that? But not Old Testament. You haven't kissed soft Bible lips.'

'I could not bring myself to kiss what you've kissed.'

'With scruples like that you don't get to kiss anybody. In fact, Gloria and I don't kiss much. We have a semi-platonic relationship. She's not really my type. She's too Jewish. She reminds me of Mutti. You won't mind that, I know. You always were the filthy incest Jew in the family – getting in too deep, like a bee in a flower.' He made a slurping noise.

'Bees don't lick their chops.'

'No, but you do.'

'Make your mind up, Isak. I can't at the same time be the filthy incest Jew and the connoisseur of foreign flesh. Which am I?'

'You're the one because you can't admit to being the other. I'm offering you a way in. Isn't that what you've always wanted? To be a real Jew? People thought I was the frum one, but all the time I was trying to get out, you were trying to get in.'

'I never knew you were trying to get out.'

'That's because you had no interest.'

'I was busy.'

'So was I. It's not easy getting out. They stop at nothing to keep you. If you hear I've been shot, you'll know it's the ultra-Orthodox who've done it. They're ruthless killers. They keep their machine guns under their black hats. But that's me. We are talking about you. Gloria will show you what you've been missing. She's slept with Israeli presidents and world-famous rabbis. They'll rub off on you. When are you coming round to meet her?'

'I've met her.'

'I mean *meet* her.'

Isak was right, by the way. I did once have a print of Judith beheading Holofernes over my bed. I'd seen Artemisia Gentileschi's famous painting in the Uffizi on a school trip to Florence when I was fourteen. Don't ask me what I liked so much about it. Let's just say a fearless woman. Wasn't I the son of a fearless woman? *Another* fearless woman, then.

I admit, anyway, to finding the subject fascinating and could have told anyone interested where the best paintings of Judith making free with the head of the Assyrian general were to be found. In the National Gallery, for example, there's a startling version by Johann Liss in which Judith turns to face the spectator with a look so brazen you have to turn your own head from it. A less muscular, more exquisitely demure Judith – not a million miles in black-eyed, soft-mouthed, still seductiveness from Gloria formerly known as Whoo – was bought by Charles I and remains in the Royal Collection. In this, Judith holds out the handsome head of Holofernes by a clump of hair as though it's a contemptible 'thing' she is about to drop in the first rubbish bin she can find. Her expression gives nothing away and is shocking for that reason. What exactly made Charles I buy this painting for his collection one can only guess. A premonition perhaps.

Charmian was waiting up for me. Had I had a good night?

A good night!

She waived away her clumsiness. 'I've been drinking,' she said.

'I thought you were working.'

'I only said that because I couldn't bear to sit through a film of people being killed.'

I told her she'd made the right decision. It was unbearable.

Yes, but she couldn't relax for thinking about me. Was I really all right? She was concerned for my state of mind.

Yes, I lied. In truth, I was very not all right.

She had been listening to the radio. Anything interesting? Yes. No. A report on the International Court of Justice's ruling against the legality of the Jews.

I waited . . . Against the Jews' what?

Not the Jews' anything. Simply the Jews. Though its findings were only advisory and so could not be enforced, the court had ruled the Jews to be in Breach of Something or Other. Nature, she thought. Or was it humankind?

Is this because we made the desert bloom? I know there are eco purists who think we should have kept it arid.

No, it goes back earlier than that.

To our eating pigs?

Earlier.

Circumcision?

Well, that is a breach of nature when you think about it.

Are you telling me the International Court of Justice enjoys jurisdiction over our foreskins?

No, that's me.

You were too late, Charmian.

Let's say I have jurisdiction over the mausoleum.

Mausoleum!

Obelisk, then. Oh, I don't know, I was only trying for a joke.

And failing, I said.

Must you be so proper about it?

I apologised. What Charmian could not have known was that I was thinking about another woman. One who, to my sense, would not have essayed phallic obelisk jokes. I loved Charmian. Nothing would ever have made me betray her other than the few words we had just exchanged. Brought up to a tragic view of life, I did not recognise bawdy as Jewish. Bawdy was a holiday from being a Hebrew. Hence my secret-sharer Chlodnik, the funny boy my mother saw, the funny man I might have been, on whom I intermittently called to release me from sanctity. The woman who had turned my head represented a rejection of Chlodnik *and* Charmian. She was the Jew – the Jewess, dared I say? – the ironic-angelic pasticheuse – of Jewish heartbreak. A temple whore, according to Isak, who transformed all that was carnal into all that was spiritual – but you can't do that unless you're in earnest. No bawdy.

Knowing nothing of what was going on in my sick brain, Charmian plunged on drunkenly with her wild contention that the International Court of Justice had ruled Israelites to be in breach of nature, starting with the Act of Creation itself.

In the Beginning was a Breach of the Natural Order, the God of the Hebrews separating earth from water, thus inaugurating the principle of apartheid, and then, relenting, inundating the land again, from which example of mass destruction His Chosen People had learnt genocide.

You tell a good joke, Charmian, I said. You'd have made a stupendous Jewish comic. But what did the International Court of Justice really have to say?

She was a great essentialiser and was disappointed that I wanted her to specify the court's ruling. Surely I had the gist of it now. But I wanted it itemised. Then you name a point at issue, she said, and I'll try to remember how they found.

The Hamas Hooha?

What's that?

Max Axelberg's phrase for the massacre.

Didn't happen.

The Gaza War?

Illegal.

The Yom Kippur War?

Illegal.

The Six Day War?

Illegal.

Not giving everything back on Day Seven?

Illegal.

The War of Independence?

Catastrophe.

Anything they liked?

The Intifada.

My head was hurting. Let's cut to the chase, I said. Jews?

Jews what?

Just Jews.

In Israel?

Anywhere.

Oh, illegal everywhere.

If she was worried about my state of mind, this was a funny way of showing it. But alcohol does that. She was not in charge of the words that came out of her mouth.

'So it looks like you're back being a pariah people,' she slurred, before turning out the bedroom light.

'Thanks,' I said.

'Have I said something wrong?'

'I think you've still not grasped it,' I answered. 'We're back to not being a people at all.'

She leaned across and kissed me where a yarmulke would have been had I worn one. 'My poor little peopleless Jew,' she said.

What more could a Jew, peopled or otherwise, want of a wife?

May God forgive the answer I gave myself.

What more could a Jew, peopled or otherwise, want of a wife? That she be Jewish, blessed, limpid, touched by divinity, and . . . a little less pissed and a little less gross.

Sanctimonious prick! But don't forget I'd had a long day, seen terrible things, returned home to hateful news from a hateful world, and was feeling feverish.

I complained of a headache, embraced Charmian more passionately than I had embraced her since Zoe ran off to join the Foreign Legion, and turned over. Because of what – or rather whom – I saw when I closed my eyes, I tried to keep them open. In the course of my twenty-odd-year marriage to Charmian I had endeavoured to maintain a clean bed and a chaste imagination. Not only had I not desired, let alone wooed another woman – Melody was not another woman; Melody was the enemy – I had not let one near the periphery of my thoughts. Not even a shirt drawer like my brother? I had made a point of hanging my shirts on hangers, let's leave it at at that. I loved Charmian, didn't doubt that any courage I possessed I owed to her example and advice, and did not for one moment imagine that her equal existed anywhere. To so much as entertain the idea that one did – or might – would have struck me as an infidelity. But now, suddenly, I was thinking of a woman who had no real existence, who had moved through my thoughts like the Blessed Damozel with three Levantine lilies in her hand, as gossamer-light as one of God's choristers, whispering low

> Baruch atah Adonai, Eloheinu Melech ha'olam,
> Shehecheyanu vekiymanu vehigi'anu lazman hazeh.

Those were the words that elevated her to a plane of spirituality and devotion unknown to a woman as athletic and rude as poor Charmian.

Why poor Charmian? Because all at once the multivarious advantages which her not being Jewish gave her – a mouth that was not bruised, eyes that were not burdened, a bearing that was not ghostly, an amused courage in her step – precluded her from the impossible idealisation my Damozel commanded. Had I ever bewailed the sorrows of my people with Charmian? I found myself remembering her first descriptions of my mother's figure and then her speculation, at my father's funeral, that I must have been dying to fuck her now she was a widow. Not Jewish things to say, Charmian, I'd told her. Not how we talk about our mothers. Not the language we use at the funerals of our fathers. Too brute. When Moses came down the mountain with his Tablets it was to warn against commenting on the sway of a mother-in-law's hips, no matter that the mother-in-law in question did not think you'd make a suitable wife for her son.

Well, we got over that. I watched her come skiing out of a

mountainous pinnacle of snow like a meteor that had lost its way and saw a magnificent recklessness of being that I would always be a stranger to myself. I knew then that hers was the chariot to which I would have to hitch my hobbled mule if I were to make anything of my life. The best recipe I know, if you're a Jew, for a happy marriage: leave the heroics to your wife. Consider yourself the most fortunate of men to have a heroic wife and be pulled along in her wake.

But then the wicked whisper of a more sinuous, sneaky sort of ecstasy hijacks your intelligence in the night and you dream your forbidden orientalist's dream of harps and angels and Hebrew melodies and a thousand fragrant consolations, under the Moorish wall.

Outcast ecstasies. Rhapsodic transports of loss. Forbidden acts in forbidden hours. Dared I? No, and I said no I won't No. Undeserved and undeserving. Maybe I said maybe. Which of the 613 mitzvot, for or against? If wrong to marry a Midianite woman, then not wrong to betray her? Especially, exceptionally, with one who shared the sorrow. Insider healing. Never mind to mend a broken world; we *were* the broken world. Yes, I said yes I will Yes. And put on the biggest yarmulke I could find.

My first ever faithless dream, from which I woke guilty of everything and nothing, perspiring with the remorse of the false and the foolish.

'Whoo!' my dreamy Damozel had cried – I would rather not say in support of what bravura performance on my part – and then 'Way to go, Ferdie boy!'

From spirit to flesh to vapour in a flash of sulphur.

The long arms I'd been caressing were Charmian's arms, for which confusion there had to be some wailing Hebrew atonement but I didn't know it, or if I knew it I'd forgotten it. and I bathed her, Charmian my beloved wife of wives, in tears so scalding, and in so many sorrowing and sanctifying kisses that she must have wondered whether, at this late stage in our marriage, I had finally decided to subject her to the ritual bathing expected of a Jewish bride.

Was this Gloria's great gift to other – to real – Jewish women, that she made repentant husbands out of back-sliders?

If only Charmian had been a real Jewish woman she might have thanked her.

THE TREADMILL OF BLOOD

'Sir,' a little boy asked me in the playground, a couple of days after the foregoing events, 'are you complicit in the genocide?'

'That's a serious question,' I answered. 'Why do you ask it?'

'My dad says you are.'

'What does your mother say?'

'She says she leaves politics to him.'

'And what do you think? Do you know what genocide is?'

He thought about it. 'Hurting people?'

'And do you know what being complicit means?'

'Not saying sorry?'

'So what do you think?' I asked him, patting his head and smiling at him in a kindly fashion. I'd have given him a sweetie had I been carrying any. 'Do I look complicit in the genocide?'

He stared hard at my face. I wasn't looking my most verdant. I had bags under my eyes – the wages of tiredness and guilt. I wouldn't have blamed him had he said yes. But trust a child to see the essential goodness in a man. 'No, sir,' he said at last, smiling warmly back at me.

We were an object lesson in international relations.

I told Charmian about the encounter. We agreed I should carry a bag of sweets in the future to be on the safe side.

'It seems to me,' she said, 'as though the best way for you to get through this period is to take life an event at a time. Trying to join things up will only end disastrously.'

'Why is that, do you think?' I asked.

'I don't know. It's like learning lines – section by section, speech by speech works best. For me, anyway. Anything else is too daunting. The world is not going to get any better, Ferdie. The marches aren't suddenly going to stop. Our daughter is not going to come to her senses any time soon. Jews aren't going to be everybody's favourite people overnight. But if you can meet a nice little boy occasionally, you will feel better about yourself. Take pleasure in small things.'

On her advice I strolled across the river, made for St James's Park and went looking for the pelicans. Had I been reading the papers for anything but the latest update on the Blood Libel I'd have known there was an epidemic of bird flu and the pelicans had been temporarily sequestered in a pelican sanatorium for their own good. One of the park gardeners told me that. 'Is there any room in there for me?' I asked him. He had no sense of humour. 'Why, have you got bird flu?' he asked.

Maybe I did. I had everything else.

Without pelicans, the park didn't do the job I required of it. After half an hour of sniffing flowers that had no scent, I crossed the Mall and headed for the National Gallery. Some people love wandering into an art gallery not knowing what they will find; I am less spontaneous and prefer to go in with a painting I want to see in mind. All that talk of my brother's betrothed enacting Judith beheading Holofernes for quivering yeshiva boys in Jerusalem had rekindled my interest in the story. Not in Gloria. Believe me, that was over. But in the art. I would go and take a look, I decided, at the Johann Liss version in the National Gallery. Not my favourite. There was something too masculinist about her for my taste. Those rippling back muscles – necessary, I accepted, if you were to cleanly hack off a head – and that look of insolent defiance as she turns to face us ('Go on, judge me if you've got the balls') – took somewhat from the shock of its being a woman who was doing this. But I was eager to look again. Some called for the death of their enemies in the street, others went to study a painting. The advantage of art, I thought, was that it gave one the chance to meddle in blood and come away with one's hands clean.

There are people you know by chance yet only ever, as though by unfathomable design, meet at the same place and roughly the same hour, in the same coffee shop, buying tickets at the same box office for the same film, in the same doctor's surgery, in the same shop doorway during a rain shower. Ultimately, if the design holds, on the same bank of the River Styx, waiting for the boatman.

Remember Melody Costello, director of Artwashingtheoccupation.org, whom I'd met on the steps of the National Gallery in the first days of the capsized world? Here she was again, on the very steps where we'd embraced. We recognised each other at once but didn't pick up where we'd left off with a kiss.

'I am glad,' she said, 'that I have the chance to resume our conversation right here where I think I overstepped the mark.'

'I don't recall your doing that.'

'I made an assumption of agreement that I had no right to make.'

'We were all confused then,' I said. 'I was grateful for your warmth.'

'Even though you hated all I stand for.'

I threw her my best Jewish shrug. The one that most profoundly expresses the philosophy that's got us through. Hated shmated. When all's said and done, none of us is wholly in the right.

Then again . . . 'Are you here to egg another painting?' I asked.

She laughed a sad, remote laugh. 'So you do hate all I stand for,' she said.

'And you, I am sure, hate all I stand for.'

She needed to think about it. 'More in sorrow than in anger,' she ventured at last, 'may I say that your decision to take a party of pupils out onto the streets to remove the evidence of opinions different from yours was . . . well . . . ill-advised.'

'Those were more than opinions, Melody.'

'Yes. And many were, I am sure, hateful and hurtful, but shouldn't the children be allowed to reach their own decisions on them? I'm sure you all had great fun tearing posters down, but wasn't that an act of political censorship?'

'In self-defence.'

She touched my arm. 'Earlier today we threw chopped liver at Pisano's *The Israelites Gathering Manna*. Would you accept that that was self-defence?'

'Not to fight with you, Melody, yes all right. But I can't speak for Pisano.'

For all the initial wariness, we had quickly moved into our earlier mode of finding each other trystfully sympathetic. If only we weren't already spoken for, if only we weren't on opposite sides of a war unto the death . . .

We looked into each other's eyes, without speaking, then she said, 'And you? Anything in particular that brings you here?'

I could have said something woolly such as Oh, you know, just a look round to see what catches my eye. But that imp of provocation that was always getting me into trouble, that leapt onto my shoulders every time I felt I hadn't fought hard enough for my priciples, loosened my tongue. 'Yes. Johann Liss's *Judith in the Tent of Holofernes*. You know it?'

Yes, she knew it. Was it the brushwork or the subject that drew me to the painting, she wondered.

I should have said that that was a distinction I found difficult to make. Instead, 'Why would it be the subject?' I asked invitingly.

Was I looking for a fight?

Yes.

Why?

To compensate for *not* looking for a fight. To beg forgiveness from the Lord of Lords for liking her, for wanting her to like me, whatever lies she told about my people and whatever acts of vandalism her politics made her commit against works of art.

'That's not for me to say,' she said. 'Perhaps you are preoccupied with representations of brutality.'

'Do you accuse me of relishing brutality?'

'Do you want me to?'

'Do I long to play the Jew-as-victim card, do you mean?'

'I don't want to fight with you, Dr Draxler.'

'I like it when you call me Ferdinand.'

Was I toying with her? What if she *had* called me Ferdinand – Ferdie even – and thrown her arms around my neck, what then? What was I offering? I was taken. Twice. Joke.

She pursed her lips and looked away. Had she accused me of relishing brutality, would she have been wrong?

Since we had no happy ending, we were doomed to an unhappy one.

'I don't know what you want of me,' she said. 'I think perhaps you don't take me seriously. You can't woo me to your views. You don't need to. I know why Judith does what she does. But not everyone who sees the world differently to you is another Holofernes. The understanding you demand for yourself you must return. My children attend your school. I don't want you turning them into gangs who go round ripping off the evidence of opposing views . . .'

'I haven't turned them into gangs, Melody. And may I say I don't want the parents of my pupils going round defacing art in support of a disreputable cause. Occupation, indeed . . .' I heard but couldn't stop myself. 'Those who don't want to be occupied should start fewer wars.'

Her shoulders dropped. Mine too. We were both tired of

this. 'I respect and feel for you, Ferdinand,' she said. 'I know these must be terrible times for the Jewish people. But you have simplified your intelligence and hardened your heart to survive and . . .' She shrugged and put her face to mine one last time. I feared she was going to cry, but if there were tears on our cheeks they were mine.

I couldn't have said who walked away first.

But the following day she removed her children from the school.

I strolled back through the park. The weather had improved and this time, when I stooped to smell a flower, it had a scent.

Not all the pelicans had been quarantined. The smallest of them had evaded capture and, as though not wanting to be noticed, was sitting on a bench, collapsed into himself like a foldaway beach bag. I was lucky. The park was quiet. I was able to sit next to him, keeping my distance. He didn't look my way.

'I don't know where you stand on this,' I said to him, 'but I think these Christians have got a nerve. They get us to fall in love with them; they kick us from pillar to post, clearing us first out of this country, then out of that, and when at last we raise a finger to defend ourselves they tell us we have forfeited their devotion and accuse us of hardening our hearts. What would they have us do? Beg to be their sweethearts? Go on capitulating?'

The pelican said nothing but showed no sign of wanting me to shut up or leave. I would have liked to stroke his spiky punk haircut but thought I had no right to touch him.

He made a strange barking noise. 'You are less melodious than that bloody Melody,' I told him, 'but I trust myself more in your company,' whereupon he did at last look at me. Then he shook himself, half opened a wing, and hopped off the bench.

I was angry with myself. I had invaded his tranquillity. Just because I had none myself.

CUCKOO

The next time I visited my mother I found Axelberg, looking the very picture of a verdant lover in a sporty, summer, light-weight yarmulke, working at his computer in what my mother had suddenly decided to call the sunroom.

'Mutti,' I said, 'you don't have a sunroom,'

'We do now,' she answered.

Axelberg was sitting on a broken office chair, so low he'd had to build the seat up with books. He looked like a small boy at the hairdresser's.

'I see you're using my family history to increase your stature,' I said.

He jumped. He'd been so engrossed in what he was reading he hadn't heard me enter.

'It would appear,' he said, not bothering to look up, 'that you had a grandmother.'

'Most people do.'

'I mean in Belsen. She survived.'

'I know. She lived in this house for many years. She made it to my bar mitzvah. A real Jewish bubbeh. I bet you'd have liked one of those.'

'Did she speak to you about her experiences?'

'*Experiences*! Experiences, Max, are what parents who don't buy books give their children for their birthdays. Going to Disneyland is an experience. Exploring eleven rooms of a haunted house pissed blind is an experience. Belsen isn't an experience.'

'It's interesting that you put Belsen in the present tense, and you a grammarian.'

'It isn't interesting in the slightest.'

'It is to me. And I also find it interesting that you speak of this – let's call it an ordeal if you don't like the word experience – as though it's yours. Do you sometimes feel you were there in person, Ferdinand?'

'In that my mother speaks of her years there with great vividness and I have an imagination, yes. Much, I hope, as you imagine yourself into the shoes of a Jew. How was circumcision for you?'

We shared the briefest moment of ruefulness that we were back to where we'd been before we showed each other our hearts in Brondesbury. But it quickly passed.

'I'm surprised you make that comparison,' he said. 'You deride my conversion to Judaism.'

'I have not converted to Belsenism. My mother was an inmate. She didn't carry me when she was in there, but it's not fanciful to believe I grew up close to an interior disturbance. But then, for all I know, your mother was startled by a Jew just before conceiving you.'

'My conversion was an act of love. Perhaps my mother fell for a Jew.'

'It would be a question, then, why you don't honour her feelings.'

'I am not a sentimentalist.'

'Unlike me, you mean?'

'I think you have pitched your camp in the heart of Jewish alarmism. To you a Jew is a once and forever Belsen boy.'

'Whereas to you it is a condition you can pop in and out of at will.'

'I haven't gone through the fires, if that's what you mean?'

'There's still time, Max.'

'Did you know your grandmother well? Did you talk much?'

'No, she wasn't a talker. She valued silence. In silence she connected to the whitened bone of calamity that befell her family.'

'She talked to no one?'

'She talked to the butcher.'

'But not to you?'

'Not much. I think she felt she owed me a candour she couldn't grant me. But I spoke to her and I believe she listened. I seemed a puzzle to her. For my bar mitzvah she gave me ten 100-krone notes, folded up in a silver money clip. But she didn't accompany the gift with words of congratulation or tenderness. Whatever was in her needed to stay in her. She had black eyes that opened just wide enough to let in light, but not to see anything. She was able to sleep standing up. But it's all in my mother's memoir. I don't know why you're acting as though you've made a find.'

'Because I have. Your grandmother was pregnant in Belsen.'

'Is that surprising? Given how they were picked up at random, many women would have been. Many would have been made pregnant on the Vienna–Belsen express.'

'But not kept alive. Pregnant women were no use to Belsen. And I doubt they had a crèche. So why didn't they gas your grandmother as they gassed the others?'

'Sweet question. I've no idea. What does my mother say in her book?'

'On this subject, nothing. Do you have a theory?'

'Yes.' I brought my mouth close to Axelberg's ear, lifted a corner of his yarmulke, and whispered hotly into the tunnel of his inflamed hearing.

'She was Hitler's mistress.'

GROSS

'Sit down,' Charmian said. 'I have something to tell you . . .'

She didn't have to finish. When Charmian asked me to sit down it was invariably to hear something new about Zoe. Most other matters I could deal with standing up.

I had just walked in from school and needed a drink. A couple of Jewish children had been to see me to complain that there was a story going round the playground that the Jews were worse than the Nazis.

'I will look into it,' I told them.

'Is it true, sir?'

I told them it most certainly was not.

Then why did they say it?

I told them that saying Jews were worse than the Nazis was a way of making out that Jews deserved everything that had ever been done to them, especially by the Nazis.

'Is that like saying there was no Holocaust, sir?'

'In a manner of speaking, yes.'

'And wasn't there?'

I needed that drink.

'Sit down,' Charmian repeated, 'and I'll fix you one. Glass of Malbec?'

'A bottle.'

When we were both seated, she arranged her hands in her lap and said, 'Right then, guess what?'

In a just world I'd have been telling her to sit down while I arranged my hands in my lap. 'Guess what, darling – I've been dreaming about another woman.' I half wished that what Charmian wanted me to guess was that she'd been dreaming about another man. Square our accounts.

'I give up. What?'

'Zoe's been in touch to say Uncle Isak has been making overtures to her.'

'Overtures! Uncle Isak! Yuk.'

'You give your age away, Ferdie. Yuk's passé. Women of Zoe's age say eew.'

'I know. Eew – a Jew!'

'That's not how you say it.'

Charmian could do wonderful imitations of our daughter's limited range of recoil. Eew. Eugh. Ew. She managed a more than passable gross as well, fishing out the dirty Jew from some disgusting pond of still water, newts' eggs, snot, piss, semen and whatever else the Jew exuded.

'Don't you just hate young people,' I said.

Charmian shook her head. 'Eew and gross are just baby steps towards discrimination,' she said.

'Discrimination isn't only an expression of disgust. You can discriminate your way into joy.'

'Rich, coming from you,' she said, laughing. 'When were you last joyful?'

'The day they arrested me for killing Jesus. Shame you didn't know me then. Those were the fun times.'

'There's a question,' Charmian ploughed on, 'that I'm surprised you haven't asked.'

'How's Zoe? Sorry. How is Zoe?'

'Addled. I think she may have fallen out of love.'

'Good. It's a long way back but dropping your terrorist lover has to be a good start . . .'

'I didn't say she's coming back.'

I was sorry. I didn't only believe her immortal soul to be in danger. I missed her. Her animal presence. The look of her. The sound of her as she had been when she had something worth hearing to say.

Immortality aside, the question Charmian had wanted me to ask was how come Zoe and Uncle Isak – and I wished Charmian would drop the Uncle – were in contact. I couldn't remember in what circumstances they'd met, if I'd ever known. Mine wasn't a family for get-togethers. And Isak had been out of the country for most of Zoe's life. That he so much as knew he had a niece disturbed me.

'My guess,' I said, 'should you want to hear it, is that they're campus confederates. Sitting round the campfire one night on the lawn of some Oxford college that specialised in Zionophobia they sang songs, compared notes, discovered they were sever- ally the undeserving children or grandchildren of survivors, maybe even narrowed the connection down to one survivor – eew a Jew! – slit the throat of a cat, and pledged eternal loyalty to pure evil.'

'Your daughter is not pure evil,' Charmian said.

I stood up. 'In her heart, no. My brother, neither. But you can only swallow so many lies before they rot your innards.'

'This is mad talk, Ferdie,' Charmian said.

To show I agreed with her I sat down again. 'You can only have so many lies, distortions, slanders, thrown at you,' I said. 'How much will you bet me that in ten years' time those kids who came to see me today will be marching in support of who- ever next wants me dead?'

Charmian agreed, but, in truth, how many lies, distortions, slanders were being thrown at me? Actually at me.

I thought about it. Yes, there was the routine 'Shame on you!' whenever I strayed, looking 'openly Jewish', into the vicinity of a march – marches were getting harder and harder not to stray into – and I was periodically stared at in restaurants when I ordered intestines and washed them down with wine the colour of Dracula's urine, but I didn't, not yet anyway, have my own security and on warm nights slept with my windows open.

'There you are, then.'

'No, Charmian,' I said. 'There I'm not. People don't have to cough directly in your face for you to go down with the plague. The stuff that kids are now hearing in the playground is a linguistic infection for which there might be no cure. When did you last hear the State of Israel not called genocidal? How long before the Nazi Jew passes into everyday speech? Nazijew – one word. Nor does it have to be you that's boycotted to feel the boycotters' boots in your back. I might end up the last unbanned, unboycotted, untraduced Jew left standing, but where will the exemption be in that? The last Jew will still be the eternal Jew.'

Having got that off my chest, I told Charmian that, in all other respects, she was right. What I had said to her about Zoe was mad talk. But there was no other sort of talk available to me. I didn't add that my dreams were troubled by the imminence of the End of the Days, the whereabouts of the nearest gharqad tree, and that sick phantom Gloria.

'I understand,' she said.

Which – because she didn't understand the half of it – only added to the burden of guilt I carried.

In bed that night I apologised to her – one of those grandiose all-encompassing apologies that immediately makes the recipient believe the worst.

Charmian put down the script she was reading. She preferred to learn her lines in bed. 'Are you having an affair?' she asked.

I couldn't lie to her. 'I had an imaginary one,' I said. 'I'm sorry.'

Charmian found this amusing.

'Did you love her?'

I shook my head.

'Is it over?'

I nodded.

'How long did it last?'

'About seven hours.'

'Where did you meet?'

'In a park.'

'Original.'

'I wasn't looking to be original.'

'What were you looking for?'

'Nothing.'

'She just appeared?'

'Descended would be a better way of putting it.'

'And was it in the park that you enjoyed imaginary congress?'

Dared I tell the truth? 'No. Here,' I said.

'In our bed?'

'Yes.'

'That's disgusting.'

'There was nothing disgusting about it.'

'I will take your word for that. So where was I?'

'Sleeping next to us.'

'Gross.'

'I know. I've said I'm sorry.'

'And what's this us! You were a couple already?'

'For about seven hours, yes.'

'Does she have a name?'

'Gloria.'

'Gloria! Eu!'

'I knew her as Whoo.'

'Who?'

Ba-boom.

I kissed her, comedian to comedian.

'Is she a barmaid?'

'I never asked her profession.'

'Age?'

'Never asked that either.'

'Do you know anything about her at all?'

This one took some pondering. 'Pass,' I said at last.

'You aren't allowed to pass, Ferdinand. You can't bring an imaginary woman called Gloria to my bed while I'm sleeping the sleep of the pure and then not tell me about her. What was her attraction — apart from her being a very quiet lover? What could she do that you've been missing all these years?'

I took a deep breath. 'It wasn't what she did but who she was.'

'Go on.'

'Must I?'

'I think you must.'

'It was her Hebraism,' I said. 'Like a woman from the Song of Solomon.'

It was all Charmian could do not to fall out of the bed I'd violated.

'Oh Ferdie, Ferdie, of all your sick fantasies this is the sickest. You can't even take an imaginary lover without her being Jewish. Is there no part of your mind that doesn't have a Jew idea or a Jew thought or a Jew perturbation or even a Jew sexual fantasy in it?'

'Yes,' I said. 'The part that reveres you.'

'Whom you have just betrayed and would prefer if she were Jewish.'

I thought about that. 'No, I would prefer no such thing.'

I thought about it for too long.

She took my head in her hands again and lightly but persistently shook it, like a blocked salt cellar. 'Your poor fucker,' she said.

And Zoe and Isak? I had too much on my plate to think that one through.

SCHNUCKIPUTZI OR THE CAKE-MAKER OF BELSEN

There's a stone relief in the British Museum showing the Israelites being marched off into Exile in Babylon — it would make a handsome bathroom tile, I've often thought — their heads lowered, their backs bent under the weight of the single bag of possessions they carry, an Assyrian slave driver, brandishing some sort of cudgel, behind. I had started to see myself in this slow procession into bondage. It was how I was beginning to walk and how — I guessed from the Exiles' expressions of resignation — I was beginning to feel. Give it another day, another month, another year, and who was to say this would not be me, not be us?

The Babylonian Exile stands as an eternal warning to Jews. It had been prophesied, and an Old Testament prophecy is as good as a promise. Fail to hearken unto the voice of the Lord their God and do all His commandments and His statutes and He would smite them with madness, and blindness, and astonishment of heart. 'And thy life shall hang in doubt before thee; and thou shalt fear day and night, and shalt have none assurance of thy life . . . and no man shall save thee.' For having done, or not done, what exactly? A little too proud, had we become? A little too convinced of our moral uprightness? A little too disdainful? Always that question: how were we at fault? Blame yourself for all that befalls you and you at least become the architect of your fate. Proud and guilty all at once. A combination that, if nothing else, makes good Talmudists and novelists.

But if another Babylonian Exile was in the offing, how would we fare?

I had become something of a prophet myself. As I wandered through each chartered street, near where the chartered Thames did flow, I had eyes only for Jews. And the signs of weakness and of woe I marked in every face omened badly should we be hauled off into another Babylon. Pride and guilt had got us through the first time, but where was that pride today? For all the seeming arrogance, the standing army and military hardware, we had grown apologetic, uncertain, repentant, a pushover in the morality stakes.

We weren't prepared to believe *everything* people said about us. Our adversaries were as ignorant of us as ever. We – the most blood-fastidious people who had ever lived, as unwilling to go near death as the Chinese are to talk about it – accused of rooting around in rotting innards to find an organ to traffic? We – the most private, least imperially minded people – suddenly become colonialists in our own backyard! We – scholars and moralists, so dedicated to the intellect and ethics that painters when they painted us drew blue veins of neurasthenia on our foreheads as though to map where an excess of mental accomplishment was endeavouring to break out through the mortal prison of our flesh – we, such as we, to be called barbaric! Only barbarians could suggest such a thing. Yet still we asked ourselves and wondered. Could it be that one-hundredth of what we were accused of was true? That we prosecuted a cruel war, whatever the justification for prosecuting a war at all. That we had become less nice about how we killed. That, in our rage, we had signed off from the 'considerate adversary' scheme we'd once championed? And if so, was that enough to make us believe we had failed in our sacred vocation to educate and enlighten, in which case, yes, we deserved to be the most detested people the world had ever known?

Because if we were not the best then it had to follow that we were the worst.

Well, there was arrogance for you, even in retreat from our own high standard. Chosen – not for special favour but unique responsibility, to be the standard bearers of ethical refinement, discrimination, reason, law. Any wonder they wanted to be rid of us? As ignorant armies pitched their encampments of know-nothingness across the lawns of learning, the hatred that beat in secret in their hearts was a hatred for civilisation. Our barbarism, in their eyes, was not to have acted barbarically. Actual barbarism they revered. Our barbarism was to believe that men could be good and wise.

But there – I hear Zoe say – our besetting sin was again: conceit. And in its wake cruelty that was the envy of barbarians the world over.

'Mutti,' I said, 'I've been thinking.'

Home, where the answers to all the questions lay hidden. Home in the leafy dark of London. Home where my mother sat like a sybil guarding the past.

'What, my son, have you been thinking?' she asked. Her sarcasm undimmed, despite her great age. How did Josef Kramer's milk not curdle in his coffee?

Maybe it did, and maybe he liked it that way.

'That things don't add up.'

'Things?'

'Stuff. Times. Dates. Hows. Whys.'

'Of what?'

'My life. Your life. Our life.'

'Your life is your life. My life is my life. What constitutes *our* life?'

'How old were you when you had me, Mutti?'

'Ah – that kind of *our life*. How do you expect me to remember that? Old enough to have known better. Nine months after your father impregnated me is the best I can do.'

'Mutti!'

'Well, you asked, Ferdinand.'

'Do you have a better memory,' I asked, 'of how old you were when you began to work for Kramer?'

She shrugged. 'It was the year I entered Belsen.'

'And how old were you then?'

'Your friend Axelgrinder has been asking me the same question. Is this some school project you are working on together?'

'What did you tell him?'

'I told him to read my book.'

'I've read your book and I still don't know.'

'Then I put it to you that you're a bad reader.'

'Mutti. What are we hiding?'

'*We*. We are hiding nothing.'

'What are you hiding, then?'

She paused. 'Which story do you want. Harrowing endurance or heroic resistance?'

'Mutti, stop.'

'I haven't started.'

'Mutti – the truth.'

'The truth, he wants?'

'You don't have to put on being Jewish.'

'Who would you like me to be?'

'Yourself.'

'My son the moron.'

'Whatever. Your son your son. Just tell me. I don't doubt anything you say. I just want us to be bulletproof.'

'Why? Who's shooting at us today?'

'The same people who were shooting at us yesterday. Everyone.'

'First you must promise not to be prim.'

'I promise.'

'And now you must make me lemon tea.'

I made her lemon tea.

Then, because the smell of lemon tea brought something back, she told me . . .

I was working as a waitress in the Café Central. We didn't need the money. I wanted the experience. The Nazis liked it there. I liked the danger. Those of my friends who had already been rounded up were caught slinking around the city, trying not to be conspicuous. No one was more conspicuous than a Jew trying not to be conspicuous. Serve Viennese coffee to an SS officer with a curtsy and a smile and, to be frank, the more Jewish you looked the better. It excited them. Jewess — yum-yum. Just don't get caught yum-yumming. I didn't dare go too far. Laws against racial shame made Germans think hard before following their desires for girls who looked like me. Virgins with sharp tongues, bright eyes and large breasts. And you could be shot not only for satisfying their lust but for inflaming it. Vienna, though, was different. In Vienna they indulged fantasies they would not have risked back home in Germany. So, if only in their imaginations, I provided a service for the soldiers of the Reich every time I leaned over them or curtsied low.

'Mutti!'

'You asked. You want me to stop?'

I wondered if she said that to the SS officers to whom she served coffee and slices of her home-made strudel. Don't ask me where I got the idea that she made strudel. All I knew was that she baked cakes. But strudel had a wicked, twisted sound that evoked bad behaviour and belonged to the darkest hours of my childhood. There was a German book of terrifyingly moralistic tales for children that Mutti gave me to read from an early age — *Struwwelpeter* which I pronounced as *Strudelpeter*. The stories in *Strudelpeter* that haunted me most were *Die Geschichte von Hans Guck-in-die-Luft*, the story of Johnny Head-in-the-Air who was always dreaming and ended up falling into a river. And Mr Snip-Snip, an itinerant tailor who cut off the thumbs of thumb-suckers with a giant pair of scissors. Though I never sucked my thumbs I lived in fear of Mr Snip-Snip. Only now does the thought that it was a circumcision fable occur to me. More than that, was the itinerant Mr Snip-Snip himself the eternal avenging Jew?

You can mess around for too long in your past. Did I wish I hadn't come to Mutti asking for the truth?

'No,' I said. 'Go on with what you were telling me.'

But I had to make her another pot of tea before she would continue.

There I was, as I have just told you, hiding in plain sight. Serving, smiling, curtsying. Your grandmother was tickled when I came home at the end of every week with a wage packet. She had never seen such a thing. 'Is this how everybody gets their money?' she asked. Her money just turned up in her bank account. I told her not to ask questions like that where she could be overheard. 'We are a stereotype,' I told her. 'Don't conform to it.' Then I emptied my pockets of tips. She grew annoyed with me. What had I done to earn those? 'Smile.' 'Well, I would rather you didn't,' she said. We were above tips. I told her not to say anything like that either. But she didn't believe anything bad could befall us. Our life was charmed. I am not going to deny it: we had wealth and influence and beauty. She woke late every morning, soaked in a hot bath, made herself up, and either went back to bed where she read romantic novels all day or put on a pinafore and baked. She had been a champion baker when she was younger. That was how she met my father who organised weddings and was always on the lookout for magnificent wedding cakes in striking colours.

My mother made five-tier wedding cakes iced in black and yellow — the colours of the Habsburg Empire — which she donated to charities who neither wanted them nor knew what to do with them. 'If you got yourself married already,' she said, 'I could bake one for your wedding.' 'Mutti,' I told her, 'I'm thirteen.' 'Not yet you're not, just hurry up and get to sixteen,' she said.

What we both feared was that we couldn't wait that long.

★

She paused to sip her tea. She had a way lowering her mouth to the cup rather than bring the cup to her as the Engish did. It was feral action that reminded me of a cheetah at a waterhole.

Was that, I wondered, how Kramer slurped his chlodnik? 'Where did I get the idea,' I asked, 'that you baked strudel?' She shrugged. 'Where do you get any of your ideas from?' 'So you didn't bake strudel?' 'Wait, wait. I'll tell you.'

My mother's cakes, I was saying before you interrupted, were my undoing. I'll explain why. I began to cut off slices and give them to the officers. I couldn't serve them in the café, obviously. But I put them in little white boxes which I slipped into their hands before they left. So we had a secret between us, which excited me and I'm sure excited them. 'Agata,' they would ask when I saw them next, 'did you bake that?' 'Maybe I did, maybe I didn't,' I answered. One called me his Schnuckiputzi — *his sweetie-pie, and touched my* toches *when I bent over to serve him his coffee. 'Untersturmführer,' I said, 'das ist verboten. I am only fifteen.' Whereupon he repeated my mother's words exactly. 'Then hurry up and get to sixteen.' I shrugged. 'Maybe you will be an Obersturmführer by then,' I teased. Which aroused him still more. My poor* toches. *You can't imagine.*

The trouble was I could imagine.

First her breasts, now her *toches*. 'See!' Charmian would have said had she been there . . .

'Mutti!' I cried.

'You promised me you wouldn't be prim. Will you just let me get to the cake?'

The toches *touching stopped immediately after Berlin reiterated the* Rassenschande — *the law against defilement of German blood — to soldiers serving outside the Fatherland who were growing more and more* sexually lax the longer they remained away from their cow-like wives. While this law was, as you know, intended primarily to stop Germans having intimate relations with us, it also warned against relations with non-Germans in general. Terrified that touching my toches might already have compromised the purity of his blood, Untersturmführer Hess withdrew his attentions and refused even to accept his nightly piece of cake from me. Could he have suspected that a Jewess baked it?

I doubt it. He wasn't smart enough. But sometimes you know what you don't know you know. So pointed in his refusal of my slice of cake did he become that it was noted by the highest high-ranking SS officer at our table, a man who had hitherto taken no notice of me. One evening, I saw them muttering together. Just before closing time, the senior SS officer asked if he could have a couple of slices of my cake, but not in the same box, bitte. These, I would soon discover, he sent back to laboratories in Berlin for testing, though whether they had equipment sophisticated enough to detect a Jewish hand in the baking I didn't know. What they did discover, however, was trace of an ingredient favoured by Jews – Gefen Ground Kosher Cinnamon. Two weeks after the sample had been sent to Berlin, as I was on my way home from the café, two SS officers stopped me in the street. Komm mit uns, they said. 'I am only twelve years old,' I told them. 'It is all right, Fräulein,' they told me, 'we mean you no harm. Don't squirm. Just komm mit uns.'

They took me to the Hotel Metropole where my mother had originally married. She sometimes took me there for tea, where she talked tearfully about my father who had disappeared. I was very frightened. The hotel, which had once been owned by Jews, was now Gestapo headquarters and had a giant poster of the Führer above the entrance. They put me in one of the beautiful glass lifts, plastered with swastikas. When we reached the top floor they led me to a door on which was the word Lebensmitteltests. I wondered if this was a cake laboratory and I would have to explain myself to a roomful of scientists in white coats. Would they demand to see the recipe? Would I be forced to tell them it was my mother who baked *the cake, not me? I didn't want to do that. I didn't want to get her into trouble, but I couldn't decide on any course of action. I didn't even know whether to curtsy to them, raise my hand and say 'Heil Hitler' or cry. What if Hitler – a man reputed to have a sweet tooth – was there in person?*

In the event there was just a single desk in the room and the person sitting behind it wasn't Hitler but a very short, very plump S S officer eating an orange. The juices were dripping down his uniform. 'Sit down, Agata,' he said. 'Don't be afraid of me.'

He opened a drawer and showed me a few crumbs of what I took to be my mother's five-tier cake on a little Dresden plate.

'There are two serious issues with this cake,' he said. 'One, it appears to be kosher. Two, it is very delicious. So what are we to do?'

'I can bake you one all for yourself,' I said.

'Are you a Jew?' he asked.

I shook my head.

'Then why is your cake kosher?'

'It can't be,' I said. 'Maybe the crumbs have turned kosher with age.'

'Very funny, Fräulein Draxler. I ask you the question again. Why do you bake a Jew cake?'

'I found the recipe,' I said.

'Where?'

'In a magazine in a dentist's surgery.'

He wiped his face. 'Was the dentist a Jew?'

'I would not have let him put his hands in my mouth if he had been,' I replied.

'That is the right answer,' he said. I still remember the words he used, 'Das ist die richtige antwort.'

He even clapped his fat little hands together. I was flattered until I realised his applause was sarcastic. He looked a long time into my eyes, reached out to touch my breasts then decided he had better not, sighed, reached into his drawer, took out two oranges and offered me one. I shook my head. 'I insist,' he said. 'I can always tell a Jew from how he – forgive me, how

233

she — eats. Oranges in particular. Jews snuffle their food like pigs at a trough.'

Takes one to know one, I thought.

I ate slowly.

'Don't bother to finish,' he said. 'We are already satisfied that you are a Jew. We know where you live. We are satisfied that your mother is a Jew also.'

I cried. He put up his hand. Like a trotter, I thought.

'Don't despair,' he said. 'We are going to send you somewhere your cake will be richly appreciated. Uberfresser Kramer has requested you as his private Kuchenbaker. We understand that it was your mother who passed on to you her skills, so we will allow her to accompany you as Uberfresser Kramer's nutritionist. Does that sound fair to you?'

'It depends,' I answered, 'whether you are sending us to somewhere we will like.'

'Oh, you will like it,' he said. 'Everybody who goes there does. Put it this way, we have yet to hear a bad word about it from people who come out.'

I wondered if I should offer him my hand. But when he saw it approaching, he fell back in his chair. 'It is enough,' he said, 'that I have allowed a cake you baked to pass my lips. Enjoy your time where you are going, remember to work hard — work makes you free — and behave yourselves.'

And with that he rang a little bell and the two officers who had led me in, led me away.

'So the Beast of Belsen was a cake-eater?'

'If I could have made a cake big enough for him to bathe in he would still not have been satisfied.'

'And you were sent there right away.'

'Without delay.'

'By train?'

'In a Mercedes.'

'How did Grandma cope with this?'

'I tried to keep from her where we were going. But of course she soon found out. "We will poison him," she said. But he was impossible to poison. She put rat droppings in the cakes. He licked his lips. Once, she caught him licking his lips over me. "Take me instead," she said. "She is mature in skills but only a child in years." He didn't argue. Either of us would do. A Jew was a Jew was a Jew. "What about the perils of *Rassenschande*?" she asked. "Are you prepared to risk syphilis?" He laughed. He wouldn't tell if she wouldn't tell, he said. Besides, it was a bit late for him to be worrying about that. When they opened him up they would discover his insides consisted entirely of Jewcake.'

'So Grandma went to bed with a Nazi?'

'*Went to bed*! Under a quilted coverlet with dimmed lights and Schubert playing? Oh, Ferdinand, what a child of peace you are. In Belsen sex was rape. With Kramer, the site of rape was the kitchen floor. He liked the smell of warm pastry. For a rapist he had epicurean tastes.'

'How often did he rape her?'

'I haven't said he raped her at all. I haven't even said he penetrated her.' She put up a hand. 'No Mutti, Mutti,' she said. 'You asked. I'm telling. So no – who knows? – he might have thought again about the risk of syphilis. They might have sat at the kitchen table playing Juckerspiel and eating cake. It's not for me to know what Grandma did. And if I knew I wouldn't tell you. Every heart must have its secrets. In extreme times people do extreme things.'

'Why do I keep thinking you're telling me he did rape her?'

'And why do I keep thinking you take too prurient an interest? If she did submit in any way to Kramer – *if* – it wasn't to save her own life, it was to save mine. It shouldn't be hard to understand why I have always wanted to save hers.'

Silence between us. Then she said, 'And if she did submit to rape to save my life, she also saved yours.'

'You can't save a life that hasn't started.'

'No, but you can make it possible.'

'Josef Kramer made me possible?'

'Possibly.'

Only possibly. That was all right then.

'And you?' I asked after an interval of time I had no way of measuring. A minute, an hour, a year? 'What extreme things did you do to make me possible?'

She held her face preternaturally still, as impassive as a South Sea Island sculpture. Then she said, 'I lived.'

'That can mean anything. What else?'

'I forget.'

'Don't forget in order to spare me.'

'I was twelve years old.'

'I assume he wasn't called the Beast of Belsen for nothing.'

'I made him soup.'

'That all?'

'I was twelve years old.'

'You were old before your time, Mutti. I understand. You had to be.'

'Do you understand? I doubt it. You've led a pampered life. You teach children for a living. You do whatever you wife tells you. Believe me – some things you have to forget. A life is not an article in a newspaper, Ferdinand. I'm not responsible to some fact-checker. Every life is a work of fiction. War-fiction even more so. Not entirely true, not entirely untrue. Did happen, didn't happen, could have happened, is still happening. I am a ghost, Ferdinand. The ghost of a ghost.'

Pretty much how I felt about myself. My *Schnuckiputzi* of a mother had schooled me well.

SCRAPING THE BARREL

Then – meaning 'next', but just possibly meaning 'as a consequence' – I did something crazy. More than crazy. Downright
insane.

Don't, Charmian had said. I had a school to run, she reminded
me. I had a job to hold down. I had an example to set.

It will be in the school holidays, I said.

Just don't, she said.

I have to, I said.

You don't *have* to do anything.

No, but I had to do this.

It's too hot. It would be even hotter in a week. You know
how much you hate the heat.

Charmian, it's not as though I'm going to the Negev.

The fucking Negev.

That's why I'm not going there. The last time they had a
festival . . .

Ferdie, stop.

It's only Edinburgh.

Tell me you're not going to Edinburgh.

What's wrong with Edinburgh? Catch a show? Take in the
Royal Tattoo? See a comedian? All right – *be* a comedian.

You! Are you completely mad?

Completely. But I won't be doing a gig. It'll be more what
you might call—

More what you might call what, Ferdie?

More what you might call busking.

You don't play an instrument.

I have a voice.

You can't sing.

I can speak.

On the street?

In a barrel. Like Diogenes.

It is sometimes hyperbolically said of people at the end of their tether that they tear their hair. Charmian did, in actuality, tear her hair. I kept some of the strands.

I can't come with you, she said. I can't be a party to this.

Don't worry – there won't be a party.

What's behind this, Ferdie? Is it Zoe? Is it your mother? Is it Whoo?

Is it Who?

Stop this. Is it me?

It's everything, I told her. It's the temperature of the times. It's the zeitgeist. It's all the fucking diabolical distortions and lies.

I arrived at my pitch wheeling a whisky barrel on a trolley I'd found in a junk shop. The barrel I bought from a garden centre specialising in transforming barrels into bird tables. I wore a false beard which in truth made me look more like Moses than Diogenes, but I hoped the white sheet, tied at the waist and leaving half my chest bare, would correct that impression. The main thing, anyway, was not whether I was meant to be Moses or Diogenes but that I was not meant to be myself. Though Edinburgh was far enough from Streatham to reduce the chance of recognition, I was still taking a risk. I hadn't been sacked yet but reports of me sitting half naked in a whisky barrel in a public place would surely tip the balance – if a decision was still in the balance – against me.

I had a script and a few jokes which I didn't expect anyone to find funny. That I wouldn't, by the common definition of a joke, be winning any fringe award for best one-liner, was a fate

I resigned myself to. But if orating the case against anti-Zionists from a wine barrel wasn't an appropriately fun thing to be doing at a fringe festival, it didn't deter the anti-Zionists themselves from taking to the microphone in church halls and jazz cellars and calling themselves comedians. I had read somewhere that the late-night streets of Edinburgh thronged with Jews fleeing comedy clubs in tears, like Masaccio's Adam and Eve leaving Eden — Adam hiding his face, Eve shielding her private parts — but I had been here a couple of nights and hadn't seen any of that with my own eyes. I'd passed a tent where a comedian who had called Zionists lice the night before and vermin the night before that was performing, but I couldn't detect sounds of sobbing coming from his show. Only the routine, regimented laughter at the routine, regimented words. *Fuck.* Ha! *Zionists.* Ha ha! *Fucking Zionists!* Ha ha ha! No matter. Since everything was a lie now, why shouldn't I try my hand at telling a whopper myself? I'd return to London and inform everyone that no Jew dared go out in Edinburgh after four in the afternoon for fear of being beaten to a pulp. Not that the truth wasn't more out-landish still. As for example that Jewish comedians were being blackballed by venues in the city because their presence made the ticket-tearers and programme-sellers feel unsafe. Good job there was just me and a barrel.

There was a brief lull in the city's eternal rain, so the streets were thronged with people looking for entertainment and busk-ers providing it. Like me. I wasn't sure what I feared most: a big crowd or a small crowd. True answer: no crowd.

A taxi-van had dropped me and my barrel several doors down from the bank outside which I'd bagged a pitch on Castlehill. I didn't want to be delivered directly to it. I preferred to wheel my trolley a few yards so as to acclimatise myself to stares and jeers. In truth, in this carnival of merriment and music, even a half-naked Diogenes attracted no particular attention. I paused at a joke shop to buy myself a comic top hat. But no one took much notice of me in that either.

What was smaller than no crowd?

Someone had painted *Boycott Israel's Apartheid – Withdraw Your Savings* on the bank's windows. I positioned myself to one side it. Let it be seen. Everyone was entitled to a point of view, even if it was always the same point of view.

I still had a choice to make. Either I could deliver my words from an upright barrel like a flowerpot man, or I could roll it onto its side and make a sort of vaulted kennel of it. By all accounts, Diogenes, who favoured the kennel approach, was in two minds about his nickname 'Dog', warning that he bared his teeth to anyone who refused to give him alms and boasting that he once passed water on a man who had the effrontery to call him a dog. 'What else did he expect?' Diogenes asked.

I let the dog stories determine my decision. Though there was every chance I'd wet myself out of terror, I wasn't planning to wet anyone else. I'd be a flowerpot man, difficult as climbing into the barrel would be. I was not an agile man even when I wasn't scared out of my wits and wondered if I should have brought a small stool to help me climb in. The Apartheid-Complicit bank was closed, so there would be no assistance from there, and I didn't want to bother any of the other buskers. That, I thought, would make me look unprofessional. Joke Number One. At last, I found a pile of fringe programmes to step on and, having tumbled half upside down into the barrel, discovered I had attracted a small gathering of sightseers eager to witness more of the same. Fighting cramp, perspiration and first-night tremors, I tried to right myself but slipped back down into the bottom of the barrel, bruised my knee and cried out. People who had not seen me climb in took the barrel to be empty and the voice to be coming from somewhere else. They applauded the brilliance of the ventriloquism. The dummy was in the barrel, but where in God's name was the ventriloquist?

A similar thought passed through my mind. Suddenly the idea of being faceless and shapeless, a small still voice at the bottom of a whisky cask appealed to me. It felt like a metaphor for something, no matter that I didn't know what. The Jewish people? The final distillation of Jew? A disconnected voice as unseen as that of the God who'd set Jews on their suicidal course to be an example unto everybody else and then left them to it when the going got tough?

Why didn't I give up on the prepared gags I knew I wasn't going to have the courage to deliver? Why didn't I just say what was in my heart? I am all that is left of the Jews – why didn't I say? – the dregs of a people whose chief sin has been an excess of piety and wordy strictures, who have probably done less harm to the world than a family of Quakers shipwrecked on a rock in the Pacific Ocean – why didn't I say? – yet whom you have chosen to saddle with responsibility for all the world's wrongs, savageries which only savage minds could conceive, we who have no history of making war, only of being warred against – why didn't I say? – while you whose legs once bestrode the oceans in your hunt for wealth and slaves and spices, builders of Christian empires, Arab empires, English, French and Belgian empires, round on us as the last and cruellest imperialists of all, though we have no history of empire, unless you go back three thousand years and find a few vassal states, no ambition to annex or subdue, no knowledge of conquest apart from the mess we're making now, which can be part attributed to our bungled inexperience in the arts of managing others under our sway – *our sway* : what do we know of that? – and part attributed to desperation, and part attributed, if you must believe this, to some overweening arrogance that, for the majority of the few thousand years we've been a scattered people – why didn't I say? – has shown itself as timidity, submissiveness, withdrawal, meekness, cowardice, that made us a laughing stock, scarce men at all, yet now, by some unfathomable transubstantiation, we parade about the swaggering Arab world like tough guys with a taste for that alien blood from which we used to run a mile. Can you explain it to me? Can you explain to me how a refugee can be a colonialist? Can you explain to me how going home – and yes, that meant, for many, going back in time, but home is home – can you explain to me how going back can be construed as invasion and theft? Explain to yourself – if you don't want to converse with me – how you can get anything so wrong, and blah blah blah words words and more words to that effect. And if you think this is self-pity speaking, then understand I am speaking from the bottom of a bleeding barrel and would appreciate it if someone lent a hand to get me out of here . . .

Thank you, you've been a wonderful audience. I'm Fred Dreck.

As if anyone could be bothered who he was, could give a fuck what took so long to explain, when truth now came in short sentences and the history of the Jews could be distilled into a single formula – $J \div Time \times Ignorance = Hate$ – that took only half a second to learn. Why wasn't there a joke that worked as well? Maybe there was but in the suffocating, fearful dark of the barrel I couldn't remember one.

Some use – like a pub with no beer – a comedian with no jokes.

Joke Number Two.

Charmian was waiting for me at the hotel. She had accompanied me to Edinburgh in the end, afraid of what I'd do after what was certain to be a disaster. She greeted me with red eyes, relieved and not a little surprised to see me alive.

'Well?' she asked.

'No, not at all well.'

'It might have gone better than you think.'

'Thank you for thinking that but it went worse.'

She didn't argue with me. Orating in a barrel about Zionism had never struck her as a crowd-pleaser. 'But you weren't attacked.'

'Not exactly.'

'What does not exactly mean?'

'Not physically. There were a few differences of opinion.'

'Well, you believe in that, don't you?'

'In the abstract. Not so much when it's my opinion people are disagreeing with. And when I'm lying like a foetus at the bottom of a fetid whisky barrel.'

'Can you remember anything that was said?'

'Yes. *Boo!*'

'That all?'

'*Don't give up your day job.*'

'I take it you told them this *was* your day job.'

'Ha ha. Good joke. You should have been in that barrel.'

'Who's joking?'

'Exactly what I said to one heckler who thought I had to be having him on. *Peace-loving people, you lot?* he shouted into the barrel. *For a peace-loving people you sure as hell are making up for it now.* But that was all. After the first minute or two of being intrigued by a talking barrel, people wandered off. There were magicians and knife throwers to watch. There was a double-jointed acrobatic strongwoman from Ukraine performing across the road to me. She tore telephone directories in half – she said, "I like to think this Putin" – and played the ukulele upside down. I think it's a fair assumption that she stole whatever crowd I might have had. Thinking it over, it might also have been unwise to put out a yarmulke for people to throw their loose change into.'

'That wouldn't have been one of Max's, would it? I know you've been collecting his casts-offs.'

'You know me too well.'

She put her arms around me. 'You smell of Scotch,' she said. 'And you're wet with it.'

'That's not Scotch, It's perspiration. It was hot down there. Next time I'll remember to bring a fan.'

'Darling, promise me . . .'

'All right. No next time. But one nice thing did happen. A homeless woman with no teeth and a dog no bigger than a mouse rolled the barrel over so I could climb out and handed me her change. "I think you need this more than I do," she said. I assumed she meant that if I pursued a career in show business I'd end up penniless.'

'She could just have thought you needed a coffee.'

'She didn't give me enough for that.'

As though I had not behaved insanely enough in Edinburgh, on the train back I savaged a quiet Japanese couple sitting opposite us for reading Roald Dahl. Not immediately. I didn't want to be on a train for four hours opposite people I'd been dementedly rude to. I waited till the train pulled out of Peterborough.

Charmian had been able to tell from the way I was twisting in my seat that I was planning an assault. 'Don't do it,' she begged.

'Got to,' I said. 'You can't have adults reading that psychopath in full view.'

Charmian knew what I had against Roald Dahl. He had said, 'Even a stinker like Hitler didn't just pick on the Jews for no reason.'

She had a low opinion of Dahl herself, disliking the spiteful little books with spiteful little twists genre, aware of his reputation as a man who cared for women scarcely more than he cared for Jews and felt safe only when meddling in the unbalanced minds of the underaged. But that wasn't a reason to berate his readers, two of whom had the bad luck to be sitting opposite me on the train. And besides, didn't I always say the man was not the work, the art was not the artist?

Yes, but there were limits to the applicability of that distinction.

Charmian had gripped my arm at Doncaster. 'Don't,' she said. 'Just look the other way.'

But as we pulled out of Peterborough I leaned across the table and addressed the couple who were sitting head to head, like dolls joined at the neck, sharing a text. 'I cannot be sure you will go to hell for what you're reading,' I said, 'but I hope that when you return home you will reflect on your rudeness in reading a book by an author who called Hitler "a stinker" and thought he must have had good reason for wanting to kill Jews, at the same table as one of the Jews he thought Hitler had good reason for wanting to kill.'

They stared at me.

It was the man who finally asked, 'What is *stinker*?'

'Ferdie,' Charmian said in the taxi back, 'you need help.'

SHLEMIEL

I returned to find a letter waiting for me from Professor Ian Ledbetter, a one-time university friend and now head of Shakespeare Studies at a university I will not name, having sworn never again to distinguish by title what passes as a university until it fires everyone teaching Post-Colonialism and Critical Race Theory. He had invited me to deliver the odd lecture in the past to students signed up to his module on the Fool in Shakespeare, a course which, without making too much of it, I believed owed something both to the many conversations we'd enjoyed on the subject over time and to my youthful *oeuvre*, *Shakespeare and the Shlemiels*, which argued that by virtue of their sad, rebarbative, rebellious souls, their social estrangement, their lowly status, the precariousness of their employment, their bitter tongue and quick-wittedness, every clown and fool in Shakespeare was a Jew.

Never mind that Shakespeare was unlikely to have met many Jews: he found the Jew where he found all his characters – in himself.

Though it never made it to the status of set text, *Shlemiels* had, for decades, been suggested reading for students doing Ian's course. It was now his sad duty to tell me, he wrote to say, that pressure from junior staff had compelled him not only to remove it from the department's library shelves but to expunge all reference to it in the course prospectus. Though it had neither given offence nor caused distress in more than twenty years, it now gave and caused both. Several students had reported falling ill after reading it. One could not stop shaking. Another was in a coma. I was, though, to rest assured that any student who specifically requested it would, on getting a clearance from two recognised medical practitioners and signing a form absolving the university of all responsibility for the consequences, be free to borrow Ian's copy. Yes, he knew what I thought. He thought the same. But the times were the times. I wasn't the only casualty. This very minute he was facing down a student rebellion against *Macbeth*.

Too Scottish? Too bloody? No – too long.

I nursed my own sad, rebarbative, rebellious soul in silence for a week then wrote back to Ian wondering if, in his view, *Shlemiels* would have occasioned the same amount of distress among the student body had it argued that every fool in Shakespeare was a Roman Catholic or a Muslim.

'Oh, Ferdie, Ferdie,' was his reply.

Was that an expression of pity or exasperation? And if exasperation – with whom?

I said nothing about this to Charmian until I could bear saying nothing to Charmian no longer.

'Oh, Ferdie, Ferdie,' she said.

'Is that pity or exasperation you're expressing?' I asked.

'I suppose neither and both,' she said. 'I don't like to see you upset. But it might just be a passing trend. Students are fickle. They might be back loving you next term.'

'That's not what Ian said.'

'What did Ian say?'

' "Oh, Ferdie, Ferdie." '

'That all?'

'He said my book had made students ill.'

'How *ill*?'

'Not terminally, if that's what you're asking. At least, if there have been fatalities, he has kept word of them from me.'

I skipped the student in a coma.

'I meant ill in what sense. Ill with what?'

'Ill with not liking my book, what do you think? Ill with there being thoughts in the world with which they disagree. Ill with psychogenic hysteria caused by seeing the word Jew on the jacket of a book someone has dared to suggest they read.'

'It's not a book, Ferdie, it's a pamphlet. It doesn't have a jacket. It's a twenty-five-page pamphlet. You gave me a copy when we met. I treasure it. But the word Jew doesn't appear on the cover.'

'The word shlemiel does.'

'And you think they'll know what that is? Ferdie, according to you, students only have a dozen words. I'm prepared to bet that shlemiel isn't one of them.'

'If I may say so, you underestimate the part played by the unconscious in matters relating to race – especially *my* race. *You* see a pamphlet written by your husband; *they* see a tract penned by the enemy. They'll smell offence in the words without turning a page. These are children of the modern inquisition. They believe scholarship consists of rooting out works by Jews who go out of their way to kill children. We have a daughter who thinks the same, remember. You are married to a killer, Charmian. I murder babies with my bare words – or at least in the gaps between them.'

'Sometimes I think you get off on the idea that you are incendiary.'

'Not me. My prosody.'

'I hate to say this to you, Ferdie, but you aren't too dangerous for anyone to read. You use nice words. I like your words. And you employ correct grammar when you remember. But you don't turn a deadly phrase.'

Should I have brought up the student with the shaking hands? Should I have mentioned the student in a coma?

'Does it not occur to you to wonder, Ferdinand,' Charmian went on, 'whether your professor friend puts a flattering gloss on the real story because he loves you? What if no student so much as noticed the pamphlet? What if it had never once been removed from the shelf? I don't mean to be cruel. I love you. But what if the truth is that your pamphlet has sat there long enough and must now give way to more modern works on the subject? The old order changeth . . .'

'Because it's taking up too much room, do you mean? You know who last used that argument against the Jews. Charmian – as you've sweetly reminded me, *Shakespeare and the Shlemiels* is twenty-five pages long. You can buy a book of stamps thicker than that.'

'There is such a thing as being too sentimental about yourself, Ferdie. Things get superseded, that's all. Ideas, like people, have their time. I don't get to play young women any more. That doesn't mean the world is out to cancel me . . .'

'So would you say the Jews too have had their time? Must we go quietly now? With our hands up? In chains? Or is that me being sentimental again?'

I shed a furtive tear. Not for myself or my pamphlet or the Jews but for Charmian. It was too sad to think that she could no longer play young women. Not too sad for me: I was not one of those men who love a woman only when she is a girl. Too sad for her.

She saw the tear roll down my cheek. I could hardly tell her the reason for it. So I had to let her think I was weeping like the prophet Jeremiah in anticipation of the destruction of his people. Or worse, weeping because no one liked the twenty-five pages on Shakespeare I'd written decades ago.

She kissed the top of my head as she often did when she was feeling protective of me.

I went to bed with the radio on under my pillow that night and learnt that activists had written an open letter to the *Guardian* calling for a worldwide boycott of any writer or penner of pamphlets who self-identified as exterminationist-apartheid-colonialist-settler-Zionist.

I shot up in bed, waking Charmian. 'Does my pamphlet on *Shakespeare and the Shlemiels* define me as exterminationist-apartheid-colonialist-settler-Zionist?' I asked her.

'Only if you want it to.'

I embraced her and went to sleep.

Lucky me. Charmian, I discovered in the morning, had remained awake. Worrying about her sick fuck of a husband.

VAI IZ MIR

Who wasn't worrying about me?

Elaine Muller, in her cardigans, stopped me at the school gates to say I looked tired.

'I'm sleeping, but not well,' I told her. 'I sleep consciously.'

'You do well to sleep at all, Headmaster,' she said.

'Are you not sleeping yourself, Elaine?'

'Only a few hours a night. I feel I have no right. I burn candles and keep vigil.'

I didn't ask her for whom. I assumed she meant civilisation. As brought down the mountain on stone tablets.

She turned to go but changed her mind. 'Do you ever have misgivings?' she asked, not looking at me.

It wasn't necessary to ask 'misgivings about what?' Jews were tuned into one another's silences.

'All the time,' I said.

'So you think we might be in the wrong?'

'I think we are always in the wrong. But not as in the wrong as "they" are. I know I shouldn't think that their wrongness puts us in the right, but I do.'

'I wonder if they think that?' Elaine asked.

'That they are always or even ever in the wrong?' I remembered Dr Magdy. 'No,' I answered.

She threw me a sad look. 'They must,' she said.

We embraced. I am starting to worry about her.

'Your hair's getting thin,' my mother observed.

'You've always said I was born with thin hair,' I reminded her.

'Well, it's getting even thinner now.'

I didn't tell her that it was because I was worrying about her. For all Max Axelberg's flattering ministrations she was begining to show signs of age. Soon she'd look middle-aged. If I'd told her I was worrying about her she'd say I was really worrying about myself. Which might have been simple psychology but happened to be true. I was still adjusting to being Josef Kramer's spiritual offspring . . . possibly. And the author of a pamphlet no one could read without going into spasm . . . definitely.

My born-again brother sent me an email. 'Just spoken to Mutti. She's worried about you. So am I. Ike.'

I get a second email from my brother. 'PS. So is Gloria.'

Then a third. 'So is Zoe.'

Zoe?

It was a measure of how not well I was feeling that it took me a minute or two to remember who Zoe was. I knew the name, I just didn't at once remember how we were related. Charmian was my wife . . . Agata was my mother . . . Ike was . . . whatever Ike was, and Zoe, ah yes, Zoe was my daughter.

Could it be true that she too was worried about me?

Charmian had said that Isak and Zoe were in contact but that seemed so unlikely I'd pushed all thought of it to one side. Not impossibly, Gloria, whom I had now stopped thinking about, had briefly crowded her out of my mind.

Infidelity was a wonderful salve.

Something else for me to worry about – was there a limit to the number of guests my brain could accommodate?

I bumped into Gillian Wallenstein in the corridor. 'I hope you are not as ill as you look,' she said.

She always reminded me of my mother. Another indomitably

harsh, unforgiving woman. Only she'd got to where she was without Belsen. How had she done that?

I asked if she was worried about me. 'No,' she said. 'Should I be?'

'No. But everybody else is.'

'Does that mean you'd like me to be? What's the matter? Is the genocide getting to you finally?'

'What genocide, Gillian?'

'You must be the last person in the world denying it, Headmaster.'

I did well, I thought, to remember how to breathe. But I'd have done better to remember how to walk away. 'Listen to me, Gillian,' I said instead. 'Any Jew who mindlessly mouths the genocide libel becomes a genocidist herself. We know what genocide means. It means removing every trace, every memory, of a people from the face of the earth. Not just the living exemplars of Jew but the very idea of it. The Nazis weren't content, Gillian, with emptying their own country of us, they ransacked the four corners of the globe in order that there would not be a single Jew, not a rack of us, our thoughts and words, our history and beliefs, left behind. When you can show me that Israel intends a comparable act of extermination, wants every memory of every Palestinian and all evidence of their culture effaced for all time, I'll let you have the word genocide back . . .'

Gillian was not afraid of me. 'According to the International Criminal Court, Headmaster—'

'Don't come to me with legal definitions, Gillian. What do fucking lawyers understand about the moral consequences of a word? There is no end to the crimes you can accuse Israel of, if you must. Truth or lies. Fill your boots. Search your horror thesaurus until the pages become thin with overuse. But saddle Jews with the specifics of this word and you give the Holocaust deniers what they've been hankering for all along. You equalise the criminal and the victim. Now we don't only deserve what was done to us, we become synonymous with the perpetration of it. We are the inferno. We are the ovens. So no one has to feel bad about what happened to the Jews ever again . . . Happy now?'

I stepped back. Another thing I did well – not to fall over.

Gillian towered under me. 'Yes, since you ask,' she said, 'I am worried about you.'

I shouted an order to a group of Year Fives playing too boisterously in the playground. They ignored me. I had a feeling that when I opened my mouth no sound came out of it. I put this down to the humiliation I'd suffered at the bottom of a barrel in Edinburgh. But it was likely that my sense of impotence had deeper roots. Who called me Jew? Tweaked me by the nose? Called me villain, killer, liar, thief? 'Swounds I had taken it, for it cannot be but I am pigeon-livered, or ere this I should have fatted the pelicans in St James's Park with the foul slanderers' offal.

'Stop that, boys,' I shouted. But they either heard not a word I spoke or were indifferent to them.

Oh yes, and the school governors turned out to be worried about me too. I received a phone call from the chairman. Warm and confidential. They didn't want to put anything in writing. These had been difficult times for everyone and they knew I had been overworked. They could see I looked tired. A term off would do me a power of good, didn't I think? Maybe two terms. My deputy Max Axelberg was, in their view, the ideal person to take over in my brief absence. They trusted I agreed.

I opened my mouth but still no sound.

Charmian booked me a doctor's appointment.

DOOM-SCROLLER

'Describe your symptoms to me,' the doctor said.

I asked him if he knew any Yiddish. Why? Because I was ill and Yiddish was the greatest of all languages to be ill in.

He had a think. Yes, he knew schmuck, schlepp and chutzpah.

I didn't correct his pronunciation. Correcting a non-Jewish person's Yiddish is disrespectful. 'Chutzpah I don't suffer from,' I said to him, 'but schmuck gets me in one. Give me an anti-schmuck pill and I'll leave you in peace.'

We laughed. He was a public-school Englishman who still blushed in his sixties. He looked the other way when I removed my shirt. I was shy too – *shemevdik* – and respected reserve in other people.

'I'm behaving strangely,' I told him.

'For example?'

'I'm shouting at the television.'

'Well we all do that from time to time.'

'I'm shouting at the television *all* the time, including when it's off.'

He wrote that down. 'Anything else?'

'I deliver religious homilies from a whisky barrel. I tell strangers what they should and shouldn't read. I accuse people I scarcely know of educating their children badly, even those who don't have children. I recently argued with an Arab about the meaning of the Koran.'

'You've read the Koran?'

'No.'

'So why do you think you're acting like this?'

'Because I'm *farbrent* and *dershlogn*,' I replied. 'I'm furious and I'm depressed, but I'm more *farbrent* than I'm *dershlogn*.'

'That's a pity. There are more pills for depression than anger.'

'Well mine's a depressed sort of anger, unless it's an angry sort of depression. I'm sleeping badly and waking badly. I'm eating badly, too. And I'm forgetting things. The other day I lost my way to the shops and when I found my way to the shops couldn't remember what I was shopping for. I don't fear Alzheimer's. To tell you the truth, I sometimes wish I had it. I don't mean that. But there's a lot I want to forget. But I've just remembered a better word for what I am. *Oysgematert*.'

The sweet Dr Passant tried to say it, but gave up after several attempts. 'Such an expressive language,' he said, smiling, blushing and shaking his head.

'We have expressive ailments,' I said. 'When you true-born English feel worn out you're either debilitated or shagged. One word's prissy, one's vulgar. *Oysgematert* suggests an altogether more metaphysically overburdened state. Not overburdened by physical labour or responsibility but by an atmosphere of hostility that seems to inhere in the very air we breathe, as though falsehoods multiply around us like microbes. So what have you got for that, Doctor?'

'For the fasehoods or for you?'

'I *am* the falsehoods. I am the Jew Judas who betrayed the Jew Jesus for a bag of clinking coins. I am Shylock who cares more about his shekels than his daughter. I am the Jew of Malta who walks abroad a-nights and kills sick people groaning under walls. I am force-fed with mendacity like a goose pumped full to bursting to put foie gras on the tables of the rich. How long does a goose go on knowing he's a goose before he confuses himself with terrine, Doctor? I am so fattened with gibberish and calumny that all I can do is sleep, wake and long to sleep again. If there were a Society for the

Prevention of Cruelty to Schmucks they would wring my neck.'

'Well I'm not going to do that, Dr Draxler.'

'I feared you were going to say that.'

We both laughed. I'm not sure why. What was so funny? All right – me without my shirt on, but what else?

'Do you take exercise?' the doctor asked.

'I walk, that's all.'

'Far?'

'My wife says not far enough, but she lives in her body while I live in my head. I walk two or three miles to school every day. And the same number of miles back. That's when I forget I've got a car. Two or three miles each way feels a lot to me. But at the moment I don't notice I'm walking. I've read that you can imagine exercise when you're not taking any. Does that make the opposite true? Can I think myself into sitting while I'm walking?'

'Why would you want to do that?'

'I don't. It seems to happen of its own accord, that's all. I am so preoccupied with what's in my head, I'm not aware I'm moving, and if I'm not aware I'm moving, maybe I'm not.'

'I don't think it works like that.'

'I'll be advised by you, Doctor. So what can I take?'

'I'm not sure you should take anything. It's more a question of what you can do. Have you considered yoga?'

'No. My wife does yoga. I don't want to muscle in. She carries a rolled-up rubber mat wherever she goes. I can't do that. People will think there's something odd about me.'

We laughed again. He blushed; so did I.

'Meditation?' he continued, collecting himself.

'You mean spending even more time inside my head than I already do?'

'Well, meditation encourages you to think outside yourself.'

'It doesn't happen that way for me. The minute I sit cross-legged on the floor and try to concentrate on something external to me I espy a lie and mentally write speeches refuting it. It's distraction I need, Doctor.'

'Do you have a sport?'

'I sometimes play patience on the computer. That's when I'm not doom-scrolling.'

'I meant sport/sport.'

'I realise that. No. As I've said, my wife does all that. She skied her way into my heart. I worried my way into hers. So far, it's worked out OK.'

'You wouldn't be sitting here if everything were still working out OK.'

I coloured. 'True,' I said. 'But this isn't about Charmian and me.'

'So what is it about?'

Hadn't he heard a word I'd said? 'It's about me being *oysgematert*, Doctor.'

'Which you go doom-scrolling to make worse?'

'Which I go doom-scrolling to confirm.'

'You're on social media, presumably.'

'I am not that crazy. I can find all the hateful madness I need just scrolling through the online papers. Press the on-button and there it is. No parental warning, nothing. Page upon page of untruths, distortion and naked abhorrence.'

'Might it not be wise to keep your computer off in that case?'

'How will I know what's going on if I do that?'

'Must you know what's going on?'

I stared at him in stupefaction. His suggestion robbed me of words. Were there a Yiddish word for wordless I'd have used it.

'The world will go on without you, you know,' he added.

'That's what I'm afraid of.'

'Try it. Just for a week. And I'll write you a prescription for something to make you sleep.'

'Will it stop me doom-scrolling?'

'Well, if you're asleep . . .'

'If I'm asleep I can't doom-scroll you think? How wrong you are, Doctor.'

Was that rude of me? We both coloured.

Suddenly, he looked weary. Too much *oysgematert*, I suspected. He was too English for the rococo elaborations of Jewish anguish. It was as though he'd been playing chequers with a grandmaster who had blocked his every move.

He looked up at the ceiling, then wrote me out a prescription. 'Try these,' he said. 'And maybe read a comic.'

I thanked him and took the prescription to the chemist. It was for beta blockers which the instruction leaflet said were especially effective in easing embarrassment and curing blushing.

I asked the pharmacist where they kept the comics.

THE GOOD DON'T HEAL

I liked the comic idea. Growing up post-Belsen I'd never been given comics. We hadn't read for fun. I'd gone from *Strudelpeter* to *The Scourge of the Swastika* in a single bound. You either fell off a cliff sucking your thumb or got gassed in a shower holding your nose.

As it happened, there was a graphic-novel-cum-wizard-candle bazaar around the corner from the school. Merlin's Well. Because black magic was largely frowned on at Strawberry Fields Primary, Merlin's Well was barred to pupils and, by tacit extension, teachers. But I knew of no other shop with such a large selection of comics of the sort I imagined the doctor recommended I read. I visited it, well scarfed-up, on a Saturday morning when the school was closed. On 'compassionate leave' or not, I couldn't afford to be seen browsing in such a place, so I quickly grabbed whatever I could find that wasn't illegal and took a bundle home under my jumper like porn. I had been a headmaster until very recently and hoped to be one again. Even a suspended master didn't read comics. Nor did he have porn stuffed under his jumper.

I got home without my feet touching the ground.

I spread the comics out on the kitchen table. *Spider-Man, X-Men, Ninja Turtles, Wonder Woman, Wolverine, Diaspora Boy* . . .

No prizes for guessing which I reached for.

I was holding it when Charmian came in from the garden.

'Christ,' she said, 'where did you find that?'

'In a pile next to warlocks made of candle wax. It's a satiric take on Zionists who denigrate diasporic Jews like me. Also seems to be an attack on Jews – again like me – who see anti-Semitism under every stone, which would be a fair objection if only anti-Semitism weren't under every stone . . .'

She grabbed it from me and swept every other comic off the table. 'I thought these were meant to give your mind a break.'

'That was the idea.'

'You might as well be reading Kafka.'

'Funny you should say that. I nearly bought an illustrated *Metamorphosis* but I thought the insect looked a bit too like Max Axelberg.'

'You've doctored that story. If the insect had resembled Axelberg you'd have bought three copies and a fly swatter. It was you it reminded you of – admit it.'

You can have too clever a wife. I tried to pull her to me. 'Or aren't you willing to kiss a cockroach?'

Hear my rhythms, talking of too clever. Too fast. Too smart. I was rattling on like a double act with me playing both roles. Sid Caesar and Groucho Marx. Chlodnik and Chlodnik.

'Slow down,' Charmian said.

'This is me slow,' I said. 'This is me neutered.'

'It's come to something,' she said, 'when even a comic shop isn't safe for you to go in.'

'Nowhere's safe for me to go in.'

'If you were a child,' she said, 'I'd ground you.'

'Pity,' I replied, 'that you didn't do that with Zoe.'

Which closed the conversation. Had we gone on talking I'd have got around to telling her I agreed with her. She was right to part me from my comic. When a man won't put away childish things it is time to put away the man.

Later, finding me sitting stimming at the dining table, twisting napkins into medieval instruments of torture and looking into remote space, both past and future, she brought out a bottle of red wine and a bottle of Scotch and plonked both on the table. And my beta blockers. 'Knock yourself out,' she said, handing me back my comics.

And that was what I did for however long I did it. Wars raged without my noticing. Rumours spread without my being around to contradict them. Jews sent their children to Oxford without a proper grounding in their own history. For all I knew to the contrary, swastikas reappeared on my mother's gateposts and nobody minded. So pleasant a place did the world become in my absence that Isak, Gloria and Zoe thought it safe to call round to see how I was and found me, so I was told later, comatose in front of a stone-dead television.

Zoe calling round! Zoe – my Zoe, Zoe the anti-Zio – in company with my meshuggener brother and his spectrally erotic companion!

Had I spent too long leafing through the fantasy section of Merlin's Well?

This needs unpicking. Not from the first syllable of recorded time, but from the hour Gloria beheld Ike in the flames, and set off a sequence of dream events that would bring Zoe back to me.

It turned out that Isak's experience of ecstatic men-only dancing at religious festivals among the Hasidim of Mea Shearim had made him something of a mover. The seraphic, foul-mouthed Gloria Wiesenthal (formerly known as Whoo) saw him when she was making pen-and-ink drawings of the ultra-religious celebrating Lag B'Omer on Mount Meron in the far north-east of Israel. Allow me – courtesy of a vivid imagination and scraps of tittle-tattle I picked up as I drifted in and out of self-willed stupor – to paint the scene:

The bonfires burned, the Haredim charged up and down the mountain in their prayer shawls, the women watched from a safe distance as their boy children got their first ever haircut at the hands of Yossel and

Moishe Snip-Snip, and there, seeming to leap through the flames like the very Devil, was Isak with his trousers tucked into his socks and his tallis over his head. 'I am in love with this diabolic fucker,' Gloria Wiesenthal thought as she moved her pen across the paper.

Isak was lying to me when he said he could not reciprocate her love. Why, I don't know. Perhaps he truly wanted to loan her out to me as a gesture of warped brotherliness and thought I'd only play along if I believed there was nothing between them. In fact, he was as in love with her as she was with him. I was told that her drawings of him dancing through flames on Mount Meron sold like hot cakes in the gift shops of Israeli hotels. In his God-driven abandon he captured the crazed, contradictory essence of the country; or rather, in her pen-and-ink drawings, she did, and she was only able to do that because of the passion they shared.

Just a few weeks before the Hamas massacre, he had brought her to London in the hope of getting Mutti to bless their union. But his nerve went. What if Mutti refused to have her in the house on the grounds that Isak owed allegiance to her alone. He'd heard that she'd barred the door to Charmian years before. Mutti didn't show love to her sons but she expected them to show exclusive love to her. He passed no judgement on his mother. She was as she had no choice but to be. Jews were as jealous as their God. The separation Jews enjoined on themselves, saying it was the Lord's will, had nothing to do with intimations of superiority. You stayed away from other people so they couldn't steal your sons or daughters.

So Isak bided his time, skittishly provoking the Zionists he met in London by telling them of the corruption of the Netanyahu administration and provoking the Arabists he encountered by reminding them of the number of times they'd lost to an army of Jews with catapults and PhDs. He took up so many warring positions for the mischief of it, he began to trip over his own contradictions. He did not, for example, subscribe to the cult that believed Jews should have waited for the Messiah before returning to Israel, but he could see the cultists' point. That was when he wasn't seeing that they had no point. He had confessed that he and Gloria had daubed Mutti's door with anti-Jewish graffiti in order to scramble my brains. But there was a good chance he had scrambled his own and didn't know what he was doing. In the end, the daubing stopped because Gloria refused to go on. She was a feminist, or had he forgotten, and feminists didn't cheer on the rape of Jewish women whatever the justice of the rapists' cause.

'Rape is not resistance,' she told Isak. 'I've had it up to here with the fucking women's movement.'

'So does that mean you finally accept the patriarchy,' he asked her, 'and won't mind sitting behind a screen with the other women at shul?'

She laughed in his face. Who knows? – that might have been when she told him she had the hots for me.

'There is one thing you can do to convince me you want the best for my family,' Mutti told her when Isak finally summoned up the courage to introduce them.

'And what is that, Mutti?'

'Now there are two things. Don't call me Mutti, for one.'

Gloria apologised. 'And for two?'

'Find Zoe.'

What Mutti didn't know was that they'd already found her. Armed with her photograph, wearing keffiyehs themselves and muttering to each other in a language which students who knew nothing of the Middle East beyond their own vanity took to be Arabic, they toured the capital's campus encampments, remembering to shout 'Shame on you!' at anyone who looked askance and 'LSE Divest' no matter that they were in UCL, when who but my daughter should come over to the bar of wherever, tell Isak that he reminded her of a sweeter version of her fucking father, and beg a smoke.

Offering her what was left of his joint, Isak looked her up and down and saw not quite so sweet a version of me. 'Zoe?'

'Uncle Ike?'

An unlikely story. So unlikely as to be miraculous. Long-lost daughter found by a chlodnik in a shepherd's smock. *The Winter's Tale*. Not my favourite Shakespeare. Not enough jokes. But bags of resurrection and restitution, and how else was I going to get a happy ending?

I was too out of things to ask questions but I gathered that my beloved wife had remained in close contact with our beloved daughter throughout her descent into criminal ignorance and disgrace and was responsible for pointing her in the direction of my brother. Why? Any port in a storm. I meant 'why' for Zoe, not Charmian. Same answer. We had all grown desperate. Did they embrace? I like to think so. Did Zoe ask after my health? I like to think that too.

Part actor in the drama, part purveyor of its progress, Charmian warned me against expecting too much. Zoe was not, at a stroke, about to be a bride of Israel or the daughter to me she had once been. Slow down, Ferdie, she told me. Read another comic. Go back to sleep.

But this much I could hold on to – Zoe had recognised from photographs one of the hostages whose remains Hamas had returned to Israel. She couldn't be sure, because she didn't want to be sure, but she couldn't doubt, because her conscience wouldn't let her doubt, that it was the same woman whose living photograph she had been filmed defacing. Poor Zoe. I both wished this on her and I didn't. However much you believe in divine justice, you don't want your children to suffer it. I was to understand that Zoe had turned to her Jew-averse boyfriend hoping for the understanding only a father could have offered her, and not finding it. She was probably not much older than me, I imagined Zoe telling him. But you are not a Zionist, I imagined him replying. Then you can go fuck yourself, I am certain she would have said. Whereupon, who should turn up smelling of weed and with a sultry angel at his side, but Uncle Ike?

Having met by whatever you want to call it – chance, design, divine intervention – they sat on the grass, smoked, held hands and allowed commiseration to take the place of judgement. Zoe found it in her to ask if Gloria's family were safe in Haifa, and Gloria told Zoe she was not to blame for any hostage's fate. There was subtext, of course. What are you doing in someone's else country, Zoe didn't ask. And how could you have shown so little womanly feeling for a girl captured by killers and for all you know tortured, raped and throttled, Gloria didn't wonder.

'Free Palestine,' Zoe would say when someone she knew walked past.

'And how will you achieve that?' Isak asked. 'By ethnically cleansing the Jews?'

Gloria dug her elbow into his ribs.

'Don't get me wrong,' Isak went on. 'I've been a Jew in Israel – I think you should get rid of the lot of us. How is the only question.'

'I am not going to stop marching, you know,' Zoe said.

'March against Israel all you like,' Isak said, 'just don't march *for* the jihadists who want all Jews dead.'

'Zionists, Uncle Ike,' Zoe said. 'Zionists, not Jews.'

Isak guffawed.

Gloria put her arms around her and told her she had a *shayne punim* – a beautiful face – an expression Zoe claimed never to have heard before though I'd told her she had a *shayne punim* a thousand times when she was small.

'I'm *still* not going to stop marching,' Zoe said. 'What's happening must stop.'

'The problem,' Isak said, 'is that your friends were asking for this to stop before it even started. You cried wolf. Now no one believes you . . . At least your father doesn't.'

'I can't care what my father believes, Uncle Ike.'

'But I think you do care. I think you march to upset him.'

'Shit psychology, I march because I have to.'

'That's a bad reason. It's not all about you.'

'You're the one who says I march to upset my father. I march for peace.'

'Which would be noble if only those in whose name you march wanted the same thing. You march for war, Zoe. I've seen you on the box yelling into a megaphone. You don't get peace through a megaphone. And you don't look peaceful when you're marching. You're an engine of war . . .'

'. . . with a *shayne punim*,' Gloria put in.

'I am personally at peace when I march.'

'I wish that were true, Zoe. I wish you were at peace now.'

'I am more at peace marching than my father is not marching.'

'That's another matter. Your father and I are second-generation survivors. We don't get to have peace. It's forbidden. We have to bear the burden of remembering.'

'For how long?'

Izak shrugged.

'Well, I can't afford to wait for the burden of remembering to be lifted,' Zoe said. 'I am not obliged to repeat my father's traumas.'

'You are not obliged to repudiate them either.'

'So you want me to be trapped in the same death cycle you and Dad are?'

'All you've done is swap one death cycle for another, Zoe. The difference being that your dad and I don't congratulate ourselves on ours.'

'That's because you have nothing to congratulate yourself for. Not marching is complicity . . .'

'Breathing is complicity, my child.'

'Don't *my child* me.'

'I am joking. Something Jews do. And now you're going to tell me that that we have a bad record when it comes to killing children. Another crime you've been crying wolf about for centuries.'

'*Something Jews do* – Jews, Jews, Jews . . . I want out of Jews.'

'I feel the same.'

'Fuck your feelings, Uncle Ike. I can't take your feelings into account when I march against the genocide – and don't tell me we cried wolf about genocide too.'

'You did, actually. You were calling it a genocide before the word was invented.'

'Pity trumps your feelings, Uncle Ike. Pity trumps your history. Pity trumps every word you utter.'

My daughter was not herself. She was weakened in her resolve. She'd ripped a murdered hostage off a wall. But she could still pack a punch with the 'p' word. Even from my sickbed I could hear the bells of pity calling. I put down my comic. Poor, pitiable Zoe.

At last, drawing Zoe close, Gloria brought out her phone and showed her a photograph.

'Who is this?' Zoe asked warily. She was unable to look, afraid it was the hostage. Or the famous video of herself, vandalising the image of someone else's daughter.

'His name is Oshri,' Gloria said. 'The younger brother of a man I used to go out with. Both artists.'

'Is he wearing an IDF uniform?'

'Yes. He was defending his country.'

'*Was?*'

'He was killed last month in an operation in the north of Gaza.'

Zoe bit her tongue. She had been well enough brought up to know that you say 'I am sorry' when someone tells you of the death of a friend. But she could not pretend to be sorry about an Israeli soldier.

'His girlfriend, Alona, was kidnapped by Hamas. We watched a video of you tearing down a poster of a hostage, Zoe. It might have been Alona.'

'Why are you telling me this? I have told you I won't apologise for what I believe.'

'Oshri hoped he would find Alona and rescue her while he was in Gaza. Every day, he called her name. On the day he was shot he left his tank to call for her. Imagine that. Her name was his final word.'

She showed Zoe Oshri's photograph again. 'Look at him. He was the loveliest man. A brilliant artist. A peace activist.'

'Peace activists don't join the IDF,' Zoe said.

'You don't *join* the IDF, Zoe. And it is no crime to defend your country. Look at him. Look at his face. Look how young. Is he not deserving of your pity?'

Did Zoe shed a tear? If she did not, I will paint a tear on her cheek for her. It's no sin to weep for someone who happens to be on the opposite bank of the river of blood.

Tear or not, she fell quiet. Tired of the fight.

Over the next days they made up, fought, made up again, danced, perspired, sat cross-legged on the asphalt, drank wine, ate chicken thighs in yoghurt, swapped anecdotes and photographs, and discussed the many differences between Isak and me, though brought up by the same mother in the same faith. Isak less principled. I less capable of change. Thin-skinned, the pair of us. Mine thinner. About her grandmother, Zoe knew dismayingly little beyond the fact that she'd survived the camps. She found her distant, imperious, enigmatic and unkind, which, not coincidentally, was Charmian's view of her as well. My fault that Zoe was so disconnected from her origins. Yes, I wanted to spare her third-generation survivor trauma, but had I been less determined to appear a free Jew myself, less afraid of being charged with catastrophe opportunism, I might have explained Mutti to my daughter in ways that would have awoken her sooner to the good fortune as well as the ills of her inheritance.

And so it was left to my crazy brother Ike the Kike to give her a crash course in who she was, which entailed teaching her who I was too. 'What you have to understand,' he told her, 'is that Jews like me and your father are dead men on leave. We don't know when we will be called up to active duty as corpses next.'

'Is that what Grandma brought you up to believe?'

'Yes. But she could hardly have brought us up to believe anything else. It was what she had seen with her own eyes. She didn't want us to grow up thinking the bad times were behind us. The bad times are never behind us.'

'If you think that, how do you ever live?'

'Well, Jean Améry – the writer who came up with the phrase *dead men on leave* – knew he couldn't live. He overdosed on sleeping pills. His leave was up.'

'I didn't pick you for a reader,' Zoe said.

'I'm not. But those fucking words were all over the house I grew up in. The only reason my mother didn't sew them into my socks was that she didn't sew.'

Zoe liked the phrase *dead men on leave*. It captured her father's temporary state of mind well, she thought. The way he was always looking over his shoulder or consulting his watch . . . waiting to be called up. She'd thought it was impatience with her. I hoped she felt she could love me a little now she knew the truth.

Gloria went with her to Foyles to buy anything by Jean Améry. 'No, no more by him,' she said as she saw Zoe's fingers twitch in the direction of Chomsky.

Over coffee, Zoe flicked through Jean Améry's *On Suicide*.
'It's so black, this stuff,' she said. 'I love it.'
'The coffee?'
'The book.'
Gloria shrugged. She wasn't a reader either.

It was by promising Zoe more talk of dead men on leave that
Isak got her to go with him to visit Mutti. 'But I'd suggest you
cover up your tattoos before we go,' he said.
'Will she cover hers?'
'Mutti! Mutti is not tattooed.'
'What about her camp number?'
'That's Auschwitz. Mutti was in Belsen. Belsen didn't tattoo
its inmates.'
Zoe, who marched against the tide of Jewish history, hadn't
known that Auschwitz and Belsen were separate institutions.
'I won't tell,' Isak said.
Mutti embraced the girl. Still the chill, but a cold embrace
was an improvement on a cold stare. Zoe thought Isak was teas-
ing her about the tattoo. Surely every Jew over eighty had one.
Mutti caught her looking at her arms. 'You won't find what
you're looking for,' Mutti said. 'Whoever wanted a tattoo, went
to Auschwitz. But I do have sentences tattooed on my heart.'
She showed Zoe a cushion on which were embroidered
the words

Man has the right and the privilege to declare himself to be in disagree-
ment with every natural occurrence, including the biological healing that
time brings about.

Zoe clapped her hands. 'Ah, Jean Améry,' she said, as though
he'd been her favourite writer since birth.
Mutti was surprised. 'You've read Jean Améry?'

'I am reading him now.'

Mutti embraced her again. A little less icily than before. 'You're a prettier child than I remembered,' she said.

More of Améry's stone-dead words were embroidered on a cushion on my mother's office chair. It supported her every day. When I was old enough to understand what Améry's words meant I told her that as a natural occurrence myself I was insulted by the idea that my mother was in disagreement with me. I recall her shrugging and saying, '*Tant pis*, but it isn't about you.' I was but a blip in the great cycle of nature – suffering and healing, suffering and healing – which she rejected. Fuck them with their healing. Which meant fuck me as well. The good don't heal.

Thus, in our family, against nature's best advice, was sorrow passed down through the generations. And thus, for all Charmian's attempts to keep Zoe free of that generational pull towards an eternal sadness, it begin to exert its fatal attraction again. Thanks to Isak and Gloria, thanks to Jean Améry, thanks to Mutti, thanks to the poor butchered hostage, thanks to the IDF soldier whose last word was the name of the woman he loved, and who might herself have been already murdered, thanks and yet no thanks to me, Zoe was returned, if not quite yet into the bosom of her family – perhaps never into the bosom of her family – then at least into that no man's land of honourable uncertainty and quiet reason where right was not reserved exclusively for your enemies, where it was no crime to know your own history and be unashamed of it.

Division had entered Zoe's soul.

LOST

As foretold, in the umpteenth week of the Peace Marches, Ferdinand Draxler – Ferdie to his friends – got lost in the middle of London.

No one knew he was out walking. He had promised Charmian he wouldn't stir from the house and had been as good as his word for longer than he could remember. But on this day he felt an unfamiliar something or other – not energy or optimism or curiosity, just a renewed sense of being, was the best explanation of it he could give himself. And that might well have been the very opposite to optimism. What if it was a renewed sense of invigorating fatalism?

He wanted to see things, anyway, rather than think things. He had spoken at length to his brother who laid an unexpectedly tender hand on his shoulder, told him Zoe was well, and repeated his warnings to Ferdinand about letting the walls of the ghetto imprison him. 'Live, bro,' he had said. 'You're not *only* a Jew, you're *also* a Jew. Tell them that.'

'Who's them?'

'The ones who don't do alsos. The either/ors.'

Zoe herself Ferdinand had not seen. He was not ready. She was not ready either. But the house felt differently on account of her having been there. The vibrating silence caused by her absence had stopped buzzing in the windowpanes. 'Hush,' Charmian said when he brought up her name. But it wasn't the old 'Hush' warning against apoplectic rage. It was a more tender, all will be well 'Hush'. A steadying 'Hush'. Let things take their time. Don't expect too much too soon. A 'Hush' to a person who needed not to overexcite himself with relief and joy as he had once overexcited himself with vexation and fury.

In a curious way, he felt guilty about the changes said to have been wrought in her. He didn't know if she'd stopped marching, but if she had – just *if* – didn't he owe it to her, reciprocally, to go on a march himself? If only for a yard or so?

She had left a note for him. At once gently accusatory and almost self-mocking. *Almost*. He made allowances. She had been in a world where doubt was frowned on and irony outlawed. All things considered, it was amazing she still had language. Yet here she was, taking on the challenge of another. She had been studying Hebrew with Uncle and Aunty Gloria. And while she wasn't far advanced, she had come to the conclusion that Hebrew grammar enjoyed an advantage over English grammar. It was more open. It invited a greater latitude of interpretation. The aim of the Talmud was to bring the Jews to the One Great Truth, but the grammatic means of reaching that Truth allowed a flexibility she hadn't encountered in all that Ridout gunk he'd force-fed her as a child. Did he know that with Hebrew you had to insert your own vowels? If he hadn't been such a dog-matic grammarian in the matter of English, if he'd allowed her to reach her own truth in her own time, insert her own vowels, so to speak, she might not have rejected the Jew in herself.

Ferdinand scratched his head. So it was Ronald Ridout's fault that she had the words KILL ALL ZIONISTS picked out to resemble needlepoint in a pinwheel design around her belly button . . . Oh, Ronald, Ronald, what damage had *English Today, Books 1–5* done to the children of the free world!

Watchfully, he stepped outside the house. Hello world, he said. But he could just as easily have been saying goodbye.

Act V is the place for reconciliations, not denouements. And silences.

A wordless, conciliatory, on the one hand this and on the other hand that maybe sort of march, then, was what he was after – for Zoe. That's if he could find a march at all. He'd been lost, in sleep and comics, without television or newspapers, for so long, he couldn't be sure marches still happened. What if the rapprochement with his daughter – if, in his virtual absence, it could be called a rapprochement – had started a trend? What if fathers and mothers the world over were gathering in their off-spring? His theory of marches and demonstrations had always been that they were more psychological than political, initiation rites for the not-yet-ready-to-leave-home into what they imagined independent adulthood looked like. Return the young to the embraces of their parents and what justification for marches was there?

Lost in the London he knew so well, he thought how changed everything was. Marathons he was familiar with, but half- and quarter-marathons were new to him. As were the roller-skating jamborees. And the E-scooter races. He didn't see how there could be room for marches. But then he heard the familiar cracked-voice cries and, after rubbing the sleep out of his eyes, he saw the warlike flags and banners that had been fluttering, it seemed, to him, from the dawn of time. Not just the marches he remembered, demanding 'Free, free . . . !' but marches in support of marches, marches bewailing the absence of marches. He thought he saw her, Zoe with her fist raised, Zoe flagged and keffiyehed up, unless that was an old prayer shawl of his she was wearing, Zoe on a scooter, Zoe on roller skates. He rubbed his face. Anyone watching would have thought he was trying to rub his face away. 'Zoe!' he called, but if she heard him she didn't answer.

He still owed her a march. Seeing him looking nervous and unsure, the March Warden pointed out a slow-footed, funereal procession of Jews he suspected might be of interest. To Ferdinand they brought to mind the stone-relief he loved, showing the Israelites being led uncomplainingly into exile. It was only when he saw they were marching behind a banner proclaiming Jews Against *something or other* – *the something or other* having been worn away by weather or years of indecision – that he realised the degree of his isolation. He too was against something or other, but he doubted it was this *something or other*

Which made him – he had to admit – even more of a sadsack Jew who didn't belong than the marchers were. Another befuddled, never-again Jew, another incorrigible casualty, to blame for nothing except being blamed, another of the sleepers of history.

He was surprised to see Elaine Muller among the marchers. He could tell she didn't want to be seen but he beckoned to her anyway.

'Fancy,' he said. He did not mean that to sound judgemental.

'I'm not surprised you're surprised,' she said. 'I don't really know what I'm doing here either. It's for my daughter.'

'I know only too well how that goes,' Ferdinand said. 'You don't have to explain yourself to me. Though oughtn't you to be teaching? It's not a public holiday, is it?'

Elaine looked away. 'In a manner of speaking it is,' she said.

'In what manner of speaking?'

'In a manner of Max's speaking.'

'Max?'

'Max Axelberg.'

'Ah yes, Max Axelberg.' Oh, how good it was to forget. 'What's he done?'

'He's given the school a day off.'

'In aid of?'

'Gaza.'

'Only Gaza? Why not Lebanon?'

'Lebanon's tomorrow.'

★

In silence he walked by her side. She for her daughter, he for his. A gust of wind blew the banner under which he was marching to reveal the words *Jews Against Genocide*.

He stepped to one side and had to jump out of the path of a marauding tuk-tuk.

And that was when something or other struck him and he fell . . .

EPILOGUE

IN OUR END IS OUR BEGINNING

Sheltered by the gharqad tree, the Jew Draxler listened to the rain fall far away.

Storm Deborah had given fair warning of her coming, flooding Venice to the height of the Last Judgement on the facade of St Mark's Basilica – leaving just Christ's fingers to flicker vainly above the stinking water from the Grand Canal like those of a man about to drown for the third and final time – sending multicoloured roof tiles from St Stephen's Cathedral spinning like frisbees over Vienna, inundating the streets of Cologne with the bones of the 11,000 virgins massacred by the Huns and housed until now in the Golden Chamber of the Church of St Ursula.

By the time Deborah made the Channel crossing, every building of significance south of London was roped down under tarpaulin and buttressed with towers of sandbags hundreds of feet high. The government described it as the greatest defensive project ever mounted in peacetime. But the truth was it had started roping far too late, dismissing all reports of cataclysmic damage as wetist alarmism, tying the ropes with single slip knots so that they could be quickly unknotted again when Deborah passed without incident and only bothering to half fill the sandbags. On the first night of the storm more than fifty great churches lost their roofs. Why Deborah went for religious edifices before any other no one could explain, but to atheists it proved that the destruction was not a punishment for man's ungodliness. If anything, it was the final nail in the coffin of religious belief, a boast they were unable to make too much of on account of the first human casualties being delegates to a weekend Rationalist Convention in Deal, a number of whom were actually blown out to sea while taking Armageddon selfies on the pier. To the satisfaction of their grieving families, images of the drowned losing their footing flashed around the world long after their demise. 'Always on my screen,' one grieving Rationalist widow posted.

Following fourteen frolicsome days of agnostic demolition, Deborah fell quiet, leading the country to believe the worst was over. The sun shone now on pastures which had never been greener. Even the heavens seemed to smile. Only shepherds refused to join the rejoicing. Normally patient sheep, they said, were chewing as though their lives depended on it. This could only mean they knew the lull was temporary. A week later, Deborah – for it was still she – kicked open the doors to her troublingly silent boudoir, unleashing thunderbolts and with them a rain that would last eleven months. This was like no previous rain. The heavens did not open. When heavens open there is hope that they will close again. This time they simply stood aside at Deborah's bidding and left the earth to cower under the ferocity of water that flew down like the arrows of a million archers. It was as though Creation had gone into reverse, changing rain back from passing phenomenon to immanence.

The longer it rained, the more questions people in high places asked. Rationalists must have been wrong in their diagnosis of Deborah's motives, they said. If her purpose in destroying churches had been to remove all trace of religious faith, why hadn't she destroyed a single synagogue? Was the storm in the pay of the Jews?

That was Question One.

Question Two: Could Storm Deborah's target have been free speech, and in particular the warlike Shabbes Peace Marches that had become a fixture of life in the capital? Was Deborah Islamophobic?

Question Three: Talking of Shabbes, where were the Jews? Had they, under cover of rain, made their escape, not waiting to gather up their valuables? And did that otherwise inexplicable seven-day pause have no meteorological function, no function at all, in fact, save that of granting those Jews who had complained about the rush sufficient time to return while the country was too busy cleaning up to notice, collect the gold and silver they'd left behind, and leave again?

Draxler had quit London for the Bethel Valley in the far northeast of the country several weeks before Deborah struck. Had he been in the know? He had no memory of what he knew. He found himself here, that was all he could say. He and Charmian were on holiday and holidays had always been Charmian's responsibility. She chose, she advised on the weather, she booked, she chose the means of transport. He had brought wellingtons, a parka and an umbrella, but those would have been normal for a late-summer holiday in the north. There was nothing to say that Charmian was aware of Deborah's intentions either. Had she known, she would surely not have rented the Old Rectory which by any account fell within the storm's apparent remit to hit religion.

As it happened, just as Deborah passed over the country's synagogues, so she passed over the Old Rectory without disturbing a slate.

So, Question Four: Was the Old Rectory spared because of the passion for the Holy Land expressed by successive generations of Bethel Valley clergy, witness to which were the fine copperplate illustrations of the Hebrew Bible adorning every wall and the mural in the bedroom of Moses coming down from

Mount Sinai and finding the children of Israel singing, shaking timbrels and dancing naked round a golden calf?

Like many remote parts of the country, the Bethel Valley had retained its Old Testament Puritan associations. There was a bust of John Bunyan in the square and a statue of Oliver Cromwell outside the Town Hall. Caleb Yates was the town's biggest landowner. His wife, Virtue Yates, was headmistress of the largest primary school. If Storm Deborah went easy on the town she had her reasons.

This much Draxler dimly understood:

Charmian had chosen the Old Rectory for aesthetic and topographical reasons, not religious. She loved reading in the brochure about its intriguing position straddling the border of two counties – the front door giving onto a tree-lined lane where foxes skulked, the back door onto a small garden with a dried-up fish pond, once fed by a turgid tributary of the river which, in olden times, locals had amusingly referred to as the Tigris. The Reverend Jabez Wolfe was said to have taken delight in the queer fact that a politician of one political persuasion represented his living room while a member of another political persuasion represented his kitchen.

But what must finally have decided Charmian on the rectory was the solitary gharqad tree that occupied the rear garden at the expense, seemingly, of any other living thing. The gharqad tree had been presented to Jabez Wolfe by an emir over a hundred and fifty years before. A plaque by the foot of the tree told how the two men had met while Jabez Wolfe was on a pilgrimage to the Holy Land, and became firm friends. Some months after Wolfe's return he received a gift of the tree. 'It is unlikely the gharqad will thrive in a climate as clement as yours,' the emir wrote to say, 'unless our Gods wish it to. But let us try.'

And behold, one or both of their Gods wished it.

The emir had not warned Jabez Wolfe that Jews congregated under the gharqad tree for protection. He didn't imagine there were any Jews where his friend Jabez lived.

Though an unfriendly, grizzled tree, it struck Charmian as likely to be sympathetic to her husband's reclusive temperament. She could imagine him sitting under it and reading with his eyes closed. She wanted this to be a quiet holiday for him, a respite from all he'd put himself through, but she wasn't expecting miracles – a reservation she would think twice about when Deborah passed over the rectory without removing a single roof tile or shaking a single one of the gharqad tree's branches.

Her husband, for his part, did exactly as Charmian hoped he would and snoozed and read vintage comics under the gharqad's branches. He laughed at the antics of Desperate Dan.

He could not remember ever being happier. The loud banging in his head had subsided. He no longer made knots of his fingers or jiggled his legs until the whole house shook. Occasionally, the idea that he owed someone an obligation disturbed his quiet, but it quickly passed. 'How is Zoe getting on in Jerusalem?' he sometimes remembered to ask his wife.

'She appears to be well and sends her love,' Charmian told him. She wasn't above telling her husband what she thought it would be good for him to hear, but this was true. Zoe had gone off to Jerusalem in the company of Isak and Gloria of whom he had made a respectable woman. They seemed to view Zoe as a daughter. Did Zoe, then, view them as parents? Never mind if she did. It was enough that Uncle Ike and Gloria had wrought so miraculous a change in Zoe's belief system that she was now as fervid, not to say fanatical, in her embrace of her half-Jewishness as she had previously been in her rejection of it.

'*Baruch Hashem*,' Charmian said. Her husband wondered how she came to know the Hebrew for Thank God. He used the Yiddish '*Gottze dank*'.

'Zoe taught it me,' Charmian said, kissing his eyes.

No, he could not remember ever being more at peace with himself.

There was no reason, either, for him to be worrying about his mother. He had a recollection of seeing her before leaving for the north. She was, she told him, in good spirits. Max Axelberg had volunteered to do her shopping and read to her. '*Gottze dank* for him,' Draxler said.

'And *Gottze dank* for Charmian,' his mother said in reply. It did her heart good to know how well her daughter-in-law looked after her son. She had always loved Charmian. Perhaps she hadn't told him often enough how much she loved him, but she did. She beckoned him to her and kissed his face again and again. They cried together. 'I shouldn't be away too long,' he told her.

'Call me Mutti,' she told him.

'Mutti,' he said, 'Mutti, Mutti.'

They embraced and cried again. 'Dear little Chlodnik,' she said, kissing his face.

Underneath the gharqad tree, Mutti's boy closed his eyes and smiled.

When, occasionally, he had the strength to brave the rain – gentler and more fitful here than in the south – he marvelled at the light, the pavements swimming in the watery reflection of the heavens, the shop windows streaming as though with pearls, the great shadow play of clouds on the hills, like a slide show put on for visitors. Never mind rainbows, to him there was no promise of peace quite equal to the moment light shuttered aside the dark mirroring of clouds on the hillside. It was as though some usually forbidding, non-mortal place opened itself to the human eye, allowing a glimpse of what normally lay hidden, the domed city beyond, the treasure vaults within – the troves of carnelian, chrysolite and emerald, topaz, onyx and jasper from which emanated a music he did not recognise but thought he'd known all his life – before retreating again into the unfeatured darkness.

Draxler paused to shield his eyes against the brightness and looked. It seemed so long since he had paused to look at anything.

He resumed walking, tentatively, as though on some glacial substance, recalling snatches of poetry he had no memory of reading. A Psalm recited at school assembly came back to him, along with memories of the faces of the boys reciting it. Which boys? Those he taught or those he had himself been a schoolboy with? He did not bother to make a distinction. Boys were boys. He believed that if he concentrated hard enough – and he had nothing else to do – he would at last not only make out all their faces but hear all their voices.

'For thou hast delivered my soul from death; wilt not thou deliver my feet from falling, that I may walk before God in the light of the living?'

He trembled, as the words flooded his recollection, just as, in the school hall, he had trembled years before. So, today, he walked in the light of the living, slushing through the waters in which the feathery sky looked down bashfully into its own reflection. He paused again to look into a bridal shop. Espenbaum's. The words of a poem he did not know by Paul Celan, a poet he had never read, returned to him.

> *Espenbaum, dein Laub blickt weiß ins Dunkel.*
> *Meiner Mutter Haar ward nimmer weiß.*

Aspen tree, your leaves gaze white into the dark.
My mother's hair ne'er turned white.

Quaking like an aspen tree himself, he repeated the words *Espenbaum* and *Meiner Mutter* over and over. A strange conjunction because his mother never trembled. Not even, he believed, when Josef Kramer did, if he did, whatever he with impunity did to her.

'Are you all right?' a kindly woman in a headscarf stopped to ask him.

'How nice of you to enquire,' he answered. 'I am more than all right. I am on cloud ten.'

She smiled at him and touched his arm. 'Do you mean cloud nine?'

'No, I mean cloud ten.'

His mother too. She'd told him so.

He wondered, as he roamed about the town, smiling at passers-by, whether the absence of swastikas and those other incitements to hatred he had grown accustomed to was a consequence of Storm Deborah. Had the rain washed the swastikas away?

Was there anyone to ask? And what form would his asking take? Libraries were the best places to go to when you needed local information but what would a librarian think if he enquired as to the whereabouts of the swastikas?

He no sooner thought about a library than he found one – a neo-Byzantine temple, was how it struck him, built of a mosaic of red and brown brick, and altogether too big for the town. For all its bulk it seemed to hover, which made Draxler think he had stumbled on it just in time, before it floated off. He pushed open a heavy, arched door that groaned on its hinges and, as the building seemed to expect, all but floated into its vaulted silence. There was no librarian to ask about swastikas and no evidence that anyone had used the library for an eternity except for a trolley by the desk on which were the most recently returned books. Draxler was quietly pleased – no more than that – to see that somebody had returned *Shakespeare and the Shlemiels*. A conscientious reader, judging by the number of yellow stickers protruding from the pamphlet – one for each page, at a rough count.

He looked around him, breathing in the quiet, content to see no one. This would be where I would pass my days, he thought, were I to live here sometime in the future. He wished he could put his name into a visitors' book, and pen a compliment, but there was no visitors' book.

Back out on the street, his ears popped. Soon, he needed to rest his eyes from the translucence of the streets. He called in at an inn to order a glass of wine. What did he drink? He tapped the bar with his fingers. 'Palwin, I think,' he said. 'Palwin Number Something-or-Other, it doesn't matter which.'

A modest barmaid with heavy, downcast eyes apologised. They had no Palwin Number Anything. It seemed to break her heart to refuse him.

'Ech!' He klopped the side of his head. He explained that Palwin was a ceremonial dessert wine, drunk by the thimbleful on Jewish High Holidays.

The young woman smiled her sad smile. Yes, she knew that. They normally had Palwin No. 4 and No. 10. There had been a run on it recently. People staying in to avoid the rain, she thought. She was so sorry.

His second choice was Chianti. Chianti had followed Palwin when he was a teenager. Palwin No. 4 or No. 10 with your parents then Chianti with your girlfriend. He felt he'd concertina'd his youth into two glasses. How many more glasses before there was no life left to concertina? This wasn't a morbid thought. He was happy. 'Ah well,' he said aloud as he raised the glass to his lips. Or was it 'All's well'?

Two men in yellow cardigans came to join him at the bar. Blue-eyed and with cheeks the colour of honeysuckle, they could have been twins. 'We've been waiting for you,' one or other of them said, extending a hand.

'But you don't know me.'

'You specifically, no. But we were certain people of your kind would start to come here for shelter. You're the first.'

Had he been back in London, Draxler would have made for the nearest exit. *Your kind*, indeed. But there were no swastikas here. No rats called Jew. No notices plastered on the doors of banks, building societies, theatres, hotels, bars, cafés and schools calling for the removal of all visible or symbolic gestures of solidarity with a state currently engaged in crimes against humanity. The town was flooded with a benign watery light. There was no sound of marching or shouting and none of the usual remnants of a march – the banners and the posters and the flyers – littering the street. Even the waste bins, he had noticed, were empty.

'By my kind . . . ?' he began.

'The southern educated.'

Draxler smiled to himself. Did he look too openly educated? He wasn't even carrying his Montaigne. Only a comic.

'I thought . . .' he said, and then thought better of saying what he thought.

'What did you think?'

Draxler put his glass of Chianti No. 7 to his lips. 'I thought that by *my kind* you meant . . . you know . . .'

One or other of the men laid a hand on his arm. This was the second time Draxl been touched by a stranger in an hour. How kind everybody was up here! 'You have nothing to worry about on that score,' the other of the one or other of the men said. 'We are all "you know" here.'

'All?'

'All.'

'The entire town?'

'The whole *megila*.'

Draxler scrutinised their features. They didn't look 'you know'. But to say that would imply there was a 'you know' way of looking and that would be what he thought was called racial profiling. 'How can this be?' he asked instead. 'Has there been a mass conversion?'

'We've been "you know" and nothing but "you know" for centuries.'

'Nothing but?'

'A hundred and ten per cent.'

'Forgive me but that makes no sense. I'm holidaying in a rectory.'

'Then you've seen the art. It only ever pretended to be a rectory. Just as old Jabez Wolfe only ever pretended to be a rector.'

'Are you telling me he was a rabbi?'

'More than that. He was chief rabbi of the Lost "you knows" of Bethel. The last chief rabbi, as it happens. The town long ago ran out of money to pay for a new one.'

Draxler shook his head.

If only he could help.

Did Charmian know all this? Did she know *any* of this? Was this why she'd brought him here?

How lovely of her, in that case, to have gone to the trouble of finding such a place.

'And when you say you've been waiting for me,' he asked the men, 'what exactly have you been waiting for me to do?'

He hoped they weren't thinking of asking him to be the new chief rabbi. He was here to rest. He couldn't take on the responsibility that went with the office. Though he would if they offered it to Max Axelberg instead.

They read his mind. 'No,' they said. 'We wouldn't dream of asking that. We want to invite you to Shabbes dinner, Dr Draxler, that's all.'

He thanked them. 'Call me Ferdie,' he said. But he'd have to check with his wife as she was in charge of their diary, though he doubted they had much else on this Friday.

'You don't,' they said, 'but it doesn't have to be Friday. We are very relaxed. We have Shabbes dinner every night up here. There seems no reason not to.'

'What about now, then?' Draxler asked. He had not long ago finished breakfast but why not have a Shabbes dinner too?

They drove him at a gentle pace to their home at the foot of the Bethel Hills where they introduced him to their wives and children, each of whom embraced him. '*Shabbat shalom*,' they said. They were all blue-eyed and wearing yellow cardigans.

'As we are eating so early there is no real need of candles,' one of the wives of one of the men said, 'but I see it as a way of welcoming enlightenment, so I hope you will allow a departure from custom.'

He was offered a yarmulke. I have my own, he said, reaching into his inside pocket.

After the wife lit the candles she put her hands over her eyes then waved her hands around the candles, a motion suggestive either of dispelling evil or welcoming good. How beautiful, either way, Ferdie thought. He had never seen his mother light candles. Not even the single memorial candle for a dead relative. 'If I had to light a candle for all those I'd lost,' she said, 'I'd never be without a match in my hand.'

Before the arrival of the food, they poured the wine. Oh look, Palwin No. 5, in deference to his declared fondness for it. They asked him to say the blessing. Something else he was surprised to remember. They watched with amusement as he downed the tiny glass in one swallow. The poor man was thirsty. Then the children clung to him and sang 'Shalom Aleichem' to greet the angels whose job it was to act as best men and maids of honour and escort the bride to the table. The bride was Shabbes herself, one of the daughters of one of the men explained to Draxler, in case he'd forgotten.

How lovely, he thought. A bride called Shabbes.

And speaking of angels, there suddenly one was, coming out of the sky – halo'd by the sun – a silk parachute above, like a parasol held aloft for her by the wind. The rain had stopped, so the party was able to pause, just as the plaited bread was about to be cut, and go out into the garden and look up. The children clapped their hands. Their mothers and fathers clapped Draxler's shoulders. First him, now the angel – it was a day of divine gifts.

Charmian had mentioned, he now remembered, her ambition, while they were up here and he snoozed under the gharqad tree, to jump from each of the famous seven hills of Bethel. Whoever paraglided from all seven in a seven-day period would be awarded a commemorative ribband. Charmian coveted that ribband. She loved sports that made her laugh aloud with excitement, Draxler remembered her telling him, recalling the sight of her flying out of the snow in Kitzbühel like a rare, silvery bird with ice on her wings. Rocking acrobatically out of the bagging rain clouds this time, laughing with fear and excitement like a giant schoolgirl on a swing, and yet with the pale light of the waterlogged sun shining through her raiments, here Charmian came again.

Could she see him from so far away, he wondered. Could she see how happy he was?

He didn't tell his hosts that the angel was his wife. But he was filled with pride and love.

They poured him another Palwin No. 5 – in a glass not a thimble – and got him to recite the prayer again. *Baruch atah Adonai, Eloheinu Melech ha'olam, boreh p'ri hagafen.* Blessed art

Thou, God, Ruler of the universe, who creates the fruit of the vine.

L'chaim, he added, gathering the children to him, the Jew Draxler, father, son, brother, loving and beloved bridegroom, patriarch, light unto nations MBE, holy in his unholiness.

Looking up into the watery light of the heavens he saw that the parachuting angel's silvery cheeks were wet with tears.

He raised his glass. *L'chaim*, he said again. To life.

He hoped he had remembered the right word.

Howard Jacobson has written eighteen novels and six works of non-fiction. He won the Bollinger Everyman Wodehouse Prize in 2000 for *The Mighty Walzer* and then again in 2013 for *Zoo Time*. In 2010 he won the Man Booker Prize for *The Finkler Question*; he was also shortlisted for the prize in 2014 for *J*.